Cece Copyright ©202
Brear
ISBN: 978-0-6488003-0-9

First Publication: 2020 AnneMarie Brear.

Cover design by Image: JB Graphics

Published novels:

Dedication

To my friend and fellow author,
Maggi Andersen.

Cece

Book 3
Marsh Saga Series

AnneMarie Brear

Chapter One

London. February 1923.

In the pouring rain, Cece Marsh hurried out of the taxi and, nodding to the doorman, entered the Savoy Hotel in Westminster. She headed into the restaurant where her grandmama said to meet her at one o'clock. It was now one fifteen.

Mr Thomas, the well-known maitre'd, took her coat and gloves with a warm smile. 'Miss Marsh, your grandmother awaits you.'

'Yes, I know I'm late.' She pulled a face. 'Traffic.'

He raised his hand, and another black-suited waiter was instantly by her side and directing her to where Adeline Fordham, her grandmama, sat nestled between a blazing fireplace and a large window. It was the table Grandmama reserved once a week when in London and had done for the last forty years.

'Oh, you remembered our appointment then?' Grandmama gave her a piercing stare, looking resplendent in olive green and white lace dress. With not a grey hair out of place and light makeup applied, she defied her eighty years of age.

'I'm so sorry. The traffic was horrendous all the way from the library.'

Grandmama's gaze rose to Cece's hair. 'Traffic? I thought you had *walked* the entire way.'

Touching her wayward auburn curls and trying to tuck them back under her hat, Cece knew she didn't look her best and sighed. 'No. I didn't walk.'

'Shall you take yourself off to the ladies' room?' The pointed remark was barely out of Grandmama's mouth before Cece quickly left the table and hurried to the ladies' room, where she half-heartedly managed to repair the damage to her hair.

She unpinned her dark blue cloche hat and stared into the mirror at the rain-frizzed red hair she'd hated all her life. In her bag, she carried a small hairbrush and tortoise-shell combs, but nothing could be done with it, especially when it was raining. She wished she had her sisters' hair. Millie's black curls were neat and fell around her face in a delightful way, and Prue's straight blonde hair was cut in a sleek short bob and always stylish. However, Cece had inherited her late father's fair colouring, which was pale skin prone to freckles in the summer and wayward hair that she couldn't control.

For a moment she stopped fiddling and thought of her sisters. Millie would be busy at the chateau, organising the rebuilding of it while running after her two little boys. She missed Millie terribly. Prue, although living in London, was so involved with working for a new ladies' magazine no one barely saw her, and even though her relationship with Prue could sometimes be a little testy, she missed Prue's laughter. In only a few years everything had changed in the family, Papa died, Mama remarried, Millie moved to France and Prue a businesswoman. They'd all gone and left her, and she didn't have the slightest idea where she fitted into the family anymore.

As other women, all elegant and sophisticated came and went from the room, Cece became increasingly frustrated. In the end, she squished her hair under her cloche hat and with a last look at her plain brown skirt and emerald cardigan, she returned to the table.

Grandmama raised her eyebrows but said nothing.

'Have you ordered?' Cece asked, giving a small smile to the hovering waiter.

'Just now. Lobster soup and a selection of sandwiches. Do you wish for anything else?'

'No, thank you, that's lovely,' Cece answered, including the waiter in her response.

'Since you're finally here, we can discuss what I want to talk to you about.'

'Grandmama, I only saw you at breakfast.' Cece unfolded her napkin. 'Why couldn't we do this at home?'

'Well, I simply assumed it would be nice for us to have some time alone for a change. With Lesley at the house, it's difficult to get a word in.'

'Lesley is fine.'

'She's a loud American who outstays her welcome.'

'She was going to go home last week, and you prevented her.' Cece shook her head. Lesley Larkin, Grandmama's friend from America, was a nice woman, but Grandmama wasn't keen on Americans even though she adored Lesley, and so she pretended to all and sundry that she was only putting up with

Lesley because she was a guest and guests are always treated with kindness and consideration.

'Yes, I prevented her from leaving because she hasn't visited enough places. I don't want her returning to America and telling everyone that we British can't entertain our visitors. I'm not having that.'

Grinning, Cece sipped from a glass of water. 'Lesley has been here for five weeks. She's seen and done more things in London than I have my whole life! And I've been coming here twice a year to stay with you since I was a child.'

'That's different. You're family, not an outsider.' Grandmama paused while the waiter wheeled a trolley to their table and set out the tea service between them.

'Thank you, Robert,' Grandmama said as he left.

Cece poured out the tea into the thin porcelain teacups. 'Where is Lesley while we are here? You've not barred her from joining us, have you?'

'No, I have not! What cheek.'

'I didn't see her at breakfast this morning. Did she sleep late?'

'No, she left early to go on a tour of Cambridge that I organised for her through a friend. She'll be back tonight.'

'Did Lesley enjoy the theatre last night?'

'She did, howled with laughter.' Grandmama's tone was disapproving. 'Most embarrassing it was. I ordered her to stop, but she didn't of course. She does it to spite me.'

Cece rolled her eyes, trying not to laugh. The whole family was amazed at how a loud American had come to be best friends with their difficult grandmama.

'Anyway, enough of Lesley. I wanted to talk about you.'

'Me?' Cece was surprised at that. When did anyone ever talk about her?

'I know you objected to my taking Prue to India and Italy.' Grandmama sipped her tea.

'I felt left out, yes.' Cece didn't deny it. What would be the point? She was hurt that Grandmama had taken her sister Prue and not included her.

'You weren't ready to go on such a trip. We both know that.' Grandmama paused again as the lobster soup was brought out and the three-tiered cake stand full of sandwiches, little French pastries and miniature cakes.

'That is your opinion,' Cece muttered, eyeing the cakes.

'And the correct opinion.'

'Is this you apologising for not taking me?'

'Good heavens, no. Why would I do that? I am not sorry in the slightest. Prue needed that adventure and look how well it has turned out for her. She's married and is now part of a new magazine business with Lady Mayton-Walsh.'

Cece fumed inwardly. Yes, Prue had the perfect life, as usual. She thought of Millie, her eldest sister, and admitted that Millie's life was also perfect, living in a chateau in Northern France with her husband and two children.

'You're thinking what about *you*, aren't you?' Grandmama sipped her soup. 'It's natural to do that. Millie and Prue are settled and happy, and then there's you.'

'Always last,' she tried to keep the anger out of her voice.

'Don't be self-absorbed. It's unbecoming,' Grandmama snapped.

Cece stared at her, a formidable woman she'd loved and admired all her life. Adeline Fordham was a force to be reckoned with and had spent her years as a young woman travelling the world and she ruled her family with a rod of iron, or once did.

'I have bought you a cottage.'

'A cottage?' Cece was so astonished her soup spoon was suspended half way to her mouth.

'In Scotland.'

'Scotland?' Cece lowered the spoon and sat back in her chair. 'Why? What purpose is there to me having a cottage in Scotland?'

'Because I reason that you need it. You'll own something that is uniquely yours. You'll have a responsibility.'

'Why in Scotland? I don't wish to live in Scotland.'

'You don't have to live there permanently. It's simply a place that is yours alone for you to escape to when you need to.'

'Escape? What am I escaping from?'

'The world, family, yourself.'

'I see.' She didn't of course. She had no clue as to why Grandmama would give her a cottage. None of it made sense.

'Are you not pleased?'

'Thank you, Grandmama, it is indeed a generous present.'

'Perhaps tell your face that then.' Grandmama continued to sip her soup.

Cece did the same, yet she didn't taste any of it. Her mind whirled. A cottage in Scotland? It sounded like banishment. Why couldn't she have a cottage in the Cotswolds, or Cornwall, or the South of France, or anywhere warmer than Scotland? Did Grandmama want rid of her? Was she tired of having her stay with her in London? She didn't understand.

When Cece could bare the silence no more, she pushed away her soup. 'Do you not want me to live with you anymore?'

Grandmama frowned and dabbed her lips. 'Why would you say such a thing?'

'Scotland is so far away.'

'It's a night's journey by train, hardly outer Mongolia.' Grandmama patted Cece's hand that rested on the table. 'I enjoy your company immensely, but I am also thinking about your future. You need to do something, girl.'

'I'm extremely busy.'

'Oh, I don't deny that. You're dedicated to your charity work, which is commendable.'

'But you feel that is not enough?'

'Do *you*?' Grandmama's blue eyed gaze never left Cece's.

Cece couldn't answer her because she didn't know. No, that was a lie. She did know and the answer was it wasn't enough, as passionate as she was regarding her causes, something was missing in her life.

'The cottage is paid for and the title deeds are in your name. I've not seen it, obviously, but a friend of mine sorted it all out for me with his land agent. They assure me that the cottage is well kept and stands on seventeen acres. A nearby farmer rents the land for his cows or sheep.' Grandmama waved her hand dismissively. 'So that will also be a small income for you.'

'Papa left me well provided for when he died.'

'As he should, and as I will also when I die, but until then, what does it hurt to have a little extra?' Grandmama lowered her voice. 'Money should always earn its keep, my dear. Your late Grandpapa was a shrewd investor and highly astute where money was concerned. Thankfully, your dear papa was the same, but he didn't instil any of that knowledge into you three girls, did he? Very lax of him.'

'He would have if we'd been boys.' Cece always believed that her papa desperately wanted her to be a boy after having two girls.

'A foolish oversight on his part. Females as well as males need to know how to make and keep money. Now, Millie and Prue have married well, but what if you don't? You need to learn how to make your inheritance work.'

Cece pushed her soup bowl away. Why wouldn't she marry well? Was she too ugly to attract a suitable beau? 'My money is looked after by Mr Watts at the bank and Mr Sparks, Papa's former accountant. They were good friends of Papa's. They'd not see us go wrong, would they?'

'Do you check your statements, your investment shares? Do you understand what it all means? You rely on them too much, girl. You need to understand money as well.'

Shoulders sagging, Cece shook her head. 'No, I do not. I don't have the slightest inclination of learning about investing and such like.'

Grandmama wiped her mouth with a napkin. 'I should have taken this in hand earlier, after your papa died, but with travelling to India and Italy, time has lapsed. Your mama has no head for business at all, so she is of no use to you.' Grandmama huffed. 'Not that Violet is in any state of mind to worry about such things, not with her now married to Jacques and living in Paris. She gives no mind to anyone but herself. How I brought up such a selfish daughter I do not know. Between Violet and Hugo, I'm well blessed.'

Cece cocked her head a little in thought. Grandmama was upset. She missed Mama, who now lived most of her time in Paris. Uncle Hugo lived in Ceylon, and she wouldn't see him again unless he travelled back to England and he didn't seem inclined to do that. Poor Grandmama was alone for the first time in her life. Cece understood the hollowness of loneliness, it was all she felt since Millie married in nineteen-nineteen and her family was never the same after.

'Have you heard from Uncle Hugo recently?' Cece selected a finger-length sandwich of beef and cucumber. Uncle Hugo was a touchy subject, but nevertheless, Cece was interested in her scandalous uncle. He'd fathered a baby with his wife's cousin, Gertie. He and his wife fled from Bombay to Ceylon in disgrace taking the baby with them and Gertie had disappeared in the night and had not been heard of since. This had all happened while Grandmama and Prue where staying with them. Prue never mentioned it, or much of her time in India, which made Cece suspicious that something happened more than just Uncle Hugo having an unwanted illegitimate baby.

'A letter arrived last week that informed me he and Daphne are fine. The baby, Samuel, is not doing as well as they would like. He's a sickly baby and needs a lot of attention.' Grandmama drank some tea. 'Obviously Samuel gets that from his mother's side, for Gertie was a pale-looking creature. Hugo was never sick as a child. He had a constitution of a horse.'

'They will not return to England?'

Grandmama took a small cake from the stand. 'No. They've made Ceylon their home. Hugo doesn't wish to bring the baby back to a cold climate when he is not strong.'

Cece knew this was the reason for Grandmama's upset. She would probably never see her son or grandson again.

'We have veered off-topic.' Grandmama gave a little shake as though ridding her mind of unpleasant thoughts. 'I would like to help educate you on the subject of money.'

'I understood that talking of money was distasteful?' Cece smiled, trying to lighten the mood.

Grandmama snorted. 'In public, yes, and speaking of how much you have is vulgar, certainly, but not the making of it, my dear. How else do people gain huge fortunes if they don't talk about making it with others?'

'Do I want a huge fortune though?' Cece selected a chocolate-coloured macaroon. 'I mean, I'm happy enough with what I have. I don't go anywhere or do anything to spend a fortune, anyway.'

'That is defeatist talk, girl. You can never have enough.'

'But wouldn't that attract the wrong kind of suitor? I don't want a man's attention simply for my money.'

'The way you're going, you should be grateful for any man's consideration. You'll be twenty-four on your next birthday.'

'Prue got married last year aged twenty-four,' Cece defended. 'Why should I be in a hurry? Because I'm not as pretty as Prue?'

'Don't start that nonsense again. You're remarkably pretty in your own right. You need to stop comparing yourself to your sisters. You're intelligent and well read, something men admire even though they don't know it. A stupid wife is embarrassing.'

'So is an ugly one.'

'Stop it. This self-pity is becoming a bore.' Grandmama dabbed at her mouth with a napkin. 'Now Lesley has been most forthcoming about her family's investments.'

Cece sighed and ate another cake.

Grandmama leaned closer. 'Oil.'

'Oil?'

'It's the way forward. I've invested in American oil shares on Lesley's advice. You'd never know it to look at her for the woman dresses like a rag-and-bone man, but she is extremely wealthy. When we met her in Positano, Prue and I understood she only bred race horses, but the main money comes from oil. I think you should invest, too.'

'If you say so.' Cece sipped her tea, finding such a conversation rather tedious. 'I'll draft a letter tonight for you and Lesley to approve of and then send it to Mr Sparks to act on my behalf.'

'Forget Mr Sparks. We'll send it to my advisor in Bond Street. Mr Goldstein is an incredible man, one your grandpapa trusted sincerely.'

'Very well. Now, can we talk of something else, please?' Cece looked over her shoulder as a party of people came into the restaurant, their muffled laughter causing a stir in the quiet room where the only noise was the tinkle of cups on saucers and subdued conversation.

The two women and three men weaved through the tables, but Cece only had eyes for the last man, the tallest of the group. Shocked, her heart thumped irrationally as she watched Monty Pattison smile at something one of the women said.

'Oh, it's Monty.' Grandmama waved to get his attention. 'I've not seen him since that Christmas we spent at Millie and Jeremy's chateau.'

Fighting her panic, Cece saw his slight hesitation as he murmured to the others and then headed for her own table. Monty looked more handsome than before, despite his scars on one side of his face, which he'd received from a bomb blast in the war. She'd never cared about his scars, they and his gentle manner had endeared him to her when he was living at Remington Court, Millie and Jeremy's Yorkshire estate.

'Mrs Fordham. Cece.' Monty kissed both of Grandmama's cheeks and then did the same with Cece.

She held her breath, taking in the sharp musk scent of his aftershave. His dark hair was slicked back neatly, his jaw cleanly shaven, and he wore a smart steel-grey suit. Him standing so close to her made her extremely glad she was sitting down. It was ridiculous the effect he had on her after all this time.

'It is a pleasant surprise to see you, Monty,' Grandmama told him. 'We won't invite you to sit as we can see you are with others.'

'Yes, I am entertaining some clients. They buy a good deal of Chateau Dumont's champagne, and they want to buy more for a ball they are hosting next month.'

'Jeremy will be pleased.' Grandmama smiled. 'Business is good?'

'It is in this country, yes. I'm marketing the chateau's champagne to more and more clients. I may need to take on another salesman shortly.'

'Excellent to hear! Jeremy did the right thing by hiring you to be his London-based man. Well, we'd best not keep you, dear Monty.' Grandmama reached for her silver bag. 'But you must come for dinner soon. I'll send an invitation to your office for next week, shall I? Will you be in the country?'

He gave Cece a fleeting glance. 'Yes, I will. Thank you. I'd like that immensely.'

Grandmama pulled out from her small bag a little black diary and skimmed through it. 'Friday at eight?'

'Perfect. I'd best go. It has been lovely to see you both.' He bowed slightly and left them.

Once he'd gone, Cece breathed more calmly. She was hot and wished she could fan her face. She also wished she'd worn a pretty dress instead of what she'd thrown on this morning without a care. Monty. The man she held all men up to and found them wanting.

Since first meeting him in nineteen-twenty at Millie's new home in Yorkshire, she and Monty had become instant friends and when she returned to York, they had exchanged many letters. She'd fallen in love with him quickly and completely. He'd been the only man she'd wanted since. He knew that too, for she'd confessed her feelings to him when they all spent Christmas at Millie's chateau.

Only, Monty had rejected her. The sting of that rejection still hurt. And now, two years later, she'd seen him again and her rapid beating heart told the same story as before… her feelings for him hadn't changed.

She had to find a way not to be home next Friday.

Chapter Two

Cece stood before the full-length mirror and hoped that her dress was suitable for tonight's dinner. Despite her best intentions to cry off tonight, it simply hadn't been possible. A migraine would have worked, but a small part of her recoiled at such cowardice. Her stubbornness had come to the fore. Why should she shy away from seeing Monty? She'd made a fool of herself two years ago. Hopefully he'd not even remember her gaff. Time to let it go.

She wore her best dress, silly she knew, for the dinner wasn't formal, just her grandmama, Lesley and Monty. Four people. At home. Yet she was wearing make-up and a deep aquamarine blue silk dress shot through with gold thread. Its drop waist and handkerchief hem, which wafted around her ankles, was of the latest style. She'd forgone jewellery to not be overly showy and instead wrapped a thin silver silk scarf around her head and let the ends drape over one shoulder. Pretty silver heels completed the outfit.

She looked the best she'd ever looked. Was it enough? Would such armour help her get through the evening? Should she even care?

But she did. Desperately. She wanted to be stunning.

A light knock and the door opened to reveal, Lettie, the upstairs maid who'd helped style Cece's hair earlier. 'You look very pretty, miss.' She placed clean nightwear into the drawers next to the dressing table. 'Mr Pattison is here. I heard Mr Kilburn announce him a moment ago.'

'I'd best go down then. Kilburn won't want his schedule put out for dinner.' Though they both knew the able butler could manage anything that happened in this house.

'No, let us hope not. I'm helping to serve tonight and he's most fierce when he's displeased.'

Cece laughed. 'I don't believe you.'

Lettie grinned. 'Well, his quiet looks can be fierce.'

Still smiling, Cece tripped lightly down one flight of stairs to the middle floor where the dining room and drawing room were situated in her grandmother's townhouse. The drawing room was wallpapered in deep green and furnished with pieces of walnut. A dark red rug was placed in the centre of the floor under the cream sofas. A roaring fire blazed happily in the fireplace and standing next to it was Monty, appearing resplendent in a black suit.

Cece took a breath and let it out slowly as she crossed the room to receive his kiss on the cheek. 'Welcome, Monty.'

'You look delightful, Cece.'

'Thank you.' She turned away before she blushed and took a seat on the sofa next to Lesley and opposite to her grandmama.

'That dress is most becoming, granddaughter.' Grandmama murmured, sipping her Madeira, as her gaze checked Cece's appearance in detail.

'I've been looking forward to this night all week,' Monty said to the ladies. 'Living alone, one soon grows tired of eating by oneself, or having to go out most nights.'

'It's extremely tiresome, I agree.' Grandmama nodded. 'I do enjoy company.'

'Back home in Kentucky, we eat outside a lot in the summer,' Lesley told them. 'It's a pleasant way to watch the sun go down and see the stars come out.'

'Eat outside? In the evening?' Grandmama stared at Lesley as though the woman had lost her mind. 'Why on earth would you do such a thing?'

'It's like a picnic but at night,' Lesley added.

'I know what it is,' Grandmama scoffed. 'I've done it myself many times as a young woman while travelling in foreign countries, as that is to be expected, standards are different in other countries. However, I thought America to be rather sophisticated. You disappoint me.'

Lesley laughed her loud cackle that made Grandmama sigh and Cece grin. 'I declare, Adeline, you are a cracker!'

'I most certainly am not!'

'You should live a little. You did all that travelling as a wild young woman and now you're an old stick in the mud.'

'I beg your pardon?' Grandmama reared back as though slapped. 'Live a little? If not allowing my staff to deposit my dining room furniture out into the street for us to sit and dine as though we are a circus performance, then yes, I'm an old stick in the mud!'

Lesley roared again and Cece put a hand over her mouth to hide her giggles. Monty, too, chuckled.

'You need to move, Adeline.' Lesley wiped her eyes. 'Find a house with a garden, or some land, even. Learn to breathe clean air.'

'You are displeased with my house, with London?' Grandmama stared at her.

'Not with London, it is a fine city, but the air is thick with smog and fog and coal fumes and smut. You need fresh air.'

'I receive plenty of fresh air when I go visiting.' Grandmama defended. 'London is my home.'

'You should come to Kentucky. Walk the hills on my farm with me.'

'You talk utter nonsense, woman! Walk the hills? I'm eighty. What is wrong with you?'

A discreet cough from Kilburn at the door, allowed Grandmama to usher them into the dining room during which Lesley kept talking.

The long dining table had been set for four at one end, creating a more intimate setting. Cece and Monty sat on one side, Lesley on the other and Grandmama at the head of the table as usual.

Kilburn poured the red wine while Lettie and Susie, the parlourmaid, served the entrée of roasted quail.

Throughout the course, Cece was acutely aware of Monty sitting so close to her. His thigh was only inches from hers and it was hard to concentrate on Lesley's descriptions of Kentucky and neighbouring states as she told Monty about her home.

The second course of grilled salmon was brought and taken away again with Cece barely tasting it, as

Monty spoke of his work. Despite being an earl's son and now a brother to one, he was eager to tell them of his working day, something he'd never considered he'd enjoy as much as he did. Marketing Chateau Dumont's champagne and meeting people from all over the country was a rewarding position and one he was profoundly grateful to Jeremy for.

Grandmama indicated for the second course to be cleared away. 'Jeremy has done tremendously well at rebuilding and expanding Chateau Dumont's estate. Millie writes that he works all hours securing contracts and making sure the vineyards are producing the finest grapes. They are still finding unexploded bombs in the fields; would you believe it? Extremely dangerous.'

'A scary business, indeed. I'm expecting to visit Jeremy and Millie next month,' Monty said, sipping his wine.

'I shall go later in the year for the children's birthdays.' Grandmama nodded. 'It's extremely convenient that both Jonathan and Charles have birthdays so close to each other. It'll be baby Charles's first birthday at the end of October. I'm sure the whole family will be there for it.'

'And his christening. I'm to be a sponsor, godfather, as it were.' Monty beamed. 'I'm deeply honoured.'

Cece looked at him. 'Christening? That's the first I've heard of it.' She glanced at her grandmama. Why hadn't she been told? 'Did you know?'

'I didn't, no.'

'Forgive me.' Monty flushed slightly. 'Jeremy mentioned it in a letter he sent two days ago, an add on to his business instructions. I'm not sure anything is official yet. Only Jeremy mentioned that a christening to coincide with Charles's birthday would be best for them after the harvest, and then he asked if I'd be godfather.'

'Well, that is charming news.' Grandmama raised her wine glass. 'A toast to Charles and Monty.'

Cece lifted her glass with the others. The christening would be another occasion where she saw Monty. Was he to always be someone she constantly bumped into?

As the third course arrived of braised chicken breasts, Monty adjusted his cuffs and sat forward a little. 'Oh, I say! I have just remembered that I have some tickets to an operetta tomorrow night. *Lilac Time* is at the Lyric Theatre. Would you ladies care to join me? Mrs Fordham you have not seen it, have you?'

'No,' Grandmama replied.

'I've heard rave reviews about that show.' Cece drank more wine.

Monty nodded enthusiastically. 'I've been trying to attend a performance for several weeks.'

'Isn't it German?' Grandmama frowned. Since the war Grandmama no longer trusted anything German or bought German made products.

'Austrian. Set in Vienna,' Monty supplied.

Grandmama's gaze narrowed slightly. 'I do not wish to see it but thank you for the invitation.'

'I would like to go,' Cece blurted out before she could help it, and instantly regretted the words.

'Excellent.' Monty's smile didn't reach his eyes.

Cece's heart plummeted further. 'Unless you wish to take someone else? I do not mind.'

'Lesley?' Monty asked. 'Care to join us?'

'I'm afraid I'm booked to attend a card party hosted by some fellow Americans who I met last week in a bookshop in Kensington.' Lesley turned to Grandmama. 'You are coming, too, aren't you, Adeline?'

'Am I?' Grandmama cut into her chicken. 'I suppose I could, yes.'

Cece played with her food and dared not look at Monty.

'It seems it's just you and I then, Cece,' he said.

She detected a slight dullness to his voice. She forced a smile. 'Honestly, if you'd prefer to go along with someone else—'

'He's just said it's you and him, child.' Grandmama gave her a piercing stare. 'Such rudeness.'

Cece swallowed. 'Thank you, Monty. I would like that.'

'It starts at eight.' Monty finished his wine and poured some more before Kilburn had the chance to top his glass up.

'I'll meet you there, shall I?' Cece couldn't summon a smile.

He nodded and concentrated on his food. 'Excellent.'

Cece toyed with a piece of carrot on her plate and tried not to be hurt by his lacklustre tone.

~ ~ ~ ~

In the freezing cold, Cece pulled up the fur collar of her black coat outside the Lyric Theatre and wondered if Monty would even show up. People were jostling to walk past her and not get caught in the drizzly rain that had continued to fall for the last two days. London's lights shimmered in the street puddles and people were miserable as they hurried to get out of the awful winter weather.

'Sorry! I didn't mean to keep you waiting.' Monty appeared from nowhere as a group of people entered the theatre. 'I had a business meeting run late.'

'That's perfectly fine.' She had to dodge to one side as another couple walked past.

'Have you been waiting long?' Monty gave a small glimmer of a smile.

'No, a few minutes, no more.'

He nodded, not making eye contact. 'Shall we go in?'

'Yes.' She stepped into the foyer with him and handed over her coat to the cloakroom attendant and received a reclaim ticket in return.

The theatre was packed. She waited for Monty to shed his coat and hat and returned to her.

'This way.' He took her elbow and guided her up the stairs.

She could smell alcohol on him, making her spirits sink lower. Had it truly been a meeting, or had he been drowning his sorrows in a pub somewhere at the thought of spending the evening with her?

They took their seats and settled as others did the same, and then the lights lowered and there was no chance to talk as the show began.

The opening musical number was uplifting and magical to Cece. Soon she was enraptured as Franz Schubert's compositions filled the theatre and took the audience on a journey of unrequited love.

When finally, the operetta was concluded to rapturous applause, Cece wiped her eyes, embarrassed she'd become so emotional.

'Wasn't it brilliant?' Monty clapped louder, as the audience stood on their feet and cheered.

Cece nodded, too emotional to speak, but smiling at how much she had enjoyed it.

It took them some time to wait and claim their coats and find their way out to the street, the show was popular, and the crowd surged out the doors into the night and the rain.

'Shall we go and have a drink?' Monty asked, donning his coat.

'I'd like that, yes.'

Taking her elbow, Monty steered her through the throng and across the street. They laughed as the rain hit their faces and they hurried along Rupert Street and turned into the first bar they saw.

Shaking off the raindrops, Monty weaved through the drinkers to the bar, pulling Cece behind him. He was so much taller than her and she saw nothing but his back until he made a space for her next to him at the bar.

'Gin and soda?'

She nodded, not really caring. She was still on a high from the performance. 'I am so thrilled that *Lilac Time* was everything I expected.'

'I had a feeling it would be.' Monty paid the barman and passed the glass to Cece.

'I do enjoy theatre productions. Prue prefers the movies, but I still prefer the theatre as the better option.'

'I agree.' Monty spotted a vacant table by the window and quickly grabbed it, laughing as he did so. 'What other shows have you seen?'

'I saw the *Cabaret Girl* a few months ago.'

'I attended that on opening night!' Monty eyes widened in surprise. 'Did you enjoy it? I thought it fabulous!'

'Yes, we did enjoy it. Grandmama and I had dinner first and then went to the show. It was a lovely night. What else have you watched?' Cece drank deeply, she was thirsty and nervous now it was just the two of them.

'Perhaps we should have had dinner too? Are you hungry?'

'No. I ate with Grandmama and Lesley before I came out.' Cece opened her coat, revealing her neck to get some air, the bar was terribly hot with so many bodies squashed into its enclosed space.

'Do you want to go somewhere else?' Monty frowned at the noisy men standing near their table. 'It's not very elite in its clientele.'

'You are a snob!' Cece laughed.

'I've reverted to type I'm afraid.' He looked around. 'Are you sure you want to stay?'

'Yes, it's fine, truly. It's just a little warm in here, don't you think?'

'Very.' He took her coat and his and hung them from the spare chair at their table. 'I've become used to the good life again.'

'I'm pleased for you.' Cece finished her drink and Monty ordered them another.

'It's all thanks to Jeremy. I owe him my life. He saved me when I was homeless and had nothing.'

'Do you miss Remington Court?' Cece asked, accepting another drink from the barman.

Monty shook his head. 'No. After Millie and Jeremy moved to France, the estate was incredibly quiet, lonely. I didn't want to have so much time to ponder over my past.'

'Do you see any of your family?'

'A few times. My eldest brother, the earl, lives in Paddington. Our meetings are not easy. Too much happened when I returned from the war.'

Cece nodded and sipped her drink. Monty's story of his fiancée marrying his brother after she saw Monty's scars was tragic, made more so by his former fiancée killing herself over the guilt she felt. Then Monty's family's estate was declared bankrupt, and they lost it. The family splintered and, in his depression, and pain, Monty walked the roads sleeping rough without a penny to his name. Then, one day, Jeremy found him.

'*The Last Waltz*. Have you seen it?'

Startled out of her thoughts, her eyes widened in question. 'No, I haven't. I must do if you think it's worthwhile?'

'I do, yes. Set in Warsaw in the year of nineteen-ten, before families were destroyed by the war.' Monty glanced down at his drink. 'A time when I believed I had the entire world at my feet.'

'You still do.'

'I was whole then.' He touched his scars.

'You still are.'

He threw back his drink. 'No self-pity tonight.'

She watched him as he ordered another round. Monty had demons and was haunted by his past. Her heart melted for him all over again.

They sat in silence for a few minutes.

'I treated you badly in the past, Cece. I am sorry. You didn't deserve that.'

'Don't!' She held up her hand. 'You were honest with me. I appreciate that. I didn't then, but I do now. You can't force someone to love you.'

Their drinks arrived, and they both drank deeply.

'You had a lucky escape.'

'I did?'

'I wasn't functioning properly back then. Too much had happened to me.' Monty gazed down into his glass. 'Two years ago, I was trying to find my place in the world. You were a complication I didn't need and couldn't handle.'

'I understand.' Could he handle it now? Hope flared for a second.

'I miss our letter writing though. Your letters were always full of information about your day-to-day activities and I adored them. Through your letters I had a glimpse of a normal family life at a time when I had no one.'

She didn't know what to say and so drank some more.

Monty drank as well and sat back in the chair, more relaxed. 'I was worried about seeing you tonight, just the two of us.'

'So was I.'

'I'm glad you came.'

'Did you think I wouldn't be incredibly fun?' She snorted. 'I don't blame you. I'm not known for being fun, that's Prue's role.'

'Then what is your role?'

'I don't have one. I'm not worthy of a classification in my family, not yet. I'm not defined by anything. Oh, except perhaps my self-pity. Grandmama says I am full of it.'

'And are you?'

'Yes.' She nodded and stared out of the rain-drenched window. 'I wish I wasn't.'

'Then don't be. Only you can change it.'

She sighed deeply. 'I simply feel my life is seeping away and I've accomplished nothing at all. I'm not married. I'm not a mistress of a fine house. I'm not a mother. I'm not an explorer, or a socialite, or run a business...' She finished another gin and tonic. 'I am simply nothing.'

'Boohoo, woe is you!' Monty stared at her with a smile. 'Your self-pity is terrifying!'

Suddenly, she laughed and got up to go to the bar. Something she'd never done in her life. 'You know what?'

'What?'

'I actually accept I'm the most boring person I know!'

He raised his empty glass to her. 'That makes you accomplished at something!'

She swiped at his shoulder, chuckling.

For hours they sat in the bar at the little wooden table by the window and talked and laughed and watched as the busy London streets grew quiet until the landlord asked them politely to leave.

Staggering out into the rain, Monty stumbled and Cece held him up. Together, arm in arm, they laughed at nothing and headed for another street where they might find a taxi as the rain fell harder.

'What time is it?' Cece asked, her hair dripping.

From his waistcoat pocket, Monty took out a fob watch and peered at it under the streetlight. 'Twenty past two.'

'Good lord!' Cece swayed, blinking to clear her fuzzy mind. 'That's awfully late.'

'We need to get you home.' Monty wiped a hand over his face.

'Where do you live?' she asked, shivering. The rain of the cold winter's night was beginning to seep through her coat and clothes as they walked along Coventry Street, which was empty save from the odd lady of the night sulking in shadows and the road cleaners sweeping up the horse droppings and litter.

'I've an apartment on Dean Street.' He waved vaguely behind him. 'Over there somewhere.'

'Is it close?'

'Not far at all.' He stopped and stared at her. 'You're shivering.'

'I'm becoming extremely cold.'

'Do you want to come to my apartment and warm up? I can scour the streets and find a taxi while you're safe and warm.'

'That would be most satisfactory, my good man.' She nodded and swayed.

He bowed and stumbled.

She laughed and grabbed his arm, then giggled again as a raindrop dripped from the overhang of a building and splattered onto Monty's nose.

He frowned and tucked her close against him. Dean Street wasn't far at all and soon he was fumbling with his keys to open the door to the building.

Drunk, Monty took several moments to unlock the door and let her in. They climbed the stairs to the second floor, groaning that it was too far.

Eventually, Monty stopped at number seven and unlocked it.

Inside, the room was dark and cold.

'Bloody hell it's freezing!' Monty shuddered. 'My apologies.'

'Is there a fire?'

'A gas one, yes.' He fumbled for a switch to turn on the gas lamp by the door and once on the small room flooded with golden light to show a fireplace, a sofa and a kitchenette off at an angle.

'What's in here?' Cece opened a door to reveal a bedroom. The bed was neatly made, and a few clothes hung over the bottom of it.

'You could sleep in here, if you wish and I'll be on the sofa. You could go home first thing.' He spoke from behind her shoulder and when she turned, she was standing awfully close to him.

His eyes narrowed, heavy with drink and something else.

'I could stay,' she whispered, suddenly acutely aware of him as a man.

'Your grandmama…'

'Will be fast asleep and will assume I'm in my own bed.' She watched his expression, waiting for his refusal, his excuses to send her on her way. She stiffened her backbone ready for the hurt of his rejection.

Instead, he pulled her into his arms and kissed her.

She hadn't been prepared for that and it took a moment for her to gather her shocked wits to act. She gripped his wet shoulders and kissed him back with an urgency that surprised them both.

Spurred on, Monty shrugged off her long black coat and his own. Cece helped him with his suit jacket and her own cashmere jacket. She shivered as his hands touched her bare arms. The room was icy cold.

Monty shuffled her backwards towards the bed, and in one movement bent down and yanked the blankets back.

Cece's body took control, and all she wanted was this man. She unbuttoned his waistcoat, and it landed on the floor as she kicked off her shoes. She pulled his shirt from his trousers and gloried in running her hands under it and touching his chest.

His intake of breath made her smile and when he pulled his shirt over his head, she kissed his chest, running her tongue over his nipples.

His groan filled the dark room and with a swift tug her dark red dress was over her head and joined his clothes on the floor.

Pushing her onto the bed, Monty followed her quickly, covering her body with his and deepening his kisses until she could think of nothing else.

His hand roamed her body under her satin slip, and he kissed her breasts and neck, moaning his need of her. Her legs curled around his back and she arched into his body, luxuriating in the power she had as her hands touched and caressed him, making him moan even more.

For the first time in her life, Cece felt wanted, desirable, and admired. She was proud of her body, pleased she was slender with a nice bust and a little waist and when Monty stripped himself of his underwear, she did the same, except her silk stockings which she kept on.

The cold, their lives beyond the bed were forgotten, as Monty made love to her. His eagerness matched her own. She wanted this like nothing else in the world. He was hers. She'd loved him for years.

She didn't hesitate when he pushed her legs open and welcomed him wholly. There was no pain, just a fullness that surprised her, before it too was forgotten as Monty moved slowly and then with increasing speed. A mounting pressure built inside her. Something needed to be reached, but she didn't know what. Just when she thought the pressure was too much, Monty groaned and stopped moving.

Cece opened her eyes, frowning. What had happened? Monty shuddered and groaned and then flopped down beside her.

All the built-up pressure and pleasure subsided. Cece lay there, clutching Monty's shoulders and feeling the cold seep over her bare skin.

Was that it?

She moved slightly. Monty snored.

Astonished, she slipped sideways out from under him and he continued to snore.

'Monty?' she whispered, shivering.

He slept like the dead.

Annoyed, bewildered, Cece grabbed her clothes and quickly dressed. She stood at the side of the bed, staring at his naked back and buttocks, and didn't have a clue what to do next.

She couldn't climb back into bed with him. The cold light of realisation at what she'd just done dawned swiftly and hit her like a hammer.

She had slept with a man who wasn't her husband. A hot blush crept up her neck. Grabbing her coat, she put it on and then her shoes, before quickly throwing the blankets over Monty's naked body.

For a long time, she stood there, but he didn't move and continued gently snoring.

What would he say to her when he woke?

Unexpectedly, the idea of facing him when he woke horrified her. She ran from the bedroom, the apartment and the building.

In the shadowy slippery wet streets of London, she ran, not caring where she headed.

Chapter Three

Cece woke to a knock on her bedroom door. Grandmama walked in, dressed in a pale mauve dress and a long black coat ready to go to church with Lesley.

'Sleepy head. You're not up.'

'No, I don't feel too fantastic.' That was the understatement of the year for Cece felt utterly awful. Her head was banging, and she was so tired from lack of sleep.

'You don't look the best at all.' Grandmama put a hand to Cece's forehead. 'You're a little hot. What time did you get home last night? It must have been extremely late for I didn't fall asleep until well after one o'clock.'

'Umm… I came home just after two. Monty and I went for a drink after the show and then it took an age to find a cab. I ended up hiring an old hansom, the horse was a dreadful nag that plodded along and the old man driving it seemed to nod off regularly. I was dreadfully cold by the end of it.'

'A hansom? Indeed, it's been a while since I was in one. We are spoilt with motor cars now.' Grandmama stepped towards the door. 'Well, we are off to church. Lesley will book her passage home tomorrow, so I shan't have the bother of her for much longer.'

'You'll miss her.'

'Apparently, so I've been told.' Grandmama reached the door. 'Stay in bed. It's Sunday and we have no visitors today.'

'I'll come down a bit later.'

'Did you enjoy the show?'

Cece thought of the operetta, which seemed like a hundred years ago now. 'I did,' she answered truthfully.

'Good. Good!'

When Grandmama closed the door behind her, Cece snuggled back into the warm covers and stared at the ceiling.

She'd slept only for a brief time around dawn, the rest of the night and morning she'd thought of Monty, of what they had done.

What would happen now?

Was he disgusted by her?

Amazingly, she didn't regret her actions. She had relished every second of being in his bed. She'd always enjoyed his company and had wanted him for so long. She thought she'd put him behind her after that terrible Christmas, yet one look from him, one touch and she was lost to all reason. She should have been stronger, admittedly. However, deep down she knew he didn't love her and last night had been her one chance to have him before he cast her aside again, which he undoubtedly would do.

She sighed despondently. If only he loved her as she did him. Last night had taken her a step further in her life. She'd become a woman, a proper woman, like her sisters. True, she wasn't married as they were, but no one needed to know what she'd done.

Did that make her a woman of loose morals now? All those times she censured Prue for being flirty, and here she was no longer a virgin and unmarried. Guilt flamed her cheeks.

Would Monty think of her differently? What *did* he even think of her?

The agonizing thoughts flew around in her head making her frustrated and annoyed. Staying in bed wasn't helping.

A walk was needed. She dressed quickly in a thick tweed skirt with a cream blouse and navy cardigan. Stockings and solid black shoes completed the outfit and a caramel-coloured cloche hat was pulled down over her hair.

She reached the bottom of the stairs, ready to ask Kilburn for her coat when the doorbell rang.

Kilburn answered it while Cece fetched her coat from the hall closet.

'Oh, Mr Pattison, welcome, sir,' Kilburn said, opening the door wider to allow Monty to step through.

Cece froze, one arm in her coat. 'Monty.'

He had the grace to look shamefaced. 'Cece, can we talk?'

She nodded.

'You were going out?' he asked.

'Only for a walk.'

'Then I'll come with you.' Monty turned and went outside again, leaving her no choice but to don her coat and follow him.

They walked to the end of Upper Grosvenor Street without speaking, crossed the busy Park Lane and into Hyde Park. A good many horse riders were out and, in the chilly air, their mounts snorted clouds of misty vapours. Church bells rang across the city to announce the conclusion of Sunday morning service and Cece wondered if Grandmama would return home or go out for lunch somewhere.

'I wasn't sure if you'd be home or had gone to church,' Monty said, his coat collar pulled up against his cheeks and his trilby hat low over his eyes.

'I wasn't feeling like it this morning. I didn't get a lot of sleep.'

'About last night…'

She glanced away over the park, watching the dog walkers. 'Last night…'

'I apologise profusely.' He didn't look at her as they walked. 'I behaved in an ungentlemanly manner, and I am extremely sorry, Cece. What must you think of me?'

'Of you?' She stopped and stared at him. 'There were two of us, you know.'

'Yes, but I should have shown more restraint.'

She frowned. 'Are you saying because I'm a woman I have no capabilities of having restraint should a man lavish his attentions on me?'

'No, I mean… You see…'

'Monty, I was fully in control of myself last night and I did what I wanted to do.'

'But we had so much to drink, it impaired our sensibilities, made us rash.'

'Perhaps, but I don't regret it, Monty, none of it.'

He watched another horse rider go by.

Cece's heart fell to her shoes. 'You do regret it though, don't you?'

'I feel I took advantage of you and I'm not proud of it.' Still, he didn't look at her.

'I gave what I wanted to give, Monty.'

'I was wrong to take it.'

'Why?'

'Because… because I know how you… well, how you feel about me. Unless, of course, that is no longer true?'

'It's still true,' she admitted. There was no point in lying.

His sigh was long and deep.

Cece turned away. 'Really, Monty, think nothing of it.'

'Wait, Cece.'

She swung back to him, expectantly. 'Yes?'

'You are a fine, wonderful woman, and I wish I loved you… However, I like you a lot, an awful lot, really, I do. So, perhaps…'

'What?' She scowled at him, not understanding.

'Perhaps we could give it a go, you know, see if it, if you and I, might lead somewhere.'

For what seemed an age she stared at him, seeing the uncertainty in his eyes. 'If you had said that two years ago, I would have pounced.' She gave a little smile. 'I would have wrung some emotion from you just by sheer will. I'd have taken anything you were willing to give, but you see I've watched my two sisters marry men they love, men who in return love them completely.' Emotion built in her throat. 'I want that, too.' Her voice cracked. 'I want a man to love me so much that he can't live without me. Why should I settle for anything less?'

He nodded. 'Absolutely. It's what you deserve. Total love and commitment. All I can offer is friendship, companionship.'

'And it's not enough.' Her smile was broken, as was her heart, again.

'I'm sorry.'

'It's not your fault. You can't make yourself love someone.'

They began walking back to Grandmama's house, the silence a wall between them.

Cece stopped at the roadside. 'There is no point in you coming with me. Goodbye, Monty.'

'I'll see you at Charles's christening.' He took her hand and smiled. 'I'm glad we can still be friends.'

She couldn't answer him and quickly crossed Park Road. *Friends.* What a weak word that was when she wanted so much more. She had friends and acquaintances galore. She didn't need Monty for a friend. Couldn't bare it, actually. After today she hoped to never see him again.

'Well, it is done. *No more,*' she murmured into the frigid air.

Enough was enough. Monty wasn't for her, that was clear. She had to find another path to take.

~ ~ ~ ~

In the drawing room, Cece sat on the sofa before the fire reading a book when Grandmama walked in holding letters in her hand.

'I'm home from that dreadful Florence Bright's luncheon. I shan't go again.'

'You say that every month, yet you still go.'

'That's because I hope each month, she has found some common sense. But it still eludes her. The woman continues to serve wilted salads and dry cakes. Her cook should be let go and allowed to work in a zoo where the animals wouldn't care that her food is unpalatable. And, worst of all, she invites Reverend Finchley and treats him as though he is some sort of demi-god. The man is an imbecile. He is the only person I know who is against education for girls. He's still living in the last century, the pompous old goat. Imagine not allowing girls to be educated?'

'What are his reasons?'

'*Girls should be knowledgeable in only household and family matters.* He said those words to me!' Grandmama's blue eyes widened dramatically.

'Incredible.'

'I had half a mind to slap him with my limp crab paste sandwich which Florence declares is the height of sophistication, yet it tastes like wallpaper glue.'

Cece laughed.

'I can't consider that she is the daughter of an admiral. She's as intelligent as a drain pipe. She might be Bright by name but certainly not by nature. And if the damned Reverend Finchley gets his way all women would turn out like Florence!'

'Thankfully, he is in a minority.'

'He'd not like it that you are reading. Heaven forbid you have some intellect.'

'Well, this James Joyce book isn't as good as all the hype makes it out to be. I can't get my mind into it, so maybe the reverend would laugh at me instead.' She closed *Ulysses* and put it to one side. She couldn't blame the book, really; her mind had been unfocused for two weeks since the night with Monty. Despite all her reasoning, all her inner rationalising, she'd still held out the hope he'd see her in a different light.

Ridiculously, she had expected a letter from him saying he'd changed his mind, or for him to call and take her out for tea somewhere or even for a bunch of flowers to be delivered. But nothing. And as each day passed and the likelihood of him calling on her grew more faint, she became more despondent and angrier at the fates that allowed her to love a man who thought nothing of her in return.

So, she threw herself into the good works she'd been brought up to do. She helped various London charities in any way she could, she answered her correspondence with the York charities she was involved with, giving them money and ideas to raise more money. She shopped, she visited friends and acquaintances, she accepted all the invitations sent to her. In the two weeks since that fateful night, she'd even been back to York twice to attend a ball and a dinner party.

Grandmama sat by the window so she could read her letters by the last of the afternoon sunlight. 'A note from Prue saying she and Brandon are off to attend a movie film tonight and wanted to know if we want to go with them? It's a comedy, apparently.'

'No, thank you.' Cece unfolded her legs, which had been tucked up beneath her. 'I'm a little tired. I've had such a busy day. I've not been home long myself.'

'I've never seen you so busy. You're hardly home. Have you joined every charity committee in London?'

'No, not quite.' She rose as Kilburn entered the room to add more logs to the fire.

'I expect you're on more boards than I am now.' Grandmama opened her next letter.

'Hardly, but I like to be busy. I've a fundraising meeting for the St Anne's School in the morning and then there's a new exhibition of Italian artists at the National Gallery that I want to see.'

When Kilburn left the room, Cece stood in front of the fire and watched the flames lick the new wood.

'And in the afternoon?' Grandmama asked, reading her letter.

'I have letters to write to Millie, Mama and Cousin Agatha, plus there are a good many invitations to answer. The committees I'm involved with in York need my advice on certain things as well.' She stared at the flames and realised none of that grabbed her enthusiasm.

Grandmama waved the letter in her hand. 'This is from Lesley, she has arrived in America and is home and settled again. Enjoying life on the ranch and her niece is pregnant. She sends her good wishes to you.'

'That's nice. I'll write to her, too.'

'We have dinner at the Thorndales tomorrow night, remember.'

Cece nodded, her mind drifting. 'Yes, and that reminds me that I shall need to call in at Selfridges and purchase some more stockings.'

Grandmama opened her last letter and after reading for a moment, gasped. 'Well!'

'What?' Burning from the heat, Cece moved back to the sofa, knowing she should start writing her correspondence but not in the mood to do so.

'Your mama is selling Elm House.' Grandmama's eyes were wide with shock.

'No!' Cece couldn't believe it.

'She says she is moving permanently to Paris. Jacques's apartment is too small, and they want to buy something else. Elm House stands empty most of the year. They can use the proceeds of the sale to buy something in Paris.'

A great sadness weighed heavily on Cece's chest. 'That is my home! She can't sell Elm House!'

Grandmama's pitying look said differently. 'It does make sense, my dear, but it will be a sorry day when it's sold, for I greatly enjoy being in York. I've been going there since your mama married your papa. Elm House is a second home to me.'

'It's not fair! Why isn't she telling me this news herself? It is my home, too.'

'Yes, I agree, dear, she should have consulted you, but since her marriage to Jacques your mama has thought of no one but herself.'

'Where will I live?' Cece murmured, close to tears.

'With me, of course, here in London, or in Paris with your mama and Jacques.'

Her vision blurred as tears gathered but she fought them from spilling over. 'No, not Paris. Jacques is a lovely man, but I don't want to live with him.'

'Come, dearest.' Grandmama rose and put her arms around Cece. 'It'll all work out in the end.'

'Will it though?' Anger replaced the tears and a hard knot of rage burned in her chest. 'Mama wishes to be rid of Elm House, my home, and I'm forced to move away from York, and none of this is considered without me? Why am I always the last to know anything?'

'I'm certain a letter is on its way to you. It'll arrive in the morning post, you'll see.'

'It makes no difference now. The decision has been made, hasn't it? There has been no thought to me at all.'

'You have a home here, Cece.' Grandmama moved away and sat on the embroidered chair at the writing desk in the corner. 'I'll write to your mama immediately and ask for more explanation as to her future plans for you.'

'Her plans for me? I'm not a child.' Cece scoffed. 'Mama doesn't have any care about me. She is mindful only of Jacques now. She has her life in Paris, I am an afterthought, as always.'

'That's not true.'

'Isn't it? Then tell me why she hasn't come back to England to see how I'm faring?'

'She knows you're here with me, that's why. Am I not taking care of you well enough?'

'I'm not a child, Grandmama! I don't need to be taken care of like an infant.'

'Then stop acting like one!' Grandmama snapped. 'Violet is making choices for her life. She's moved to Paris to be with her new husband. Elm House is now redundant. You're a grown woman with many options on where you wish to live. London, Paris, Millie's chateau, for I'm certain she'd love to have you. Or simply spend your days travelling between all three, even Prue would want you.'

'I'm going home, while I still have one.' Cece ran from the room and upstairs to pack. She rang for Lettie, then emptied the drawers of her clothes.

'Yes, miss?' Lettie asked, coming into the room.

'Ask Kilburn to bring my suitcases, please, and to have Higgins bring the car around. Then come back and help me pack, please.'

'Yes, miss.'

During the hectic packing, Grandmama came into the bedroom. 'When will you return?'

'I don't know. When the house is sold.' Cece pinned a hat on and changed her house shoes for sturdy warm boots.

'You'll get the night train to York?'

'Yes.'

'Send me a note when you get there. I'll have the kitchen make you up a hamper for the journey. Oh, and I've sent Kilburn out to telegram Forbes at Elm House to expect you. The last thing you want is to arrive to no welcome.'

'Thank you.'

'I see you going to Elm House as a clever idea. You can help ready it for sale. Your mama will want the furniture sold as well, I should imagine.'

'Then Mama should get back over here and oversee it herself.'

'Why should she? There's you to do it.'

Cece clenched her jaw, not wanting to say something she'd later regret.

~ ~ ~ ~

From a chilly York Station not long after dawn, Cece hired a taxi to take her to the outskirts of York and the grand house that was Elm House, her family home. Since her mama's move to Paris, the chauffeur had been let go and Papa's motor car sold, which had saddened Cece for she'd learnt to drive in the motor car, and it was another part of Papa lost to her.

The morning was grey and overcast as she walked up the front steps to the door, but Forbes, the family butler, opened the door with a warm smile.

'Miss Cece, so lovely to have you home again.'

'Thank you, Forbes. It's good to be home.' She left him to pay for the taxi and bring in her luggage.

In the drawing room, a cheery fire blazed in the grate. The furniture and ornaments were as they should be, clean, ordered and in their rightful place. The room was comfortable, familiar. Under this roof so many memories had been made. She pulled off her gloves and unpinned her hat, staring at the portrait of Mama and Papa on their wedding day, which was hung on the wall beside one of the long sash windows. What was to be done with it? Mama wouldn't want it.

Sally, the parlourmaid, passed the doorway and took her luggage upstairs, while Forbes came in and waited for her to give him instructions. However, what could she tell him? Had Mama sent word about the house being put up for sale?

'Has Mrs Marsh, I mean Mrs Baudin, Mama,' she stumbled over her words, 'been in touch lately?'

'Yes, miss. Just yesterday I received a letter from her with the shocking news that Elm House is to be sold.' He stood with his hands behind his back, his expression one of sorrow.

Cece bit back the remark that even the staff had known before her. Instead, she summoned a forced smile. 'You mustn't worry, Forbes, and let the other staff know that your references will be top quality and there will be a generous bonus given to you when you leave.' She'd just made that last bit up but damn it, if she had to oversee the selling of her beloved home and be the one to put these good people out of work then she'd make sure her conscience was clear.

'Thank you, miss. That will put the others at ease somewhat. Have you had breakfast, miss?'

'No, that would be wonderful. There is a lot we must do in the next few weeks, you and I are going to be busy.'

'Indeed, miss.'

From her bag she took out several letters and handed them to him. 'Will you post those for me, please?'

He bowed and left the room.

Cece sighed. On the train, she'd written letters to Mama asking for instructions, and then wrote to Millie and Prue imploring them to change Mama's mind. During the night she had lain awake on the narrow bed in the carriage and pondered the situation. She could stretch out the sale of the house for at least a year, perhaps, if she took her time sorting out the personal belongings and selling of pieces of furniture. She'd ask her sisters if they wanted items from the rooms.

Going upstairs, she entered her bedroom and gazed around the pretty room she'd always found to be her sanctuary. It's pale pink flowery wallpaper, the soft bed with its large padded bedhead. The cream damask curtains and the sturdy walnut wardrobe, drawers and dressing table, all of which held her possessions from since she was a small child. Shelves of books and trinket boxes lined one wall and below the window was a cushioned window seat where she'd spent hours reading and daydreaming.

A knock on the door interrupted her thoughts. Sally came in and bobbed her knees. 'Excuse me, miss, your breakfast is ready, and Mrs Hood asks if it pleases you would you spare her a moment afterwards to sort out the meals for while you're at home?'

'Yes, that is quite all right. I'll send for her after I've eaten.' Cece left the bedroom and walked along the gallery to the staircase. 'Oh, and, Sally, where are Iris and Enid? Why are you working up on this floor as well as downstairs?'

'They've left, miss. Last week. Iris got married and Enid found a job at Rowntree's Chocolate Factory.'

'And they've not been replaced?' Cece asked, again annoyed that she'd not been told that their two upper bedchamber maids had gone.

'No, miss. There seemed to be no point, and the mistress said not to bother in her last letter to Mr Forbes.'

'Thank you.' Cece went downstairs and into the dining room. A fire had been recently lit, but it wasn't throwing out enough heat to make the large room comfortable.

As Forbes entered the room, Cece paused in scooping up scrambled eggs from the warmer on the sideboard. 'Forbes, after I've finished my breakfast, I would like to see both you and Mrs Hood, please.'

'Yes, miss.' He poured her a cup of coffee.

Cece ate with her mind not on the food. She was ravenous but the task ahead gave her much to think about.

In the end, she pushed away her plate and asked Forbes to bring a fresh pot of coffee into the drawing room and fetch Mrs Hood.

'So,' Cece started as she faced them, 'I am waiting on further instructions from my mama about the sale of the house, but, until then, we must continue as normal. I've been informed that Iris and Enid have left us. Are there any more staff shortages I should know about?'

Mrs Hood, a plump, kind woman, coughed discreetly. 'Well, miss, I've lost two girls in the kitchen to the chocolate factories in town. Better wages and shorter hours they said, and I couldn't argue with that as the mistress wasn't able to match the wages, and as she said, and rightly so, no one barely lives here any more so there's no need for a large number of staff to run an empty home.'

But I live here… Cece wanted to cry out, though she didn't, of course. 'Yes, understandable. Anyone else?'

'One of the young lads who worked in the garden has gone, miss,' Forbes mentioned. 'We have Sally in the house, and myself, Thomas, too, but his role is unspecified. He does a bit of everything now. I was training him to be an under butler, but well…'

'Yes, I see.'

'Then in the kitchen there is Mrs Hood and just one girl, Rose.'

'Indeed, we are in a sorry state, are we not?' Cece tried to make light of it, but it was hard. Before, only a few years ago, the house had been so full of family and staff it was difficult to find a quiet space to yourself for more than a minute.

'Will you be entertaining, miss?' Mrs Hood asked.

'No, I shan't be, unless it's my cousin, Miss Agatha. So, order the food as you would normally, Mrs Hood, for the staff. I will eat the same. There is no need for you to make fancy meals just for me.'

'Very good, miss.'

'Is there anything else you wish to discuss with me?' Cece wrapped her hands around the coffee cup, feeling desolate.

'Only that,' Mrs Hood glanced at Forbes, 'only that we are unsure of when to apply for our next positions. How long are we to remain here, miss?'

'I do not know, Mrs Hood, I'm sorry. However, there will be no hard feelings if any of you find new positions before the house is sold. As I told Forbes, you will receive a reference and a bonus when you leave.'

'Thank you, miss.'

Cece stood, bringing the meeting to a close.

Cece

Left alone, Cece stepped into her papa's study and shut the door. This room had no fire in it and coldness penetrated her clothes making her shiver. She ran her fingertips along the desk, her gaze dropping to the framed etching of Cece and her sisters when they were small girls, which had always sat on Papa's desk. She picked it up and hugged it.

Sitting on his big leather chair, she absentmindedly opened the desk drawers, finding papers and ledgers. There was a faint smell of cigar and the mustiness of an unused room. This room reminded her so strongly of her papa it was as though he would walk through the door at any moment. Tears built hot behind her eyes. Soon she'd have nowhere to go to feel close to Papa. This house was his home, bought for his new wife when they married. He and Mama had left their marks in each room. Every room had a memory.

How could she part with it?

Chapter Four

With her head covered in a scarf and wearing an old apron Sally had given her, Cece was in the dusty attics sorting amongst the trunk and crates. Years of storing things no longer needed had created a multitude of items, which at first overwhelmed her but now, two days later, she was making some head way with.

Forbes and Thomas, along with Sally, were her team as she sifted through the dust-covered treasures.

'Miss, this crate is full of musty clothes, for little girls it looks like.' Sally pulled out little cotton and linen dresses in white with coloured sashes and flounces of lace.

'Charity pile.' Cece had grown hard at seeing reminders of yesteryear. The first day she had cried when finding nursery toys, and small pairs of ice skates, drawings and books, dolls and spinning tops. Memories had flooded her mind, taking her back to when she was a small girl following her sisters around, waiting for them to notice her.

'This rocking horse, miss?' Thomas asked from the corner of the attic.

'All children's things are going to the Ashton Home for Women and Children. I know Mrs Victoria Ashton will be grateful for anything we give them.'

'I heard Mr Joseph Ashton hasn't been well,' Sally piped up. 'My cousin works in the laundry at the Home. She says old Mr Ashton refuses to rest, despite his wife telling him to.'

'They both must be in their seventies,' Cece said, sorting through a box of former household ledgers. 'They are good people. I'll send a note to Mrs Ashton and ask when the best day would be to deliver all this.'

Forbes climbed up the steep steps. 'Excuse me, miss, but your cousin, Miss Marsh has arrived.'

'Oh splendid!' Cece scrambled from the debris of the attic and down the narrow stairs to the gallery, untying her apron as she did so.

At the bottom of the staircase Agatha waited, looking up. 'What on earth have you been doing, Cece?'

'Sorting through the attic.' Cece hurried down to her and hugged her tight. 'It's so good to see you, Aggie.'

Her cousin remained the same. When everything else changed in the world, Agatha Marsh still wore dowdy dark coloured skirts or shapeless tunic dresses. Her brown mousy hair was always worn in a bun at her neck and her poor eyesight rendered her half blind without her glasses. She hated fuss and arguments and never got a word in when Cece and her sisters were about. Yet she was loved unconditionally by the whole family.

'And you, Cousin. I was incredibly happy to receive your note saying you were back in York.'

Cece led her into the drawing room. 'How is Uncle Edmund?'

'He's well. Why are you in the attics?' Agatha asked, sitting down on the sofa.

'Mama wants to sell the house.'

'No!'

'Yes. A terrible blow I shan't recover from.' Cece still hadn't completely accepted the decision.

'How utterly awful. Where will you live? In Paris with Aunt Violet?'

'No, in London.' Cece shrugged. 'I've not completely made up my mind yet. However, it seems Grandmama's house is the only sensible choice, really.'

'Gosh. I'm stunned. This house is like a second home to me.' Agatha took a handkerchief out and dabbed her eyes.

'Do not cry, Aggie! I beg you!'

'I'm sorry, it's just so sudden. I will barely see any of you again.'

'Yes, well you can thank Mama for that.'

'Can you not buy the house yourself?'

'I have thought of it, but to live here by myself would feel so sad and lonely. It's such a wretched decision!'

A knock on the door preceded Forbes who carried a tea tray. 'I've put the second post on the tray, miss.'

'Thank you.' Cece selected the letters. 'Will you pour, Aggie? This letter is from Mama.'

Opening her mama's letter, Cece began to read.

Dearest Cece,

Cece

Darling, do not be angry with me for my decision.
You know as well as I do that living in York is no
longer beneficial when Jacques's home and work is in
Paris. The little time I would spend at Elm House
hardly makes it worthwhile to keep it on. Please
understand. It was a difficult decision to make, and
one I talked over with Jacques and Millie, and they
both agreed it was a sensible thing to do. Millie, like
yourself, is sad that the house will no longer be ours,
but as I explained to her, life goes on. Elm House was
your papa's home, and without him, I felt lonely and
rather miserable living there. It made me miss him
even more. I expected him to come home each
evening, and he never did. I know I might sound silly
to you, but the house gave me no comfort, and only
worsened my despair of losing him.

For that reason, I would rather not return to York
to oversee the sale. I hope, and would be eternally
grateful to you, my dear daughter, if you would do
this one task for me? I leave it all at your discretion
with regard to selling the furniture. I have no need for
any of it.

Your papa's belongings can be distributed
between you and your sisters. My personal things can
be sent to me here in Paris. I'm certain Millie and
Prue will write to you and between the three of you,
things can be divided as needed. I've enclosed a card
and details for an agent to sell the house. He comes
with a highly-recommended reputation. I have
already written to him and asked him to call on you.
We have discussed the price, etc.

I know you must be disappointed by this decision,
but you'll always have a home in Paris with Jacques
and I, or in London with your grandmama.

Sometimes we must let the past go, my dearest. Forgive me.

> *With love,*
> *Mama.*
> *Paris.*
> *March 5ᵗʰ 1923.*

Cece glanced at the little card in the envelope and gave the letter to Agatha to read, while she opened the next letter from Prue.

Darling Cece.

Goodness, I don't know what to say to you, but changing Mama's mind isn't going to work. She wants Elm House gone, and I cannot in all honesty blame her, she has moved on with her life. It is difficult to imagine, however, that we no longer have a childhood home. I shall miss it dreadfully. I spoke to Brandon about buying the place, but I decided it would hold too many memories and wouldn't be the same without Papa and everyone being there. After his death nothing was the same, was it? Also, Brandon's family already have a house in Yorkshire, so we wouldn't need another one.

I'm sorry this has fallen on your shoulders to sort out. I would come and help but I am travelling to New York tomorrow to meet with some fashion designers for the magazine. I know you'll do a magnificent job of closing up the house and selling it.

My personal things from my bedroom can be forwarded on to me here in London.

We must catch up as soon as I return from America.

> *Much love,*

Cece

'It all seems very final, doesn't it?' Agatha sighed. 'Aunt Violet has no intentions of returning to York.'

'No, and neither does Prue. She's left it all to me to sort out while she goes to New York.'

'New York? How wonderful.'

'Yes, that is Prue's life.'

'Don't be too hard on her, she does have a particularly prominent position within the magazine.'

'You seem very informed about it.'

'We write as often as we can, and she tells me all about it.'

'Indeed, she would. She'd love to inform you how amazing her life is. The perfect husband, the perfect and very modern job in a woman's magazine and living in a perfect house in London.'

'Stop it, Cece. Don't be bitter.' Agatha's sympathetic tone grated on Cece's nerves.

'I'm *not* bitter.'

'Really? You've always been jealous of Prue. It's time to let it go.'

Cece jerked from the chair. 'Don't lecture me, Agatha. I can get that from Grandmama any time I wish!'

'You will never be happy if you continue to compare yourself with Prue, or Millie, or anyone.'

'I don't wish to discuss this. I have enough to worry about.'

'Cece, you are my dearest cousin, the one person I am closer to than anyone else, and I want you to be happy.' Agatha stood and clasped Cece's hands.

'Look at me, for heaven's sake. There are four Marsh girls, and I'm the plainest of us all. Imagine how difficult it has been for me growing up amongst you three beauties. It was torture.'

Cece stared at her. It was the first time Agatha had ever mentioned such a thing.

Agatha gave a watery smile. 'I had to learn to live with it or be forever miserable. It hasn't been easy, and I hated the balls and parties we attended together for I was never picked to dance with until last. But now, well, I've come to the realisation that comparing myself to you three didn't change anything except my mood. So, I gave up on it.'

'I never knew that. I'm sorry.' Chastised, Cece squeezed Agatha's hands gently. 'You are too good, Aggie.'

'Not really. There are times I curse my life, but then I do charity work and see how others in society suffer so cruelly and I simply force myself to be content.'

'I wonder if I'll ever be content.'

'You will. One day. Now, I'll come back tomorrow and help you list everything in the house. After cataloguing Papa's library, I'm an old hand at writing lists!'

'Thank you. I'd like that.'

~ ~ ~ ~

Cece stood in the library, placing books into crates that were being sent as donations to York Library. Special volumes had been chosen to keep by Uncle Edmund yesterday when he'd come with Agatha for dinner and he was happy to take them, having admired them for years.

With each shelf becoming empty, the character of the room paled. Unlike the bedrooms upstairs which had been stripped of personal affects when Millie and Prue and Mama left to be married, the rooms downstairs had held on to the memories and familiarity she'd always known.

Paintings, ornaments, lamps and furniture were going to auction next week. The agent selling the house, Mr Roth, visited last week extolling the virtues of the house and gardens, exclaiming the sale wouldn't take long as he was advertising in major newspapers up and down the country.

Cece hoped he was wrong, and the sale wouldn't go through for years. She decided she'd stay in York and at Elm House until the last possible moment. With the house packed up, she'd re-established her volunteering duties at different charities and calling on old friends.

Soon her diary was full of invitations to parties and dinners, race days, morning teas and afternoon visits. Mama's friends called, wanting to learn the latest gossip and dismayed by the fact the house would be sold and Mama was not returning.

Aggie was a constant visitor and Cece took advantage of having her company all to herself. Together they attended plays and the newest movie film release, they listened to brass bands in the parks as the weather warmed heading towards April. They went shopping and even caught the train to Scarborough to have a day by the seaside.

But as April dawned and spring blossom filled the garden enticing fat bees to come out of hibernation, Mr Roth began showing more people around the house. Cece knew it wouldn't be long before an offer was made, and Mama accepted it.

Strolling along the path in Rowntree Memorial Park, along the banks of the River Ouse, the early April winds blew blossom about like confetti at a wedding. Cece walked with her arm tucked through Agatha's, idly watching the barges chugging on the water, black plumes of smoke coming out of their little chimneys as they hauled coal and other produce in and out of the city.

'Shall we walk by the lake? There have been some more gardens created since we last came here,' Agatha mentioned, steering them away from the river walk and the strong breeze which threatened the lace of her parasol.

Cece flapped away a flying insect. 'Yes, I read in the newspaper that more work has been carried out. They've done so well establishing a lot of gardens since the park opened less than two years ago.'

'I don't assume the mayor would want to let the Rowntree family down. It's not every day the city is given acres upon which to create a park.'

They walked for a while in silence, watching children run about on the grass, while some older boys kicked a football.

'I've been meaning to tell you something,' Agatha said, a worried look in her eyes.

'Oh?' Cece noticed a new garden design and gardeners on their knees busily planting.

'I have wanted to tell you this for some time, but well, at first I wasn't sure, not completely set in my mind, and then you've been so preoccupied with the house sale, and everything.'

Cece stopped and looked at her, holding the brim of her straw hat as the breeze tugged at it. 'What do you want to tell me?'

'I've been courting, I suppose that is what you call it.'

'Courting?' Surprise drove Cece's voice up a notch.

'Yes. Mr Josiah Backhouse.'

Cece stared. 'You've never mentioned this man's name before, yet you tell me you are courting?'

'I know it must sound strange, but I wasn't certain whether I wanted to take it further with him.'

'Who is he?'

'He's a friend of father's really.'

'Uncle Edmund's friend? Are you telling me he's an old man?'

'No, no, not as old as Papa,' Agatha quickly denied. 'He's in his late forties. He is a solicitor who works in the partnership of Papa's solicitor's firm. Mr Backhouse was married before, but his wife died two years ago. He has a daughter, Cynthia who is eleven and genuinely nice.'

'You've met his daughter?'

'Yes, we enjoyed an afternoon tea a few weeks ago. Cynthia and I took to each other rather quickly. She has only a maid-come-cook in the house and attends a local ladies' college daily. She's a shy quiet little thing and reminds me of myself at that age.'

Cece watched the emotions flicker across Agatha's face. 'You feel sorry for the child? That's why you are courting the father?'

'No! No, that is not the only reason. Mr Backhouse and I have much in common and he's gentle and kind.'

'Do you love him?'

'I suppose so.'

'Suppose so?'

'I'm not like you or Prue or Millie, I don't have this burning desire to be dramatically in love and all the heartache it brings with it. Look at you and Monty Pattison.'

'What about us?' Cece spun to glare at her. 'There is no me and Monty Pattison!'

'Exactly. You were in love with him from the first moment you met him two years ago and no man has come close since then and look where that has got you? Alone. Prue fell in and out of love since turning sixteen and Millie saved herself for one man, she didn't even know she wanted. All three of you are so dramatic!'

'Whereas you will simply settle for whoever comes your way?'

'There is nothing wrong opting for a gentle approach to marriage.' Agatha continued walking.

Cece stared after her, wishing her cousin hadn't mentioned Monty and Agatha didn't know the half of it. She'd been unable to tell her of the night she spent in his bed, knowing Agatha would be ashamed of her. Cece had done so well to put him from her mind the last few weeks. She needed no reminders of her feelings for him. She had to forget her foolishness.

Cece hurried to catch up with Agatha. 'So, do I get to meet Mr Backhouse?'

Agatha smiled, a small dimple appearing near her mouth. 'I'd like that, as long as you don't judge and just accept. Can you do that for me, please?'

Tucking her arm through Agatha's, Cece nodded. 'If he is the man you want, then I'm happy for you, truly.'

'Good. As I'd like you to be a witness at the wedding next month.'

Cece jerked to a stop. 'Next month!'

'There is no point in waiting. I'll be twenty-five on my next birthday, and I'd like a baby. Besides, Papa will not be here forever and then I'll be on my own. I want to take my chance while I can.'

'It sounds like you have it all worked out,' Cece commented as they walked past a nanny pushing a pram.

'This is my chance, Cece. I may not get another. I don't want to be an old maid. I want to be a wife and a mother and run a house that belongs to me and not my papa. Do you understand?'

'Yes, I do.' In truth Cece wanted the same, but the possibility of obtaining all that was becoming more distant with each passing day. She had no wish to just settle. She wanted love, proper deep love, that she'd read about in books and seen in plays. She wanted a man who would do anything for her. Was that too much to ask?

'Come for dinner tomorrow,' Agatha said as they strolled beside the lake. 'You'll like Mr Backhouse.'

'Yes, very well.' She watched the ducks swimming and thought how much life was changing and how fast. Next month Agatha would be married. That left her more alone than ever.

Chapter Five

Cece entered the house and gave Forbes a small smile.

'How was the wedding, miss?'

'Lovely. Miss Agatha looked beautiful.'

'Indeed, she would, miss. The Marsh girls always make beautiful brides,' he replied loyally.

She gave him a white box. 'Wedding cake for the staff. Miss Agatha, I mean, Mrs Backhouse, sent it especially for you all. Goodness, I'll have to get used to her new name, won't I?'

'How delightful, miss, thank you.'

Cece walked into the drawing room and unpinned her pale-yellow silk hat with its array delicate white roses tucked under the upturned brim. Her linen dress of pale lemon and fine white lace was a smart choice as the day had been very warm for the first week of May.

'Tea, miss?' Forbes asked, following her in.

'No, thank you, I've had enough tea to last me the rest of the day.'

'Very good, miss.' Forbes departed, leaving Cece pondering what to do next.

The morning's wedding ceremony and breakfast had not lasted as long as others she'd attended in the past, as Agatha and Mr Backhouse didn't invite many people to the wedding. Also, they were honeymooning with his daughter in the Lake District and had wanted to set off just after midday. She'd liked Mr Backhouse. He adored Agatha, she could tell just by the way he gazed at her. She was pleased her cousin had found a decent man.

Now, Cece was at a loose end. She could change her dress and go for a walk, or start on another room to pack, but neither idea interested her. The weather was too warm to walk and in the last two months she'd packed the attic and most of the rooms. The main room still to do was this drawing room, which she'd left until last so she could still entertain visitors.

The peel of the front doorbell made her turn. She listened to Forbes answer it and the muffled voices.

'Miss, are you at home?' Forbes asked, coming into the drawing room.

'Yes, who is it?'

'Mr Roth, miss.'

The house agent. Cece nodded. 'Show him in.'

She shook Mr Roth's hand as he entered the room with a smile. She'd met with him on two previous occasions when he came to Elm House to take down the exact details of the listing and when he had shown a couple around the house a week ago. She'd liked him instantly.

'Thank you for seeing me at such short notice, Miss Marsh. I should have sent a note ahead.'

'I've just returned from my cousin's wedding, Mr Roth, so you have found me at a good time.'

'Excellent.'

'Please, do sit down.'

A tall man, his knees stuck out when he was seated. 'I won't stay long, Miss Marsh, for my news is all of the best kind. We have had an offer on the house.'

'Oh, I see.'

'I telephoned the details to your mother, Mrs Baudin, yesterday, and she has accepted the offer.'

'She did?' Annoyed that yet again she'd been the last to know, Cece inwardly fumed.

'The buyers were extremely taken with the house when they came and were most sincere about its charms.'

'It is a beautiful house.'

'Absolutely. They are also interested in keeping Mr Forbes and Mrs Hood on in their current roles. Do you think that would be possible?'

'I'm sure it would be. Forbes and Mrs Hood have yet to obtain positions elsewhere. They didn't want to leave me unattended, you see, not knowing how long the sale would take.'

'Very noble and loyal of them.'

'They are, yes. They've been with the family for many years. I will speak to them both.'

'Thank you. I also have letters for them from the buyers.' He took two envelopes out of his small leather case and passed them to her.

'I will see that they get them.' Cece held the letters tightly, hating that Mr Roth, as nice as he was, was bringing more change to her life. She thought she had more time.

'The buyers would like to finalise the bill of sale with the solicitors and the banks within the next two weeks. Is that satisfactory to you?'

'Two weeks?' Suddenly it was all too real.

'Do you care for more time, Miss Marsh?' His expression was one of sympathy. 'How much time would you need?'

Cece glanced down at the floor. She didn't need any time, not really. What was left to pack would only take a day or two and then all she had to do was board the train to London. In previous weeks she'd sent trunks of personal items to Mama, Millie and Prue, and even a trunk of clothes that Grandmama kept here for when she stayed.

'Miss Marsh?'

She raised her head, fighting the sorrow. 'Two weeks is sufficient, Mr Roth. I'll have the house empty by then.'

'Are you sure? If you need more time, please don't hesitate to say.'

'No. I'm certain. What are the new people like?'

'They are good people. A family who have out grown their old home. They have four children, three boys and a girl.'

'That's nice. The house will ring with children's noise again.'

'Yes, Miss Marsh, and I deem Elm House to be perfectly suited for that purpose.'

'I hope the family is as happy here as we have been.' She rose, wanting him to leave. 'Thank you for coming to tell me in person, Mr Roth.' She shook his hand and walked out with him into the entrance hall, where Forbes stood holding the man's hat and gloves.

'Thank you, Miss Marsh.'

'I'll have the keys dropped off to your office in two weeks, will that be all right?'

'Certainly, Miss Marsh. Good day to you.' Hat and gloves retrieved, Mr Roth left the house and Forbes closed the door on him.

'Well, Forbes, that is that. The new owners will be here in two weeks, a family of six. Tell the others, will you? Oh, and the buyers wish to keep you and Mrs Hood on in your roles.' She gave him the letters.

The old man's eyebrows shot up. 'They do? I wasn't expecting that.'

'Will you stay on?'

'To begin with, yes, miss. I have not applied for another post. This house has been my home for thirty years. Mr Marsh hired me to run his home even before he married Mrs Marsh. So, yes, I'll stay.'

'I'm pleased.' She left him and went upstairs to her bedroom. Sally was in there putting away fresh washing.

'Afternoon, miss. Did you enjoy the wedding?'

'I did, yes.' Cece sat on the padded window seat and stared out over the gardens that were bursting with spring colour. 'We have to pack this room now, Sally.'

'As you wish, miss. I have the packing boxes ready for you.'

Cece let the tears roll over her lashes as she glanced around her bedroom. She was lost, adrift.

Sally came and stood close to her and gave her a white folded handkerchief. 'Don't cry, miss. It's a new beginning. Me mam says that some things happen for a reason, we just don't always know what that reason is.'

'I certainly don't know.' She wiped her eyes.

'Look at it this way, you're going to have a whole new life in London with Mrs Fordham, and she's a character if ever there was one.' Sally smiled.

'That is true.'

'And maybe in time another house will come to mean a lot to you just as Elm House does. One day another house will hold new memories for you. We have to be positive, miss.'

'I don't feel very positive right now, Sally, forgive me.'

'Why don't I run you a nice bath? Mrs Hood has made delicious lamb roast for dinner and currant sponge and custard for dessert. You can have it on a tray up here in your room, so you don't have to get dressed after your bath. I'll bring it up and tell Mr Forbes you've retired early.'

'That sounds perfect, Sally, thank you.' Her kindness made Cece cry again.

'I'll run that bath. I'll be back shortly.'

Lazily, not inclined to rush at anything, Cece unbuckled her shoes and rolled down her silk stockings. Tears and anger mixed together as she undressed and donned her robe.

Why was she the only one to mourn the loss of the family home, and why did Mama constantly neglect to inform her of what was happening? A few lines on a telegram, or a quick telephone call was all it took to keep her updated.

Was Mama so busy with Jacques that she simply forgot Cece existed?

With the anger simmering, Cece paced the bedroom. She had a good mind to telephone Mama and have it out with her, but her courage failed her. Mama would loathe such a discussion over the telephone where the operator could easily listen in. Cece knew that the telephone Jacques used wasn't in his apartment but situated in the foyer of the apartment building, so anyone walking by could hear the conversation, and Mama would be horrified to speak publicly about a family matter.

Cece stopped by her writing desk. A letter? Put all her feelings down in words? Would that help? She doubted it, for Mama would only reply and say thank you for all her hard work and invite her to visit Paris.

She didn't want to go to Paris. Jacques, as lovely as he was, wasn't her papa. She didn't want to live with Jacques. She didn't want to live with Mama either. She'd grown tired of accompanying Mama to her friends' homes for tea parties and reading nights or joining Mama and her friends as they attended musical recitals, card nights and dinner parties. She'd spent enough time as Mama's companion when Prue was travelling, and Millie was in France.

Did she want to do all that with Grandmama? At least in London Grandmama gave her freedom to do as she pleased, she'd have none of that in Paris with Mama. Besides, Grandmama enjoyed her own independence and didn't need Cece with her every day as Mama requested.

Sighing, she sat on the edge of the bed. She caught her reflection in the long mirror. Her robe had come open and Cece frowned at the little tummy she had on show. Looking down, she sighed again. She'd put on weight eating Mrs Hood's wonderful meals and done little exercise to combat it. At least in London she'd start walking each day again. Walking around the city was one of the few highlights to living in London. Horrendous traffic often made the task of walking to one's destination a better option than going in the motor car.

Sad and lonely, she went to have her bath. Perhaps she should plan a trip away? Somewhere hot and exotic!

Cece

~ ~ ~ ~

The following morning, Cece dressed in a plain brown skirt and cream blouse and headed downstairs. After breakfast she'd start packing up the drawing room with Sally and Forbes.

'Good morning, miss,' Forbes said, placing a fresh pot of coffee onto the table.

'Good morning, Forbes. It's the drawing room today.'

'Very good, miss. I'll have Thomas roll up the rug and start taking down the last of the paintings.'

At the serving board, Cece lifted the first silver cloche. The aroma of mushrooms hit Cece, and she gagged. Quickly, she put the lid down again.

'Are you all right, miss?'

'Yes, absolutely.' Cece moved along and lifted the cloche of the next dish. Kippers. Cece retched three times.

'Miss!' Forbes was beside her in an instant.

'I'm fine.' Eyes watering, Cece sat at the table. 'I must be coming down with something. I'll just have some coffee.'

Forbes served her himself.

The first sip of coffee settled her stomach, and she smiled. 'Goodness. I don't know what came over me.'

'It isn't any wonder, miss, that you're all upset. There has been much to contend with in the last couple of months since you arrived home.'

Cece nodded. 'You are probably correct, Forbes.'

'I'll get Thomas and Sally started on the drawing room, miss. You wait here and rest a bit.'

An hour later, feeling better, Cece was in the thick
of packing delicate porcelain ornaments, and felt
ravenous. 'Forbes, could we stop and have morning
tea, please?'

'Certainly, miss.' He departed the drawing room
carrying a box.

Cece strolled outside into the garden for the warm
May weather was magnificent. She sat at the white
wrought-iron chairs and table near the rose garden.
The roses were in full bud, some even opening early.
The ornamental trees had lost their blossom and new
leaves where bright green against the blue sky. She
watched the bees buzz amongst the flowers. She'd
miss the garden, the place she'd played in all her
childhood.

She wandered over to the old wooden swing which
hung from an old oak tree that she and her sisters
used to climb when the governess wasn't looking.

Sitting on the swing, it creaked from lack of use
but held her weight and she rocked to and fro looking
up into the sparse green canopy. Tears gathered hot
behind her eyes. It was painful saying goodbye to the
house and garden, her home. Why weren't the others
as upset as she was? Why weren't they here to walk
the rooms with her one last time?

Sally came out of the conservatory and placed the
tea tray on the wrought-iron table.

Cece couldn't push the sadness away as she
strolled back across the lawn.

'I'll fetch the other tray, miss,' Sally said.

'Have you found work, Sally?'

'No, miss, not yet. I thought I had, but the position
fell through at the last minute.'

'Perhaps the new owners will take you on. I'll put
a good word in for you.'

'Thank you, miss. I'd hate to leave. Mr Forbes tells us that the family has children. It'll be good to see the house full again.'

'Yes, it will.' Cece sat down and poured out the tea.

When Sally returned, she carried a tray of delicious cakes and tarts. Cece sat in the sunshine and indulgently ate cake and sipped her tea. In a few days she'd be finished with the house and, with Agatha on her honeymoon, she had no reason to stay in York. It was time to move on. To go to London and start again. The prospect didn't fill her with excitement.

'Miss, the mail has arrived.'

'It is late today.' Cece took the letters off the silver plate Forbes carried.

'Mr Tanner from Carpenter's Auction Rooms has arrived to transport the last of the furniture to their warehouse.'

'Very good. I've tied a tag on everything that is to go. All that will remain is my bedroom furniture. Ask him to return tomorrow for that and then I'll go to a hotel for tomorrow night once I've concluded all my business. I shall travel to London on Saturday.'

'As you wish, miss.'

Left alone with only the birds' twittering for company, Cece opened the first letter, one from Millie.

Dearest Cece,

How busy you must be in organising the house ready for sale. I would come and help you but it's such a trial for me to leave the boys right now. Charles is teething and refuses to be held by anyone but me at the moment and Jonathan is learning to be

70

*potty trained and not very successfully. Nanny and I
are at our wit's end with the pair of them. I thought I
was pregnant again, but thankfully it was a false
alarm. I was late and worrying unnecessarily, but the
scare shocked me. I am not ready for another child
for some time — if ever. I have enough to do with
rebuilding the chateau and the boys and helping
Jeremy expand the business, another child would be
overwhelming for me at this time, I don't mind telling
you.*

Cece stopped reading and put down the sponge
cake she held in her other hand. Millie had been late
with her monthlies and thought she was pregnant.

A shiver ran over Cece's body. Late. Like
clockwork, Cece had been regular every month since
she was thirteen years old. Last month she had
vaguely wondered when she needed to be prepared
for her monthly show, but with the upheaval of house
packing, the thought had gone soon after.

Now it returned with full force.

Dashing inside and up the staircase, she passed a
surprised Sally as she rushed into her bedroom. On
her writing table was her diary and skimming through
the pages, Cece flipped back to where she had last
marked a little 'm' which was the symbol for when
she got her monthlies. She had to go back as far as
February twelve before she saw the 'm'.

February?

Had she been remiss in marking the date for March
and April? And now it was May!

A tingle of fear clutched her heart. She'd been
with Monty towards the end of February…

Good God!

No. It couldn't be possible, could it? It had only been the one time.

She touched her stomach, there was a tiny mound there when usually she was reed thin, like all the Marsh sisters were. The Marsh sisters weren't known for being curvaceous. None of them had a claim to decent size breasts or curving hips. Childbirth had given Millie a little more in the breast department, but Prue had a boyish figure, especially after being struck down with Malaria in India.

Cece stood in front of the full-length mirror and pressed her skirt flat against her legs. There definitely was a tiny mound, but nothing anyone would notice. Hell, *she'd* not even noticed until last night before her bath.

Was she pregnant?

A whimper broke from her throat. It could be her body reacting to the stress of packing up the house. She was merely late, that's all.

She nibbled a fingernail, but what if she was? Who could she ask? Certainly not Doctor Morris, the family's doctor. That would be too embarrassing. Another doctor in York had to be sought.

Quickly, from the top shelf in her wardrobe, she took out a brown velvet hat and put it on. Grabbing her small handbag, she hurriedly left the bedroom and went downstairs.

Forbes was instructing Mr Tanner and Thomas on removing the furniture.

'I'm going into town, Forbes,' she called, leaving the house.

At the bottom of the road, she spied an omnibus taking on passengers. She hurried to jump on it before it left the stop.

Once in the centre of York, Cece thought hard, trying to think where there could be a doctor's rooms.

'Miss Marsh?'

Cece turned and despite her worry she smiled at the old lady who walked up to her. 'Mrs Ashton. This is a pleasant surprise.'

'It is good to see you. How are you?' They stepped to one side to allow pedestrians to go by.

'I'm well, thank you. And you and Doctor Ashton?' Cece raised her voice over the noise of the motor cars and horse-drawn vehicles plying York's cobbled streets.

'For our age we are doing exceptionally grand.' Mrs Ashton's warm smile was familiar. 'However, I do miss not having your dear mama and you and your sisters visit me. I heard only this morning that Elm House is sold!'

'It is.'

'I can't bear to think of never having a member of the Marsh family to dinner or seeing one of you attend a fundraising again.'

'I cannot bear it myself, Mrs Ashton.' Cece's chin quivered as emotion built.

Mrs Ashton placed her hand on Cece's arm. 'What is wrong, dear? When I saw you just now, you looked terribly troubled. Your mama is a dear friend, and I'd like to know I've done the right thing by her in watching out for you, while you're here in York, alone.'

'Thank you for your concern, but I was simply wondering where I could find a doctor, that's all. It's nothing serious.'

'Then come home with me and see Joseph, stay for something to eat.'

Cece shook her head. 'Thank you, but no. I have much to do. I leave for London in two days.'

'Isn't Doctor Morris your family's doctor? Oh, but wait, he is in Edinburgh, isn't he? Joseph was meant to go to the lecture at the university there as well, but his age gives him a perfect excuse not to attend.' She laughed softly.

'Oh, I see. I simply have a question I need to ask, that's all. Nothing really worth bothering anyone about and I'm extremely busy trying to sort everything out.'

'Yes, of course you must have a great deal to organise, but I cannot let you go on your way unsatisfied. Doctor Wilks is in Coney Street, a good man and a friend of Joseph and me.'

'Thank you.'

Victoria Ashton kissed Cece's cheek. 'If you ever need a friend, remember me.'

'Thank you, Mrs Ashton.' Cece watched the old lady walk away slowly, using her cane, and again squashed the urge to cry. She'd probably never see the Ashtons or any of their friends again. To keep returning to York would be too hard. She'd have to resign from the committee she was on, too. Once she left York, a clean break would be needed.

Once in Coney Street, Cece found the doctor's office easily and entered. Four people sat waiting in the front room. After enquiring at the desk, she was told to take a seat, and she'd been seen when it was her turn.

For over an hour Cece waited and so many times in that hour she forced herself to remain seated when instinct told her to run. For an hour her mind whirled with questions and possibilities until she brought on a headache and felt sick.

Eventually she was invited into the office by Doctor Wilks, a young doctor barely thirty years old, but, thankfully, Cece didn't know him.

Nervously, she explained her reason for the visit. Doctor Wilks examined her and asked questions. Then confirmed her worst fears.

She was pregnant.

Chapter Six

In a daze, Cece walked all the way home, and by the time she'd reached Elm House, she had a blister on one foot and a thunderstorm was brewing replacing the sunshine.

The drawing room was empty, stripped bare of every comfort, reducing the memories to ashes.

'Miss, would you like a light luncheon?' Forbes asked as she passed him on the way up to her bedroom.

'No, thank you, Forbes.' Then she thought of the baby she carried. 'Actually, yes, I will, thank you. I'll have a tray in my room, please.'

'Very good, miss.'

Once in her bedroom she slumped onto the bed and slipped her shoes off, wincing at the blister. If only a blister was all she had to worry about.

What was she to do?

A baby!

All the way home, those two words had scrambled her brain. She couldn't find an answer to the problem.

She thought of Monty. Would he want to know about the baby? Would he marry her because of it?

She shivered as thunder rolled overhead.

Did she want him as a husband knowing he didn't love her, and he'd only married her because it was the decent thing to do? Could she live with a man who no doubt would resent her and the baby for the rest of their lives? No. To be Monty's wife when he didn't love her was selfish. She loved him too much to do that to him.

Should she try and get rid of it? She had read about backstreet abortionists, the risks, of authorities shutting them down only for more to spring up in dubious areas. What if she found a doctor who would do it? Surely there must be good doctor who would do the procedure in a safe way if she paid him enough? In London she'd have a better chance of finding one privately than in York. Could she achieve that without anyone knowing? Did she really want to do that? Could she go through with it? She might die.

God! What was she to do?

She wanted to cry, and she wanted Mama.

A knock preceded Sally, who carried a tray. 'Beef and pickle sandwiches, miss, apple pie and custard for afters.'

'Thank you.' Cece waited for Sally to leave and then taking a triangle sandwich she sat on the window seat and ate it without thought.

If she didn't go to a doctor, or if she couldn't find one who would do the deed, then she'd have to give the baby away at birth. Adoption. Yes.

She ate another sandwich. She'd have to go away. America? No, Grandmama would want her to visit Lesley and she couldn't do that. France was out as Millie would want her to visit her, as would Mama.

India was out of the question also, as uncle Hugo would want her to visit him.

A cottage by the sea, perhaps? But where? Cornwall? Devon? Her family would think it odd her going to the coast alone.

Cece paced. She needed to go somewhere that wouldn't cause too much comment and no one knew her.

She glanced at the tray, the custard was cooling, congealing with a skin forming. Suddenly, Cece rushed for the bathroom and brought up the sandwiches she'd just consumed.

Sitting on the cold tiled floor, she leaned against the bath, feeling clammy and hot. She couldn't go to London when the slightest thing made her vomit. Grandmama was too clever not to work it out.

Resting her head back, she stared at the wall, its flowered wallpaper in hues of mauve and blue. She stared at it, picking out the different flowers in the pattern: roses, pansies, thistles...

Thistles. Scotland. She had a cottage in Scotland.

As though a huge weight had been lifted off her shoulders, Cece scrambled out of the bathroom and back into her bedroom. At her writing desk, she once again flipped through the pages of her diary to find the page in February where she had written the information about the cottage in Scotland.

There, the address. Willow Cottage, Resslick, Scottish Highlands.

Never had she thought she'd ever visit that cottage. She'd cursed the gift originally, believing she'd been short-changed by Grandmama. Yet, now, she had her hiding place. She could stay there, have the baby and then organise for it to be given to a good family somewhere, there was bound to be an orphanage in Scotland who'd take the baby.

She took out a piece of paper and pen, waited a moment for her hand to stop shaking and then began to write.

Dear Grandmama,

Now Elm House is sold and packed up, I'm taking the opportunity to travel to Scotland to see the cottage you bought for me. Then, I shall spend the summer touring the Scottish Highlands. I might as well while I'm there, I've never seen Scotland's Highlands. Also, I have a friend in Edinburgh, whom I might visit while up in the north.

All mail for me can be directed to the cottage, and I shall collect it when I stay there between tours.

I'll write when I can.

With love,
Cece,
Elm House
York
May 1923.

Content that message would prevent Grandmama or anyone going to Scotland to visit her, she wrote a similar brief note to her mama and sisters. She'd invented the friend in Edinburgh, but no one would know that.

Once the notes were in envelopes, Cece sighed, and in a break in the clouds, the sun poked through and shone brightly into the room, but not into her heart.

Cece

Exhausted, Cece lay on the bed and closed her eyes. Tomorrow, she'd say goodbye to the staff and her home. There was no reason to stay longer, and every reason to travel to Scotland before her secret became known.

~ ~ ~ ~

The train rocked and rattled towards the station of Fort William, a Highland town on the east side of Loch Linnhe. Steam jetted out from under the carriages blocking the view of the mountains on Cece's right. A fellow passenger had pointed out the tallest peak and told her that was Ben Nevis. She didn't really care but had smiled and thanked him anyway.

On the long journey from York Station, she'd changed trains and sat in first class completely uninterested in her surroundings or fellow passengers. Her mind wouldn't let her think of anything other than being with child and the enormity of her situation. It was any wonder she'd made it to the right destination at all.

The conductor walked past calling out that Fort William was the termination of the line. Cece stood and gathered her bag and coat and opened the door to the corridor. Like-minded passengers were doing the same and a steady stream of people walked down to the carriage door just as the trained pulled into the station.

On the platform, Cece waited until a porter was free and then gave her ticket to him to retrieve her trunk from the baggage carriage. While she waited, she stared around, noting the surge of people making for the exit out into the street.

When the porter eventually brought her trunk to her on a trolley she smiled tiredly. 'Thank you. Can you tell me how I can get to Resslick, please?'

'Resslick?' He scratched his head under his peaked cap. 'You'll need a pony and trap, miss. Old Fred has left for Resslick already. He only goes once a day and he leaves after the four o'clock train. He never stays for this one as there's never anyone on it for Resslick this late normally. Are you sure it's Resslick you want?'

'Yes, that is the town I need to go to.'

'Town?' The porter laughed. 'Resslick isn't a town, miss, it's barely a village.' He laughed some more.

'Oh, well, anyway, I need to get there as soon as I can.'

He scratched his chin. 'I canna see how you will, miss. You'll not make it before dark, that's if you do find a lift.'

Deflated, Cece fought back a wave of disappointment. 'Is there a hotel I can stay at?'

'Aye, there's a couple in town.' Then he raised his head. 'Hang on a minute. George!' He hollered over the noise of the shutting carriage doors and the snorting steam.

The porter darted away to talk to a portly older man.

Annoyed, Cece stood waiting for him to return as she couldn't drag her trunk by herself.

'All fixed up, miss.'

'Pardon?'

'George lives beyond Resslick, so he says he'll take you, if you don't mind sitting in a farm cart.'

Did she even have a choice?

'I just need to get there, so I don't mind.'

Her words came back to taunt her hours later, as
with the sun slipping behind mountains, she sat on the
hard wooden seat of George McMurray's farm cart.
His Scottish accent was so thick she hardly
understood a word he said and reverted to simply
nodding and smiling when she thought it was
required.

Once away from Fort William, they crossed River
Lochy and the Caledonian Canal, where she glimpsed
the impressive Neptune's Staircase, a series of locks,
which George informed her was the longest staircase
lock in the country and currently undergoing many
repairs after years of neglect.

At the northern end of Lock Linnhe, they turned
westwards.

On the rutted dirt track that snaked through fields
and trees, always hugging the bottom of a mountain,
George pointed out various landmarks, their names
going over her head. Yet, as they followed the shore
of Loch Eil, she couldn't help but find it beautiful as
the setting sun glimmered gold over the water.

'Willow Cottage, hey?' George rubbed his chin in
thought.

'Yes. Do you know it?' she asked hopefully.

'Aye.'

She waited for something more, but he remained
silent and flicked the reins.

Ten minutes later, George made a clicking noise to
the horse and slowing, they turned in between large
willow trees onto an even more rutted and overgrown
track. The long wooden gate sat open, drunkenly
lodged in the thick grass. A small painted sign
declared 'Willow Cottage'.

In the last of the evening light, Cece stared at the
cottage in disbelief. Whenever someone in her social

circle spoke of having a cottage, it usually meant a small manor. Many of the family's friends had cottages by the sea, cottages in the country and so on, and Cece had stayed at many of these and each 'cottage' was a neat medium-sized manor, or at worst a hunting lodge of only seven or eight rooms. That is what she had expected her cottage to be.

Instead, she stared at an actual farm cottage. Constructed of grey stone, with only one window on either side of the door, the cottage had three dormer windows jetting out of the slate tiled roof. Cece imagined that a mistake had been made.

George pulled the cart to a stop and jumped down to come around and help her from the seat.

'This is Willow Cottage?' She stood, unable to take it in. The house was so small. 'Are you absolutely certain?'

'Aye, miss. The one an' only.' George heaved out her trunk and small bag from the cart.

'Where is the village of Resslick? Perhaps there is another Willow Cottage?'

'There's no other Willow Cottage, miss.' He handed her a lantern from the side of the cart and lit it for her. 'You'll be needing this more than I will. It's full of oil so it'll last ye a few days if ye careful.'

'Thank you.'

'Ye've a key?'

'Yes.' She held the lantern and walked with him as he carried her trunk to the white wooden front door. From her bag she took a large iron key and, after a moment or two of struggle, opened the door.

Lantern held high, Cece stepped to one side in the small square entrance so George could put down the trunk. Directly in front of her rose a steep staircase and beside the stairs a narrow corridor led to the back of the cottage.

There was one door on the left of the entrance and one door on the right. The shadowed light showed two small rooms with a window and a black iron fireplace in each. The room on the left was empty but the room on the right held an emerald green horsehair sofa, which had seen better days. Thick purple curtains hung at the window and on the wooden floor a faded patterned rug was placed between the sofa and the dirty fireplace.

She turned as George came in carrying a tray of vegetables and placed them on top of the trunk. 'I guess ye'll be needing these, miss, until ye get yeself sorted.'

She blinked at his offering. 'Thank you,' she murmured, squashing the urge to cry. 'You are most kind.'

'Do ye want me to take the trunk upstairs?'

'No, no, thank you. I'll manage.' How she would do so she had no idea.

'Right, well, I'd best be off then. The village is a couple of miles to the east.' He pointed in the direction. 'I'll be passing by on Thursday, if ye want a lift into Fort William.'

She nodded. 'Thank you so much.'

'Right ye are then.' He doffed his cap and closed the door behind him.

Full darkness had fallen, and the lantern provided pitiful light. With it held high, Cece crept down the narrow corridor past the stairs, her heart in her throat as the shadows flickered and swayed on the walls. The end of the corridor opened into a large room, which ran the width of the cottage. One side held the kitchen range and a deep sink under the window, and at the other side of the room stood a large pine table with mismatched chairs.

A door led out to the back of the cottage but Cece didn't have the courage to open it and wander out into the dark.

Returning the way she'd come, she slowly ascended the stairs, her nerves on edge. The landing at the top of the stairs was small and square, showing only two doors. One bedroom was small and empty, but the other bedroom was large with two of the dormer windows and a decent size iron framed bed and mattress and a fireplace.

The bed squeaked as Cece sat on it, the noise loud in the quiet house. She placed the lantern on the floor. She stared around, her mind blank, uncomprehending. She was in an old cottage, devoid of warmth or comfort, in the middle of God knows where. How had she come to this? Every instinct told her to run, to leave the cottage and walk into the village and beg someone to take her in until the morning, when she could catch a train back to London and Grandmama.

No, not to her grandmama. She'd never forgive her grandmama for this unwanted and unthoughtful present. Grandmama had bought her this cottage – this rundown, unfurnished, dreadfully old cottage while Prue had been given a year long trip to India and Italy and Millie had received a piano and money for the restoration of the chateau.

Cece's chin wobbled as she stared around her. She'd not been worth a decent liveable home. Did her family think so little of her? Mama didn't care, she was too ensconced with Jacques and Millie was too busy being a wife and mother and Prue was engrossed in the magazine, and Monty didn't love her…

She was as unwanted as this cottage.

And stupidly she'd become pregnant!

In her predicament she had no one to turn to. Her shame would embarrass the family. Mama wouldn't accept her disgrace and the burden would be too much to place on Grandmama's elderly shoulders.

There was nothing else to do but stay here in this unkempt hut and wait her time out.

Pulling her coat around her, she unpinned her hat and slipped off her gloves. Then allowing the tears to fall, she turned out the lamp, curled up on the mattress and cried until tiredness overwhelmed her and she fell asleep.

Chapter Seven

Cece woke to sunshine streaming into the room. Stiff and a little achy from sleeping in the same position all night, she stretched and gingerly sat up. Her stomach rebelled at the motion. Taking deep breaths, she fought the nausea. There was nowhere to be sick up here. She slipped on her shoes.

Downstairs, she stepped around the trunk and went out of the front door. Standing on the step, she gazed over the long length of lawn bordered by mature trees down each side, with the drive coming up the slope on the left.

Cece walked down the track, for calling it a drive was a stretch of anyone's imagination. She paused at the broken gate wedged in the overgrown grass. The sign definitely said, 'Willow Cottage' and willow trees bordered the front fence of the property.

Breathing in deeply, her stomach settled a little. On the other side of the dirt road, the wide expanse of the loch's dark waters shimmered in the morning sunshine. Seeing it, Cece noted its beauty and the serenity. The cottage's one redeeming feature was that it overlooked the loch.

Strolling back up the lawn, she studied the front of the building. A creeper of some sort grew along the west wall, and in front of the windows garden beds were choked with weeds. Tall grass hid the flagstone path to the door.

Walking around the side of the cottage, Cece saw a swing tied to a branch in a large tree. She smiled. A tree swing like the one back home.

Continuing, she ventured further up the slope into the barn type building behind the house. Inside, the scent of hay and old leather filled her nose. A horse stall and manger were towards the back of the barn and above her head was a storage floor. Dust and cobwebs coated all surfaces and straw littered the packed dirt floor. In one of the corners a small stack of cut wood leant against the wall.

Between the large barn and a smaller one were disused animal pens of some description, and she found the smaller barn empty. Directly behind the barns, the slope grew steeper, leading into a stand of trees and beyond that a mountain rose majestically, covered in heather and bracken in hues of mauve, green and brown.

On either side of the mature trees that bordered the cottage, open fields stretched as far as she could see.

Returning to the back of the cottage, Cece was thankful to find a water pump and bucket. When she pumped the handle, clean fresh water shot out of the tap. With the bucket filled, she tried the handle of the back door and it opened easily.

'Not locked,' she murmured. 'I could have been murdered in my sleep.'

The thought made her laugh nervously for seriously she was alone, stuck between a loch and a mountain and not a person in sight.

In daylight the kitchen looked worse than the glimpse she had of it last night. A door on the other wall opened to reveal a larder. All the shelves were bare. The black iron range didn't shine like the one in Elm House, and there was no warming glow of a good fire to cook by or heat water with either. Not that Cece had ever cooked or heated water in her life. The thought overwhelmed her. All her life she'd had devoted staff tending to her every need. She was trained in how to be a lady, and how to order staff to perform the duties needed to run a large house, but none of that was useful when one had no staff.

How could she stay here not knowing anything about anything!

In a fit of anger, she slammed the door of the range shut and a shower of coal smut and ash floated over the red stone flags of the kitchen floor.

'What am I doing here?' She stamped her foot, hating the cottage, hating her life, and hating the child that grew inside her.

For several minutes she stood in despair, not knowing what to do or where to begin this new challenge.

Perhaps she should walk into the village and see if she could hire a maid? And a cook? And a gardener? What if there was no one to hire?

Did she need to purchase a motor car? Did she have enough money to do all that she needed to do? She wished she had listened to Grandmama about money. Was she able to afford to run a home of her own with staff and a motor car? How much did all of that cost? Did the stipend she received in her bank account each month cover such expenses? She'd never in her life paid a bill or an account. Her papa had done all that and after his death, then her mama or Grandmama had seen to it all.

Again, she was assailed by doubts. She hadn't thought any of this through properly. Anger at Grandmama swiftly became her focus.

If Grandmama had only bought her a decent house, furnished and with staff she'd have none of this worry. Why was she gifted a rundown cottage with no one to help her? No one in their right mind would live here! What was Grandmama thinking when she agreed to purchase it? Or did she not care since it was only for Cece, and the family didn't care about what she needed or thought.

Her stomach rumbled. Being pregnant was stupid. One minute she was ready to heave and the next minute she was starving. She couldn't wait to give this child away and get on with her life.

Shoulders slumped, she returned to the front door and peered at the vegetable tray. What the hell was she to do with potatoes, carrots, onions and... Cece picked up the round white and purple root vegetable. She didn't even know what that was.

Carrying the tray into the kitchen, she placed it on the benchtop beside the sink with no tap. She searched the cupboards under the sink and found a scrubbing brush.

'That's no help,' she muttered in disgust.

Next, she searched the tall cupboard beside the range and found a drawer containing a few rusty knives and a spoon. Taking them out she put them in the sink. Another cupboard held a ball of twine and an old picture frame with no picture and right at the back was a box of matches.

The range stood cold and quiet and she knew she'd need to get a fire going. She'd watched the servants many times light and tend to a fire. She just had to think practically. She'd need newspaper and small pieces of wood.

Out in the barn, she filled her arms with the smallest pieces of wood she could find and carried them into the kitchen. The lack of a newspaper was a problem. Instead she returned to the barn and scrapped up handfuls of straw from the floor.

In the kitchen, she shoved the straw into the grate of the range and placed small pieces of wood on top. She moaned when opening the match box and saw only three matches inside.

'I *can* do this,' she mumbled, lighting the first match to the straw. A flame grew quickly and caught all the straw alight. In an instant the straw was burnt and the wood untouched.

Hurrying to the barn, she collected twice as much straw and repeated the process. The straw burned brightly and fast, too quick for the wood to catch.

For the third time, she tried again, stuffing as much straw into the grate as it would hold. She lit the last match and watched, her fingers twisted in hope that the wood would catch and burn. But just as before, the straw burned quickly, sending white smoke up the chimney and out into the kitchen before spluttering and dying out.

Coughing, Cece sat back on her heels. She wouldn't cry. She *refused* to cry!

Utterly deflated, she walked outside to the pump and filled the bucket with water to wash her face and hands. There was nothing for it but to walk into the village.

Cece

Half an hour later, Cece stood in the middle of a grassed area surrounded by of a scattering of cottages. She'd strolled the two miles along the road, keeping the loch in sight. On the edge of what she assumed was the village she'd spied a small stone church and after that a farm set back from the road. Then the road became more defined and split into a fork around a village green. She counted six cottages on the right and on the left was an inn and what seemed to be a tiny school house for she could hear the chanting of children's voices. More cottages lined the lane. She couldn't identify one single shop.

A man wearing a flat cap, sitting on a bench in the sun outside of the inn, took his pipe out of his mouth and waved it at her. 'Ye lost, hen?'

Cece walked closer to the inn. 'No, I don't believe so. This is Resslick?'

'Ahh, English.'

'Yes, I am.' She stated the obvious.

'Ye looking for somebody, hen?'

'I've just moved into Willow Cottage.' She pointed in a vague way behind her. 'I'm in need of some help.'

'Help?'

'Yes. I wish to buy some things. There is nothing in the cottage for me to use to cook or light a fire…' she finished lamely. She doubted her ability even if she did have all the tools she needed to build a fire.

'Alf!' the old man suddenly shouted, making her jump.

Another equally old man came out of the inn, wearing a white apron and squinting as though the sunshine was alien to him. 'Oh aye, Murray, who's this then?'

'Yon lass needs things for Willow Cottage.'

'Willow Cottage?' The innkeeper whistled through his teeth. 'I wonder what Ross Cameron will say about that?'

The two men lapsed into what Cece thought to be Gaelic.

'I'm Cece Marsh,' Cece interrupted and nodded hopefully to get their attention again.

'Cece Marsh? I don't know of any people called Marsh,' Alf told her.

'Well, you wouldn't, would ye?' Murray scoffed. 'She's a Sassenach... English.'

'Ah, right. That'll be why then.' Alf nodded wisely.

'Is there a shop close by?' Cece asked.

'A shop?' Murray, the old man on the bench laughed. 'No shop here, hen. Ye need to get to Fort William, or better still ride up to Inverness, plenty there.'

Cece's shoulders slumped. 'I haven't the transport to get to either of those places.'

'What do ye need?' Murray creaked up from the bench.

'Food, matches, that type of thing. And bed sheets, pots and pans...'

'Come away in, hen,' Alf beckoned. 'We'll fix you up with something.'

Hiding a small smile at being called 'hen', she gratefully followed the two men into the dark interior of the ancient inn. Smoke-stained walls bulged with age and, not very high above her head, thick black beams ran the length of the tap room. The smell of stale ale filled her nose.

'This way.' Alf lifted the end of the countertop to allow her through into the back area of the inn. Murray hobbled behind them.

In a kitchen area, a large fire burned with suspended pots bubbling with something that smelled delicious.

'What do you need again, hen?' Alf asked, poking around the room as though the deep corners held hidden treasures he was only exploring for the first time.

'Newspaper and matches, to light a fire, firstly. Then food...' She stared around the cramped kitchen that was filled to the brim with so much stuff she could only stand by the table without knocking something over. Chairs held stacks of newspapers and ledgers, on the floor were crates of vegetables and buckets, a milk churn stood by the back door. Coats and boots littered the other old sofa, which was pushed up against a wall dresser that was brimming with cups and plates and bowls. Books wedged open another door, showing a steep staircase behind.

'You've nothing at Willow Cottage?' Murray asked, leaning against a stone sink.

'No, I assumed it was fully furnished but when I arrived, I learnt that was an oversight on my part. I shall never assume anything again. It was silly of me to expect it would have furniture.'

'Everything was sold off.' Murray sucked nosily on his pipe. 'McInness sold up and went to America.'

'I see.' Cece had no idea who he was talking about and was more interested in watching Alf.

Alf grabbed a wooden crate and tipped out a load of rubbish, or treasures depending on your point of view, and gave the empty crate to Cece. As she stood there holding it, Alf began to fill it. He gave her a pile of newspapers and a box of matches he found in a draw and added to that four candles and two candle holders. Murray placed inside the crate two plates, cutlery, a couple of bowls, a teacup and teapot.

Alf sorting through another cupboard gave her a small bag of tealeaves and another of sugar, oats and a bottle of milk. 'The milk is from Mrs Durie's cow, over yonder. She makes good butter, too.'

'Thank you, thank you so much!' Cece put the crate down on the edge of the messy table and pulled out some money from her coat pocket.

'Wheest! Put that away.' Alf turned his back on her outstretched hand clutching money.

'But you've given me so much. I must pay.'

'Just tell ye friends to come and have a pint here, that's payment enough.'

'I don't have any friends. I'm on my own at the cottage.' She wasn't sure if that had been a smart thing to say. A single woman alone far from anywhere, but the locals would soon learn the truth soon enough.

'On ye own?' Murray's eyes widened. 'A lass?'

'Yes.' Cece withered under their looks of astonishment. On the train travelling north she'd come up with a story to tell any strangers who she'd meet. 'My husband is away. His business takes him all over the world,' she lied.

'And ye not go with him?' Murray frowned.

'No, not this time. I thought to come here and stay at the cottage for the summer.' She picked up the tray. 'Thank you very much for all this.'

They followed her outside just as the bell rang at the little school house. A stream of children of all ages rushed outside and began running around the small field to the side of the school house. A tall suited man followed the children out and strolled up to the gate.

'Ho there, Mr Evans,' Alf called. 'We've a newcomer to the parish, another of your lot. We'll have more Sassenachs than Highlanders at this rate.'

Embarrassed, Cece shifted the weight of the tray in her arms.

Coming out of the school gate, Cece watched the man walk towards them and was taken by his friendly smile.

'Mrs Marsh, this is Mr Evans, our teacher,' Murray boasted proudly. 'Resslick only managed to have a teacher in the last year or so, haven't we, Mr Evans? Before that the wee bairns had to walk miles to the next village.'

Mr Evan's tipped his boater hat. 'Good day to you, Mrs Marsh, and welcome to Resslick.'

Cece's eyes widened at his English accent. 'I'm pleased to meet you, Mr Evans.'

'Are you visiting relatives, Mrs Marsh?' Mr Evans had an easy manner as he glanced back at the playing children.

'No, I own Willow Cottage. I've come to spend some time here.' She made sure she held the tray in front of her stomach, not that the small bump could be seen underneath her coat. The warmth of the sunshine was making her sweat, that and the men calling her *Mrs* Marsh. She was a fraud.

'Ye'll need a maid or two, won't ye, Mrs Marsh?' Alf enquired, scratching his head.

A cry came from the schoolyard and Mr Evans excused himself.

Cece turned her attention to Alf. 'Yes, I do need help in the house.'

'I'll ask about for ye.'

'Thank you. I'd best go. Thank you again.' Cece smiled at Alf and Murray.

The long walk back to the cottage nearly brought her to her knees. The weight of the tray grew so heavy she had to stop several times and rest her arms. Sweat beaded her forehead and trickled down her back. She'd need a bath tonight.

Did she even have a bath?

Depressed, she turned into the gate, hating the sight of its leaning state, and walked up to the cottage.

Thankfully, she dumped the tray on the kitchen table. A fly buzzed against one of the windows, the noise loud in the quiet room. She stared at the cold dark range. Thirsty and hot, she couldn't even make a cup of tea.

She didn't want to make a fire or cook her own food. Her lack of experience made her frustrated and angry. Could she get by until a suitable maid of all work was found? How long would that take out here in the middle of nowhere?

No. It was too much. A maid wouldn't be of any use for there was nothing in the house! She didn't have a pot or a blanket. She had nothing. What kind of place was this to not have shops nearby?

She couldn't stay here. Resslick was too remote.

Impulsively, she left the kitchen and grabbed her bag. She'd go somewhere else and to hell with it. A train to Edinburgh, or Inverness or anywhere but here was the answer. She'd live in a hotel until the baby arrived, then find an orphanage and give it to them. Then she'd be free to return to her life.

She opened her trunk, searching through her clothes for a change of underwear and another blouse, which she'd crammed into her bag. The rest of her things would have to be left behind. She'd buy more in the first city she came to.

Closing the door, she locked it and put the key in her coat pocket. With the decision made, she felt better. She'd walk back into the village and ask Alf where she could stay until someone was heading to Fort William and could give her a lift to the train station.

As she walked down the drive, she frowned on seeing a boy sitting on the broken gate. 'Can I help you?'

'I'm just resting. Can I have some water, please?' His accent was Scottish but not strong.

Cece glanced around. No one else was about. 'Are you from the school?'

'School?'

'In Resslick.'

'No, miss. I've just come from Edinburgh way.' His gaze shifted away and Cece knew he was lying.

'Edinburgh? That's a long way.'

'Certainly is.'

'You've come all that way on your own?'

'I'm looking for work.' His over-long light brown hair fell forward over his dark blue eyes.

'And there's no work in Edinburgh?'

'I don't like cities. I want to be in the country.'

'Where's your family? You seem a little too young to be wandering the countryside by yourself.'

He looked her straight in the eye. 'My family is dead.'

She didn't know what to say, but she'd seen a glimpse of pain in his expression. He wore trousers too short for him, and a knitted pullover in dark grey that had a hole in the arm. His face was filthy, and she'd dread to guess when he last had a decent wash. Then she realised he wasn't wearing any shoes. At that moment, Cece lost her heart to the skinny boy sitting on her lopsided gate.

'I ain't running from the police, miss.' He jumped down from the gate. 'I only stopped here because I thought the cottage looked nice and friendly.'

'Really?' She turned and looked back at the cottage that she hated. Nice and friendly? With the sun shining on it, warming the grey stonework, she could see that to another person it might seem welcoming. If you ignored the unkempt garden and dirty windows.

'I can work for bread and board, miss,' he said hopefully.

'You can?' she asked shocked. 'How old are you?'

'Thirteen.'

'You don't look thirteen.'

'I'm small for my age.' He shrugged.

'And painfully thin.'

He stared at her, his eyes not pleading, but nevertheless sending her a message. She could never resist a sad story and was known in her family to be the soft touch.

'Can you light a fire?' she asked.

'I can. I can chop wood and work in the garden, as I grew up doing that. I know a lot about vegetables.'

'Very well. You can stay and we'll see how you get on.'

His grin brightened his face. 'You won't regret it, miss.'

'I'm *Mrs* Marsh. What is your name?'

'Finlay.'

'Do you have a last name, Finlay?'

He paused ever so slightly, a wariness in his manner. 'No. I never knew me dad.'

Cece

Cece had spent many years helping her mama with charities in York and knew of the thousands of children who had no one and lived by their wits on the streets. Finlay was obviously a child of the Parish, an orphan. Unwanted and rejected and left to fend for himself.

Turning on her heel, Cece pulled out the key from her pocket. 'Come along then. You can make me a cup of tea.'

Chapter Eight

The following morning, Cece woke to early morning sunshine streaming through the bedroom window. She stretched, dislodging her coat, which was her only covering. For the second night she had slept on a mattress with no bed linen. The quietness was broken by the sound of chopping.

Rising slowly, so as not to feel sick, she stepped to the window and looked down. Finlay was in the yard, chopping wood on a stump with a small axe.

Watching him, Cece's heart softened. Yesterday he'd made a fire in the range and brought her a cup of tea, then he'd cut up vegetables and boiled them in an old pot he found out in the barn, that had been their evening meal. Finlay had been surprised to see the cottage empty and bare of any comfort, but once the fire was going, they'd dragged the table closer to the range and sat and talked while they ate the plain boring vegetables, which despite its blandness, she was so hungry she devoured every mouthful.

She told him, her husband was away, and she'd only just arrived at the cottage. He told her that he grew up in an orphanage and worked in the kitchen garden. Cece judged he had more to his story, but he grew tired after the meal and she didn't press him. He'd slept on the sofa and she'd gone up to bed as the sun was setting.

Her stomach rumbled, drawing her away from the window. Last evening, Finlay had dragged her trunk up the stairs, and she took from it a clean blouse and a chestnut brown skirt. Once changed, she left the bedroom and sauntered down to the kitchen just as Finlay brought in an armful of wood.

'Good morning.'

'Morning, Mrs Marsh.'

She winced when he said Mrs Marsh. She really wasn't used to it and doubted she ever would be. 'Did you sleep well on that old sofa?'

'Yes, it was all right. I've slept in worse places.' He dumped the wood in the corner and then stirred the simmering pot.

'What is in there?'

'Porridge. The milk was going off, so I made porridge with it and the bag of oats in the tray.'

'Oh, well done. Good thinking.' She would never have thought to do that.

'Does this cottage have a cellar?'

'I've no idea. Why?'

'We can keep food for longer in a cellar.'

'Oh, I see.' She looked around the kitchen. 'There's a larder there.' She pointed to the door by the range.

'What's this?' Finlay walked to the other side of the kitchen where the table once stood and pulled at a ring in the floor. A hatch door lifted. 'There are steps going down. It's a cellar of sorts. Not a very big one though. I think it's more a storage area, but it's better than nothing.'

Cece peered over his shoulder at the dark square dug below the floor roughly four feet wide and six feet long. 'How amazing.'

'It's lined with stone, see?' Finlay pointed, getting on his knees. 'The stone is cold. We can keep meat and milk in there.' He closed the door hatch.

After their breakfast of unsweetened porridge, which Cece managed to keep down, Finlay beckoned her outside. To one side of the large barn a large area was bordered off with a small stone wall. Inside this area was a jumble of overgrown weeds and even weedier narrow paths.

'What are you showing me?' Cece asked.

'Look.' Finlay bent down at the edge of a slender garden bed. 'There is a garden in here, on either side of these footpaths. See the timber borders?'

'Yes.' Cece stood at the gate to the area and didn't venture any further.

'And see this?' Finlay pushed back some weeds. 'Strawberries.'

Intrigued, Cece carefully stepped to where Finlay crouched. All she could see was green grasses and weeds and broken wooden stakes. 'Where?'

'See these leaves, and the little white flowers buds? Where there is a white bud that will be a flower and then a strawberry.'

'Are you sure?'

Finlay nodded eagerly. 'Definitely. I told you I used to work in the kitchen garden at the orphanage. And see here?' He moved on to another area thick with dandelions. He pointed to a few bushy green plants. 'Self-seeded potatoes they are. They won't be ready until the end of summer though.'

He rummaged along, expressing delight at other plants. Cece kept up with him, delighted by his enthusiasm.

'There are carrots sown here and look at these old cabbages! They are past their best now, probably last years and have gone to seed and the bugs have got to them. This must have been a grand kitchen garden. We can make it neat and useful again, Mrs Marsh.'

At the end of the stone wall two medium-sized trees grew.

'I bet they are fruit trees!' Finlay said, sounding like a wise old man. 'You need more than one, so the bees can pollinate, otherwise you won't get fruit.'

'Really?' Cece peered beyond the wall at some other trees growing behind the barn, totally unnoticed by her yesterday. 'There's more here.'

The faint buzz of bees reached them.

'We should get some chickens. Can you buy some?' Finlay jumped over the wall and waded through the long grass near the barn.

'I suppose I can. But you'll have to look after them.' Cece stayed where she was.

'Mrs Marsh!' Finlay's voice squeaked, not yet fully broken.

'Yes?' Cece watched him run across to the tall trees lining the field.

'Bees!' he called between cupped hands. 'Beehives.'

She smiled, enjoying his happiness.

Finlay ran back to her. 'There will be honey in the hives. We need to extract it.'

'You'll be stung!' she warned, suddenly feeling like his mother, and not wanting to see him hurt.

'We had beehives at the orphanage, well not in the kitchen garden where I worked with Mr Graham, but next door at the vicarage, they had beehives and I've watched Mr Graham harvest the honey.'

He talked as they walked back to the cottage. 'Do you have a spade and a hoe? We should buy some seeds. We're late getting planted, but we can still grow a lot.'

Stopping by the pump, Cece picked up the bucket. 'We need more water for inside.'

As Finlay pumped the handle and water sloshed into the bucket, he continued. 'If we could get a milking cow and calf, then we'd have milk, and later you can sell the calf. I need a better axe, too. Are you going to buy a motor car? I wonder if there are fish in the loch. I've never fished before, but it wouldn't hurt to try, would it?'

'Slow down, Finlay.' Cece laughed.

'We have to make the most of the warmer months, Mrs Marsh.' He carried the bucket inside. 'I bet its freezing up here in winter. We'll need to store wood.'

Cece followed him into the kitchen. Panic seized her. Finlay talked of making the cottage a home. Did she want that? Could she hide away here as she grew big with child and hope no one would notice? Hardly possible.

That meant she'd have to leave when the child was born and not return, for what would she tell people in the village? They expected a husband to claim her eventually. A man who didn't exist. She'd have to sell the cottage, take the child and give it up to an orphanage before anyone found out.

What would happen to Finlay?

She groaned and sat down at the table. None of this had been her plan. She was to hide away, have the baby, give it up for adoption and then return to London. It sounded simple. Doable. Only she hadn't imagined a youth coming to live with her, looking for a home himself.

'Yoohoo!'

Cece jerked at the call from the front door. She stared at Finlay, who stared back.

'You expecting someone?' he asked innocently.

'No.' Collecting herself, Cece stood, straightened her skirt and patted down her short hair into what she hoped was presentable. Without a mirror in the house she was at a loss to know what she looked like.

Taking a deep breath, she walked through to the front door and opened it.

'Good day,' said the small, plump woman standing on the step.

'Good day,' Cece replied, nervously. The cottage was in no state to entertain guests. She looked past the woman to see a horse and buggy on the drive.

'I'm Miss Isla Cameron. Aren't you bonny? They said you were.' The woman was younger than Cece first thought, perhaps only in her early thirties, and most pretty with an endearing smile, which revealed two dimples.

'How do you do? I'm Mrs Cecelia Marsh.' Then because she'd been brought up to be a sociable lady, Cece swung open the door. 'Please, won't you come in?'

Cece blushed with embarrassment as Isla entered the front room, with it only having a sofa and no other item of comfort or pleasing quality. 'Forgive me, I've just arrived and didn't realise the cottage didn't have furniture.'

'Oh, I'm certain you'll soon sort that out.' Isla smiled and offered Cece the lidded bowl she held. 'I heard that you'd arrived when I was attending church in the village this morning. Everyone is talking about you being here on your own. So, I went home to fetch you this wee lamb stew. I thought you might not have sorted yourself out enough to cook as yet.'

Cece took the bowl, not realising it was Sunday and she should have gone to church. 'Thank you so much.'

'It only needs heating up.' Isla glanced around the room. 'Do you have furniture coming?'

'No. I... I need to go and buy some... from somewhere...' Cece's blush grew deeper. She was sure her face was beetroot by now.

'Inverness is the best place.'

'Yes, I simply must make the journey...'

'It's not too far if you have a motor car. Do you?'

'A motor car? No.'

'Oh, well then, I'll have Ross take you.'

'Ross?'

'My brother. He's away at the moment, visiting our cousins. He took a dozen of last year's wee lambs to Donald's farm, to introduce them into his flock and then Ross will bring back one of Donald's wee rams.'

'Shall I make some tea, Mrs Marsh?' Finlay asked from the doorway.

'Oh, yes, yes, thank you, Finlay.'

'And another wee new face!' Isla beamed. 'How lovely. The village needs fresh faces, even if they are English ones!' She laughed at her own joke. 'I was happy to hear the tidings that someone had taken on Willow Cottage. I was so sad to see it sit empty after our cousin, Callum left. Ross kept an eye on it, of course, but he has so much to do, and as he said we have no claim to it now it's been sold, but he ran some sheep on it to keep the grass under control and he'll pay you to keep them on your land if you want to. He was terribly mad at Callum for selling and not letting us buy it. Callum always was spiteful and resentful towards Ross, being the son of only a Cameron *sister* never sat well with him. I'm glad he's gone!'

Cece was so lost that she wordlessly ushered Isla into the kitchen where the other woman sat at the table and looked around.

'Heavens! You really don't have anything, do you?'

'No, forgive me. We are not equipped for visitors.'

Isla laughed. 'You're not equipped to live here yourself, never mind visitors.'

'There's only one teacup, Mrs Marsh.' Finlay shrugged as if to say it wasn't his problem.

Ashamed and feeling a failure, Cece hung her head. 'Pour the tea for Miss Cameron, please.'

'No, hold the tea, Finlay.' Isla stood. 'We are neighbours, Mrs Marsh, and neighbours never see each other go without. I have spare wee bits and pieces at my farm. Will you let me give them to you?'

'I couldn't, Miss Cameron.'

'Why?' Isla's forthright question stumped Cece. 'Because…'

'I have too much, and you don't have enough. I couldn't be a true Cameron and see another person struggle when I have the ability to help. I insist. Come along.'

Like sheep, Cece and Finlay followed Isla out to the horse and buggy and climbed aboard. Cece hadn't even stopped to put her hat on.

Isla turned the horse about and set off down the drive. 'My brother Ross has the wee farm lorry, he loves it and believes it was the best purchase he ever made, for our father still had horses and carts right up until the end of the Great War. When Father died,

Ross immediately bought the lorry, but I decided to keep the horses, buggy and Father's cart, because a horse doesn't need filling up with petrol.' Isla smiled, showing her dimples again. Her accent wasn't harsh and Cece understood every word she said and found it endearing that she used the word 'wee' so much.

'Do you live far away?' Cece asked as they followed the loch towards the village.

'No, not far. We are up in the hills.' Isla guided the horse off a well-worn track to the right. One that Cece had noticed on her walk yesterday.

After a mile of slowly ascending, the loch fell away behind them and gorges and purple heather and gorse-covered hills became the view. Flocks of sheep blanketed the slopes. The dirt road dropped down a little into a shallow valley studded with trees and at the bottom a narrow stream trickled over rocks on its way down to the loch. Crossing a stone bridge, the horse picked up its pace, sensing home, and the road cut through another stand of tall trees and then climbed up again before breaking out into an open field with the mountains beyond. A substantial white stone farmhouse dominated the landscape. To the right of the two-storey farm house were outbuildings, barns and holding pens, stables and a cobbled yard.

But it was the view that took Cece's breath away. At this height, in every direction she looked was a stunning scene. To the south, a river could be seen like a ribbon of silver below them, and which must end in the loch, and in the north rising majestically in the distance were bluey-pink mountains of the Highlands.

'It's simply beautiful, Miss Cameron,' Cece breathed.

Isla nodded and gazed out. 'It is, though I sometimes curse the isolation in deep winter when I can't leave the house for days on end.'

They followed her to a side door that led straight into a scullery and through that into a bright and warm kitchen, smelling of fresh bread and meat roasting.

Cece had never been in a proper farm kitchen before but if she'd been asked to describe one, this is what she have imagined. Isla's kitchen had sunny yellow painted walls, dark beams, and solid oak furniture. The cooking Aga was a shiny forest green, and dull red flagstones covered the floor. A working table stood in the middle of the floor and at the far end of the room a large dresser was stacked with plates, bowls and cups. Beside the fire on the other wall, sat an old woman in a brown armchair, turning a spit that held sizzling meat over the flames.

'This is Fi,' Isla introduced. 'Fi was the housekeeper and cook here for fifty years. Now she is retired, but she hasn't slowed down, have you, Fi?'

The old woman, dressed all in grey, bobbed her head at Cece. 'Pleased to meet ye, madam.'

'Fi, poor Mrs Marsh and Finlay don't have a thing down at Willow Cottage. Not a scrap! We must help!' Isla darted about taking jars out of the larder and placing them on the table.

Fi rose to put the kettle on the Aga to boil. 'That'll be because Callum McInness sold everything. Och, a rum one he was. Good riddance to him.'

'Now, I'll got fetch a wee hamper.' Isla left the room as Cece and Finlay stood by the door.

'Come away in, madam.' Fi beckoned them to sit at the table. She swiftly placed a plate in front of them both and filled it with slices of rich fruit cake and wedges of cheese.

Finlay ate as though he'd never eaten before and although hungry, Cece knew how to behave at another person's table and nibbled at the cake with the fork Fi provided.

Cups of tea were poured as Isla filled the hamper with jars of preserved fruits, a small basket of eggs, wax paper wrapped bacon, a loaf of bread, flour, sugar, tea and lastly a tin of jam. She added cutlery, a frying pan and a kettle, apologising for the dent in its side.

With the lid of that hamper closed, Isla left the room again, firing questions at Cece. Did she have bed linen, towels, curtains, lamps and so on.

Cece blushed deeper each time she said no, she didn't.

Soon the table was unrecognisable covered with so much stuff, Cece couldn't see over the other side of it.

'This is too much, Miss Cameron.'

'Och, don't be silly. My late mother, Elizabeth, never threw anything out. It's all sitting idle in a wee cupboard and only used once a year. Our family don't come to stay until the end of the summer when we always have a wee harvest party, but they are gone before the snows arrive and then we are marooned up here for months.'

'You have a large family?' Cece enjoyed the richly flavoured tea and cake.

'It's only me and Ross, but we have many cousins scattered around. Ross is the eldest son of the second eldest son, that's why we live here in the family home, and the other brothers have other farms in the area, except our uncle the clan chief, he lives in America now. Then of course we have our wonderful helpers like Fi, who is a part of our family,' Isla smiled fondly at the old housekeeper, 'and the men out in the fields.'

'And who is Callum McInness? Your cousin?'

'Our cousin, yes. He owned Willow Cottage, inherited from his mother, our Aunt Moira, she was a Cameron before marriage. Ross and Callum fell out years ago and Callum took his revenge by selling up and not telling Ross about it, so Ross couldn't buy the land, which has always been Cameron land.'

'That must have been remarkedly upsetting for him.'

'Ross doesn't say much, he's a quiet man, but the day he found out, well, let us just say he took himself up into the mountains and didn't come back for two days and not another word was said about it. That's his way.' Isla shrugged and finished packing another large hamper with linen. 'Come, young Finlay, you can help me put this into the buggy. It's a good job it's all down hill for Pansy. She has a weight to pull today.'

'Thank you so much, Miss Cameron.' Cece followed them out, feeling useless, as watching Isla, who seemed to be clever and able to do anything she put her mind to, was inspiring and Cece had none of her skills.

'Oh, Ross is back early,' Isla said, tying down the hampers.

Cece turned to watch a wood-sided lorry rumble up the dirt road to the house. Its engine turned off, restoring the quietness of the farm. The door opened and down climbed Ross Cameron, Isla's brother.

He took off his hat and his handsome face frowned at Isla. 'What's happening here?'

Isla gave the rope a final tug. 'This is Mrs Marsh and Finlay, they've come from Willow Cottage. They've arrived to find it has no furniture so I'm lending them a few things until they are on their feet.'

'Willow Cottage?' He turned his narrowed gaze to Cece. 'Are you renting it?'

'No, I own it.'

'Will you sell it?'

'No.' She stared back at him. His brash manner and lack of decent courtesy made her hackles rise.

'I'll offer you a fair price.'

'Ross!' Isla warned. 'They've only just arrived. Where are your manners?'

'In America with Callum.' He gave a sharp nod of his head to Cece and strode into the house.

'I'm so sorry,' Isla said as they climbed into the buggy.

Cece smiled, not knowing what to say or to make of Ross Cameron. The man was attractive in a rugged brooding way, but his rude questions instantly marked him as an arrogant oaf. She didn't give him another thought as they headed down the hill.

Chapter Nine

The little comforts, generously donated by Isla, gave Cece a small amount of ease as she struggled through the next few days. She constantly fought an inner conflict whether to stay or go. She'd met such nice people, strangers who had been kind and generous, would she get that treatment elsewhere? Did she want to be alone?

Finlay was her knight in shining armour, and she knew that without him she'd have left Scotland and never looked back. He had a simple trust in her that they would manage living as they did. She wished she felt the same. Finlay's constant happy chatter kept her doubts buried during the day, and usually at night she was so tired after doing physical work for the first time in her life that she fell asleep the instant she got into bed.

The sun continued to shine and for that Cece was also grateful. Finlay found an old spade in the back of the barn buried beneath empty hessian sacks, old harnesses and rusted pieces of iron. In the hayloft he found a pitchfork and with those two tools he set to work in the vegetable garden.

Cece watched him the first day, bringing him cups of water, but generally staying out of his way as he turned over the soil and cleared away the weeds. She rejoiced with him every time he found a self-seeded vegetable and that night bathed the blisters on his hands.

She felt useless. It was a continual feeling. On the second day after meeting Isla Cameron, Finlay said he didn't need her help, as they only had one spade to dig with, she returned indoors and made sure the fire was kept healthy with wood. Filling a bucket with water and using her own personal soap she cleaned the filthy kitchen windows, but they dried smeared and worse than when she started. How did people achieve sparkling clean windows? It was a mystery to her.

By the third day they'd eaten most of Isla's food and Cece knew she'd have to try her hand at cooking. The idea daunted her. With Finlay's instructions she'd mastered making a pot of tea, simple really, hot water and tea leaves and last night she had cooked boiled eggs. Finlay announced they were great eggs with a runny centre. How she'd managed that she didn't know, but it pleased her to please him.

Cece looked at the range and tried to pluck up the courage to put something in the pot. She could peel and chop the vegetables that were left, but plain boiled vegetables were not overly exciting. She longed for something sweet, and soft bread, succulent pieces of meat and a glass of wine. She had to hire a cook, for she and Finlay would starve otherwise.

She was about to pick up the knife when she heard the unmistakable sound of an engine. She hurried out of the kitchen and opened the front door and stopped.

Ross Cameron climbed down from his lorry and walked towards her. Taking off his hat, he pushed back his deep brown hair with one hand. 'Good day, Mrs Marsh.'

'Mr Cameron.' She pulled her cardigan over her stomach, not that he would notice her tiny bump for what it was she was sure.

'I've come to beg your forgiveness and apologise for my rudeness a few days ago.'

'Oh.'

'My sister hasn't stopped lecturing me, and when she isn't nagging me, she's giving me the silent treatment. For my own sanity I thought it best to come and see you.' His lips quirked into a half smile and he also had dimples like his sister.

Cece smiled back despite herself. 'Would you care to come in?'

'Thank you.'

Aware of him walking behind her through the empty cottage, Cece took him straight into the kitchen where there was a semblance of homeliness, with the table and chairs and the teacups and teapot on the table.

'You really don't have a thing.' He frowned. 'I thought Isla was exaggerating.'

'I expected the cottage to be furnished when I arrived. An oversight on my part.' She found it interesting that his Scottish accent wasn't as strong as those in the village, or even his sister's.

Through the opened back door, she could see Finlay adding more weeds to the pile to be burnt.

'I'm ashamed my cousin left the farm in such a state. It was once, many years ago, rather pretty. My Aunt Moira lived here.' He gestured out of the door towards Finlay. 'You seem to have a good helper there.'

'Would you like to come out and meet him?' Cece was keen to move out of the kitchen, for Ross Cameron seemed to dwarf the room with his size. She hadn't realised on first acquaintance just how tall and broad he was. He could adequately be described as a mountain man. His clothes were excellent quality but undoubtedly working clothes, his hair was a little overlong and when she'd first met him, he had stubbly growth along his jaw, but today he was clean-shaven and for some silly reason Cece's stomach clenched a little when she glanced at him.

Standing at the wall of the vegetable garden, Ross Cameron spoke to Finlay on the other side. Finlay was keen to show off his knowledge and quickly outlined his plan for the area to Mr Cameron.

'You're short on tools, lad.' Ross indicated to the old spade Finlay rested on.

'I'll buy some more as soon as I can find a way into Fort William or Inverness,' Cece put in. 'We are short of a great many things.'

'Fort William holds a market every Thursday, and there's a good variety of shops.'

'That's where I need to go then.'

'You'll be needing to transport all your goods back here. I can take you in the lorry, if you wish it?'

His offer shocked her, and it took a moment for her to reply. 'That would be most kind of you.'

'Although from our first meeting you'd never know it, I am a decent person. However, mention of

Callum or this place brings out a reaction in me that I'm not proud of.'

'Families have a habit of doing that to us unfortunately.'

'Until Thursday then. I'll pick you up at seven. I like to get to the market early. I'm sure you have a list as long as your arm.' He nodded and left them.

Cece watched him go and felt the need to breathe as though she'd been holding her breath the whole time he was there. Instinct told her Ross Cameron was a man she could grow to like, a lot, but did she want that?

'Did you want me to fetch you more water, Mrs Marsh?' Finlay asked.

Cece shook her head. 'I can do it myself. You're busy enough. Oh, and, Finlay, I'd like you to call me Cece. Mrs Marsh is too formal when we are living together as we are.'

His grin stretched wide. 'Great!' He jogged off to the far end of the vegetable plot and attacked the weeds some more.

Content she'd made him happy, she headed back to the kitchen. She would make a go of this place, if only for Finlay. She'd deal with the problem of the baby closer to the time.

~ ~ ~ ~

Cece was waiting for Ross Cameron's lorry and was delighted when it pulled up to find that Isla was also in the cabin.

Cece turned to Finlay who stood with her in the morning mist that shrouded the cottage, fields and loch. 'Are you sure you don't want to come?'

'No, I'll stay here and keep an eye on everything,' he said seriously.

Cece patted his shoulder, inwardly smiling at his grown-up attitude. 'Have a good day then.'

'Good morning, Mrs Marsh.' Ross came to open the cabin door for her and assisted her up into the seat.

'Good morning, Mr Cameron, Miss Cameron.' Cece hoisted herself up onto the seat beside Isla, noticing in the back of the lorry were crates of produce.

'Are you ready for a day of shopping?' Isla sat between Ross and Cece.

'I don't really have a choice!' Cece laughed as they bumped along. She'd not been in a big vehicle since she drove the old ambulance on Millie and Jeremy's estate in Northern France. She had a flashback of driving in the snow with Monty helping her negotiate the track to the field where they had selected a Christmas tree to chop down. Her heart did a little skip at the thought of Monty. She tried ridiculously hard to keep him out of her mind. No good would come of thinking about him, but it was hard to ignore the fact she carried his baby, and it was that very reason why she was now in this lorry with two new friends.

All the way to Fort William, they chatted about Resslick and its people, the area and the harsh weather of the Highlands, the scarcity of jobs for people and how many were emigrating to other countries to start again. Ross and Isla were part of the Cameron clan, which had lost many families to distant parts of the world.

The sunshine of the past few days failed to materialise as they entered the busy streets of Fort

William. Low clouds threatened rain and a cool breeze came off Loch Linnhe. Cece was pleased she wore her coat.

'Right, I'll park on the other side of the market,' Ross said, pulling the lorry to a stop and letting them out.

'We'll walk the market first, and then I'll take Mrs Marsh to the shops,' Isla answered as they scrambled down.

Cece heard the hawkers of the market stallholders before she saw them. Turning a corner, she was surprised to see such a large farmer's market. 'I need to find a bank, Miss Cameron, at some point this morning, as my money will run out that I have with me.'

'They'll not be open just yet, but if you run short, I've money.'

'What are you looking to buy?' Cece asked as they joined the throng of shoppers.

'Nothing really, I just wanted to come and help you.'

'You are too kind.' It touched Cece deeply that this woman was so eager to be a good friend.

'What do you need then?' Isla stopped by a stall selling handmade leather goods.

'What don't I need!' Cece chuckled. 'Everything.'

'That's true.' Isla grinned. 'Let's get started then.'

It took them two hours to shop at the market. Cece couldn't remember when she'd enjoyed a shopping experience as much before. She let Isla haggle the prices, for she was a master at it, and soon they were making extra trips to the lorry to dump all the bargains Cece bought.

Leaving the last load of purchases in the back, Cece took stock of what she'd accumulated. Pots and pans, jugs, bowls, plates and cups. Two kerosene glass lamps, plus a can of kerosene, cheap bed sheets and blankets, crates of vegetables, jars of jam, bread, cheese and a kidney and potato pie.

'Now, to the shops.' Isla led the way into the surrounding streets.

Cece's stomach grumbled and Isla laughed.

'Perhaps a wee cup of tea first though?'

'Yes, definitely.'

They found a little café where Cece paid for tea and scones. They sat by the window as the first drops of rain fell.

'That was good timing.' Isla took off her coat.

Cece kept her coat on put pulled off her gloves and glanced around at the other diners. 'I can't thank you enough, Miss Cameron, for helping me.'

'I enjoyed it, but I'd like you to call me Isla. Miss Cameron sounds so formal. I'm not used to it.' Isla chuckled. 'I get Miss Isla at home from Fi and the men, so to hear you calling me Miss Cameron makes me feel terribly old! So, Isla will do nicely.'

Cece grinned. 'I'd like that, thank you. And I'm Cece.'

'Lovely. I'm ready for this cup of tea, but it's such fun shopping for so much and not spending a penny of my own!'

'I've never bought so much in my life.' Cece groaned at the amount she'd spent.

'At least your wee home will be more comfortable now. Once you've got it as you want it to be then you'll not have to keep buying things. Aunt Moira had the cottage looking lovely in her day. The gardens in summer were a riot of flowers, and she grew the best vegetables in the area and sold them here at the market. I adored spending time with her.

She was like a mother to Ross and me. We lost our own mother when we were teenagers, you see.'

'That must have been hard for you. My papa died only three years ago, and I miss him terribly. I couldn't imagine losing a parent so young.'

'It wasn't easy, but we managed.' Isla smiled at the waitress who brought their tray of tea and scones. 'Where are your family from?'

'York, in Yorkshire. Do you know it?' Cece spread butter on the fruit scone.

'Only from history books. We have one wee room that is full of books. Father called it the library, but Mother called it Father's study of dust collectors.'

'I love books. I had to part with a great many when we sold the family home just recently.'

'Your husband's home?'

Cece cringed at the mention of her non-existent husband. She didn't like lying to her new friends. 'No, I meant my parents' home. Mama has remarried and gone to live in Paris and my sisters have also married. The family home wasn't needed any more and was sold.'

'How dreadful. I'd hate to sell our home. I couldn't imagine saying goodbye to it.' Isla ate some scone. 'When I was engaged to Robbie, I made him promise that we wouldn't move far from Resslick, so I could go home and see Ross. In the end I didn't have to worry about that issue because Robbie was killed in the war and I never married.'

'That's so tragic, but you're young and can still find someone else to love, perhaps?' Cece felt terrible for Isla, knowing the pain of loving someone and they are gone. Not that Monty was dead, but the feeling was similar, she was sure.

'Hardly young. I'm in my thirties. I don't meet many young men any more. Resslick is deserted of decent fellows. Those who came back from the war quickly soon left again to move to cities and even other countries to find work.'

'You are too pretty and nice to be left on the shelf,' Cece said, sipping her tea. She'd devoured two scones and could easily eat another.

'Well it's looking that way. What is your husband like? Where is he? Will he be arriving soon?'

'He's away, on business. He works for my brother-in-law, Jeremy. Monty... Monty is a champagne salesman based in London.' She hated the lies she told, but she had to protect herself. If people knew she was having a baby out of wedlock, her life would become a misery.

'Will he be coming to Willow Cottage?' Isla poured them more tea from the teapot.

'No. He's too busy. He'll not come. I only came to Scotland for the summer to stay at the cottage as I'd not seen it.'

Isla's expression fell. 'You mean you'll be leaving, returning to London?'

'At some point, yes.' Cece instantly felt like she was betraying Isla.

'Oh. That's a shame.' Isla pushed away her half-eaten scone. 'I was hoping you'd be a friend.'

'I can be. I will be. No matter where I am, we can be friends.'

Isla nodded and stood, pulling her coat on. 'Shall we finish finding what you need?'

Cece stood, hating that she had disappointed Isla. She touched her arm. 'I'm truly grateful for all your help and friendship. We can spend the summer and possibly the autumn together if you wish.'

Isla brightened. 'I'd like that.'

Taking a deep breath, Cece followed her out into the street. Eventually, she'd have to tell Isla about the baby for she'll not be able to hide it soon. Then she'll have to say goodbye to Isla and never return to Resslick. In the future they'll only be friends by letters, and she'll have to keep up the pretence of her marriage and the child. In time, she'll stop writing completely. The thought made her sad. She liked Isla enormously.

They visited the bank where Cece was able to withdraw money and from there Isla took her to a furniture store.

Overwhelmed by how much she needed, Cece bought a single bed for Finlay, a small dressing table with mirror and a narrow wardrobe for herself, and finally a kitchen dresser. The young man who served them was happy to have the pieces ready to load onto the lorry in an hour.

'Are you sure your brother won't mind hauling all this stuff back to the cottage?' Cece asked as head down against the drizzly rain they hurried up another street.

'Och no.' Isla ushered Cece into a bookshop. 'He offered. Now, in the absence of a cook, I think you're going to need a wee book or two to help you create meals.'

Cece snorted. 'I need more than a book. I didn't know how to boil an egg until yesterday.'

'You come from a privileged family, why would you know these things? Unlike me, I've grown up on a farm all my life and although we've had helpers in the house, my mother did a great deal and she instilled that into me, too. Elizabeth Cameron had a reputation of always having a pot of food on the go in case anyone turned up at the house, and they often did. So many aunts and uncles, cousins and friends.'

'I feel I need to hire someone, a housemaid who can cook.'

'You'll find that difficult from the small population of Resslick, or even getting anyone to come out that far from the towns. We are too isolated for town people. They hate the winters.'

'I need to find someone. I can organise a large house and a sizable number of servants, I just can't actively do anything more than that.'

'You'll learn.' Isla picked up a heavy tome. 'This is a bit old-fashioned, but particularly useful.' She gave Cece a book titled, *Mrs Beeton's Book of Household Management.*

'Do I need this? I just said I can manage a household. That was one thing I was taught by my governess and Mama.'

Isla laughed. 'You had a governess, too? Yes, you need this book. It has an introductory to cookery. Read every page.'

After paying for the book, Cece walked with Isla along another street, but stopped outside a cobbler's shoe shop. 'I want to buy Finlay some boots.'

'Yes, I saw his bare feet,' Isla said sadly. 'He has no one I suspect, an orphan boy from a workhouse?'

'He hasn't told me much, perhaps the subject is too raw for him to discuss.'

'Poor wee lad. You go in, I need to drop in on Florrie, an old friend of my mothers. Poor wee Florrie calls me Elizabeth thinking I'm my mother. Old age hasn't been kind to her. I'll meet you back in the market, yes?'

Cece nodded and entered the shop. Discussing her needs with the spectacled man behind the counter, she bought a pair of sturdy black boots that the cobbler told her would fit the feet of a youth. She hoped he was right.

With the boots bought, she went next door to the general grocery shop and bought items she couldn't find on the market. Ticking off her list she bought essential items like washing soda, Reckett's Blue, salt and pepper, vinegar, a sweeping brush, more flour and tea leaves, all for the first time in her life.

Walking back to the market, the rain eased, and the breeze dropped a little. Once more, Cece strolled along the stalls, stopping to buy the odd item, more candles, gloves for the garden, a sewing kit and going cheap from a clothing stall, she bought two pairs of trousers and a blue shirt for Finlay, plus three pairs of socks.

Satisfied she could carry no more for the net bags she'd bought that morning were bulging and heavy, she decided she'd done enough for one day. She reached the last of the stalls where the animals and larger items were for sale. There, sitting under an umbrella, she encountered George the man who had first taken her to Willow Cottage. He was selling chickens, the poor creatures were wet and looking decidedly miserable. Finlay would like caring for the chickens, and she knew how to boil an egg, so they'd not starve!

~ ~ ~ ~

Ross Cameron left the pub at the far side of the market after enjoying a delicious meal of meat and potato hotpot and a pint of beer. As usual this Thursday treat was something he did weekly, and it was a good chance to catch up with locals and friends, and the odd Cameron relative.

'Catch ye next week, Ross,' Tom McNeill called to him as he also left the pub.

Ross raised his hand to his childhood friend, then spotted Mrs Marsh talking to old George. He watched her juggling all the parcels and bags in her arms. Her easy laughter carried to him and hit him in the chest. Never in his life had he been attracted to a married woman. They were off limits, he knew that, but Mrs Marsh had something about her that caught his attention. It made him smile that her light red-blonde hair was a little messy, that she wore no make-up and she was utterly clueless about how to survive living on her own. She had a fragility about her, but also a hidden strength beneath that she probably didn't even recognise she had, but Ross saw it. There was something about Cece Marsh that spoke to him and he wished to God it didn't.

Isla talked nothing but about Mrs Marsh and her English ways. Her cultured English voice gave away that she came from money. He'd met many a woman like that when he was studying at Cambridge. He was just thankful she had no airs and graces, or felt she was above him and Isla. She seemed genuine and usually he was a good judge of character.

However, he didn't understand why such a woman would come to the middle of nowhere and live in a cottage stripped bare of all comforts, and then take in a boy off the streets. None of it made sense and where was her husband? Ross couldn't understand it. If she was his wife, he'd never be far from her side.

He couldn't watch her struggle for another moment and strode to where she was listening hard to

George talking about raising chickens. 'Here, Mrs Marsh, let me take some of those things from you.'

'Oh, thank you, Mr Cameron.' She gratefully handed over the heavy book and a basket of goods.

'You've been bus.' He chuckled.

'You should see the lorry. Isla and I have made several trips.'

'That's what it is there for.'

'I've also bought some furniture from Henson's Furniture Shop. Isla said you wouldn't mind collecting it on our way home?'

'Not at all.'

George creaked up from the chair he was sitting on. 'And Mrs Marsh is buying a wee six chickens from me.'

'Yes.' Mrs Marsh blushed, then leaned closer to Ross. 'He did say six, didn't he, and not sixty? I can barely understand his accent.'

'Yes, six.' Ross smiled, liking that she was humble and shy. It made such a change from the women he knew. Isla was full of life, noisy and always dashing about, old Fi was bossy and snappy, despite her heart of gold. In fact, most of his aunts and cousins were also loud, demanding and controlling. It was a pleasant surprise to see a demure woman for a change.

George plucked six hens from a crate and put them into another smaller crate. 'I think she should get some wee pigs, too, what ye say, Ross?'

'I'm assuming Mrs Marsh has had enough to contend with today. I'll come back for them in a moment.'

Cece paid George and thanked him and followed Ross to the lorry. 'Why is it that I can understand you and Isla but hardly anyone else?'

Ross placed the book and bags on the front seat. 'That's because I spent several years in a boarding school in England and then university. My uncle is the clan chief and all male members of his family and his brothers' male children were sent to English boarding schools and then onto university to be educated.'

'How interesting.' She climbed up into the cabin and rearranged the goods she'd bought. 'What did you study?'

'Architecture, geography and languages. I might only be a Highlands farmer, but I am an educated one.'

'I would have loved to go to university, but it was never something my parents encouraged.'

'I'm thankful now for my uncle's ruling, but at the time I was terribly homesick for my mountains.' He grinned.

'Everyone should be educated. I'm a big believer in that.'

'Me, too.' He turned on hearing Isla calling out farewells to several people she passed. 'Right, now my sister is here, shall we go to Henson's?'

Happy to be of help to Mrs Marsh, Ross enjoyed the drive home, listening to the two women chatting about cooking and managing a house. Isla was full of hints and tips, which Mrs Marsh wrote down in a notebook she took from her bag.

'I suppose it would be simpler to hire a cook, but I have begun to enjoy learning new skills,' Mrs Marsh said as they neared Willow Cottage.

Isla nodded. 'Yes, it would be, of course, but until you find someone, it'll be good for you to have some basic knowledge of cooking. I'll come down tomorrow and give you a wee hand at making something.'

'Thank you.'

Ross steered the lorry through the gate and up the drive. 'You need a man or two to help get this place back into shape.'

'Yes, I agree.' Mrs Marsh climbed down from the cabin as Finlay ran around the side of the house, smiling a welcome.

Ross, with Finlay's help, unloaded the furniture and carried it upstairs to where Mrs Marsh wanted it. The whole time Finlay gushed about having his own bedroom and how he was keen to take care of the chickens.

Finlay ran down the stairs. 'I'll mend the chicken coop this afternoon. The wire is full of holes and we don't want Mr Fox to get in.'

Following him into the kitchen, Ross ruffled the boy's hair. 'You'll find in the back of the lorry some more tools, a new spade, a hoe and a rake. They are yours.'

'Really?' he whispered, his eyes wide.

Ross was moved by the boy's reaction. 'A hard-working man should be rewarded, and Mrs Marsh tells me you've been a miracle worker on the vegetable garden and a tremendous help to her.'

'He has,' Mrs Marsh agreed.

'Thank you, Mr Cameron!'

'That's not all.' Cece gave Finlay a parcel and placed the boots on top of it. 'I hope they fit.'

In awe, Finlay held the boots as though they were something precious. 'Boots? My own boots?'

'Yes. I can't be seen with you walking about barefooted.' Cece chuckled, happy to see Finlay's response.

He opened the parcel of clothes and gasped. As he lifted out the trousers, shirt and sweater, socks and underclothes, tears welled in his eyes. 'It's like Christmas.' Finlay threw his arms around Cece's waist. 'Thank you.'

'You're very welcome.'

'I'll go get changed.'

'You need a good wash before you wear clean clothes. We'll heat some water later and then you can wear your new clothes.'

Finlay nodded, touching the leather boots.

'Don't forget the tools,' Ross joked, slightly emotional by the boy's happiness.

'I'll do that first.' Finlay disappeared to fetch the tools.

'I must pay you for those, Mr Cameron,' Mrs Marsh said to him.

Ross took a deep breath at the lovely smile she gave him. 'There is no need at all. I wanted to do it.'

'But you and Isla have done so much for me already. A few days ago, you didn't even know me and look at your generosity.' Tears gathered in her eyes.

Isla rushed to put an arm around her shoulders. 'We like helping people, Cece, it's what us Highlanders do, and just like you've helped that young lad. There will be a time when you'll help us and that's how it works. It's a circle.'

'I don't know how I could possibly help you both.'

'By being our friend,' Isla added. 'And stop calling Ross Mr Cameron. He's Ross and you're Cece.'

'I can't tell you how happy it makes me to have you two as my friends.' Cece squeezed Isla's hands but her smile was for him.

Ross tucked his hands into his trouser pockets needing to leave the kitchen and the delicate smile of Cece Marsh. It was twisting his innards to think she was another's wife and he could never pursue more than friendship. 'Come harvest time, it's all hands-on deck. You'll be needed then. We all help each other at harvest time.' He frowned as Cece's expression altered.

'You can count on me in some way,' she murmured.

Cece's answer intrigued him. There was more to this woman than she let on.

As he drove up the mountain towards home, Isla's chatting flowed over his head as he thought about Cece Marsh.

'Where is her husband?' he asked his sister, stopping her flow of talk about the prices in the market.

'London, I believe.'

'Is he coming here at any time?'

'No, not from what I can gather. Cece said he was terribly busy. She came to Willow Cottage for the summer to see the cottage.'

'And Finlay?'

'Just someone who turned up, and she took him in as he had nowhere to go. He's a wee orphan and God knows she needs his help. I'll ask around and see if there's anyone wanting a housemaid or cook position for the summer.'

'Why only the summer?'

'Because then she's leaving and returning to England.'

Ross hated the thought of that.

Chapter Ten

Cece bid goodbye to the mailman and glanced through the bundle of letters which had arrived. She had a letter each from her sisters, Mama and Grandmama. She opened Mama's letter first.

Dearest Cece,

I am much surprised by your decision to travel and stay in Scotland. I fully expected you to return to London after Elm House was sold, or if not London then come to me here in Paris. Jacques and I would gladly welcome you and would be pleased to spend some time with you. Millie too would have been delighted to see you.

However, you must do what you wish to do, of course, and visiting the property in Scotland will remove that spark of curiosity as to what it is like. I do hope the property your grandmama bought you is adequate in size and comfort. I'm certain it must be. I do wish to hear all about it.

*My concern is you travelling around Scotland
alone. I do not understand why you would do so. I'd
feel calmer if you were accompanied by someone we
know. I have a friend, Elsie Chambers, in Edinburgh,
should you wish to go there? I'll put the address on
the back of this letter.*

*Jacques is extremely busy, as usual. He has left
this morning to journey to Rome to talk with some
hoteliers about supplying Chateau Dumont's
champagne. He is meeting Monty there for a few days
before Monty moves on to Athens. Did you hear the
news that Monty is courting a London debutante? I
cannot remember her name. She's from an
exceptionally good family, naturally. We are jolly
pleased for the dear boy. He deserves his piece of
happiness and how good must this lady be to overlook
his scars.*

Cece crushed the letter into her fist. She was torn
by anger and hurt. Monty had moved on so quickly
after their little liaison. Obviously, he thought nothing
about her. He wasn't spending his days pining for her.
Why couldn't Monty be courting her? She was having
his baby! She should have told him about the baby.
He'd marry her then. He'd be hers...

But would he? The same questions and
uncertainties filled her mind once more. Did she want
a man who was with her only out of pity and duty?

No, she did not.

And she loved him enough to want him to be
happy. He'd not be happy with her, she knew that
deep down, and she wouldn't be able to live with
herself if she made him do the right thing only
because he was a decent gentleman. She couldn't ruin
his life.

Depressed at her situation, she strolled along the front of the cottage, pausing to stare blindly at the odd yellow rose that had managed to bloom in the tangle of weeds.

Tears dripped off her lashes, and she dashed them away impatiently. What was the use of crying? Would it change things? Would it make Monty come and take her away with promises of marriage and a happy ever after? No. Grandmama said self-pity was unattractive. She placed a hand on her stomach, hating the predicament she was in. She rarely thought of the child in her womb. It was an unwanted thing, like a blister on one's heel. By December the blister will be gone, and she could get on with the rest of her life.

'Cece!' Finlay came around the corner of the cottage, hot and sweaty. After two days of miserable weather, the sun was shining, and he was back out in the vegetable garden.

'Yes?'

'The chickens laid a couple of eggs!'

She smiled as he opened his hands and showed them to her. 'Wonderful!'

'Are you all right?' He squinted at her.

'Yes, perfectly fine,' she lied. 'I was simply thinking about tidying this garden up to make the front of the cottage pretty. I'm tired of being in the kitchen.'

'I'll go fetch my spade.' He ran off and Cece sighed. What was she going to do about Finlay when she returned to London? Perhaps he could go and work for the Camerons'?

Yesterday Isla had returned as promised and helped her to sort out the cottage and Isla and Finlay had rubbed along together well, each helping Cece to clean the kitchen before the cooking started in earnest. Cece's purchases made the cottage more of a home, especially the kitchen, which, with more items on show, now looked homely.

Throughout the day, Isla had given her basic cooking lessons. How to cook and mash potatoes with lots of butter, how to pan fry the fish Isla had brought with her and to make a simple white sauce to go with it, a meal the three of them had enjoyed at midday. They made two loaves of a brown coarse bread and an egg custard tart.

Then Isla had gone through a list of practical jobs. Noticing the filthy windows, she showed Cece how to clean them with lots of hot water, clean cloths and a wee bit of vinegar. Next, she helped Cece with the clothes washing. Filling a bucket with hot water and washing soda and adding the Reckett's Blue on the last rinse. The practical work had exhausted Cece. She'd fallen into bed not long after seven o'clock, but she'd felt a sense of accomplishment she'd never felt before, except perhaps learning to drive. It astonished her that she'd gone through her life so far achieving so extraordinarily little.

Finlay returned with the hoe and spade. Cece pushed her letters into her skirt pocket and after retrieving the gardening gloves she'd bought, she started the laborious task of weeding the flower bed.

'I wish I knew more about flowers,' Finlay said, pulling up a weed. 'They didn't grow flowers at the orphanage, just vegetables.'

'An orphanage wouldn't have a need for flowers. Their priority is to feed you all.'

'They didn't do a very good job of it. I was always hungry.'

'Where was this orphanage?' Cece asked, digging around an exposed rose bush.

'Edinburgh.'

She stopped and stared at him and he wouldn't make eye contact. 'The truth, if you please. I think I deserve that, don't you?'

He nodded and kept hoeing for a moment. 'Dumfries.'

'Dumfries?' She wasn't sure where that was.

'Me and my sister were left there by my father when we were little. He was English, like you, but after my mother died having my sister, he took us on the road with him to find work. Something happened and he couldn't look after us. He left us in an orphanage in Dumfries.'

'How old were you?'

'Four.'

'And your sister? Where is she?'

'Dead. She died a few months ago. That's when I left the place. She got sick, and they didn't make her better. The nuns said it was God's work. Well, God is shit and so are the nuns and their beech canes and going to bed without food! It is all shit!'

'Finlay!'

'Well, it's true. My sister did nothing wrong. She was good and everyone loved her. She shouldn't be dead.' He stormed off around the side of the cottage.

Cece rose from her knees to follow him but saw Mr Evans, the school teacher, coming up the track. She dusted her gloves together and pulled them off. She smiled at him as she pushed her hair back from her face. 'Good day, Mr Evans.'

'Good day, Mrs Marsh. I was taking a walk and thought I'd pop along and see how you were settling in.' His smile was warm and friendly, his pale blue eyes wrinkled at the corners when he smiled.

'How kind of you. Would you care for a cup of tea, or a glass of water?'

'I would indeed, thank you. The sun is warmer than I thought it would be.' He wore a thick tweed suit and a boater hat, which he took off and held in his hands. Under his arm was a folded newspaper.

'Come inside.' Cece took him into the kitchen, for the front room was still too bare for entertaining.

She placed the kettle over the hob on the range and then set out the cups and saucers. 'Would you care for some egg custard tart?'

'Thank you, that sounds lovely.'

She busied herself adding tea leaves to the teapot and cutting slices of tart. 'Do you often walk this way?'

'Yes, along the loch usually.'

'It's a beautiful area to walk. And where are you from originally?' She took the kettle off the heat as it boiled.

'Lancashire, near Preston.'

'And what made you decide on Resslick?' She mashed the tea and passed him a plate with a slice of tart on it.

'I studied at Edinburgh and when I graduated, I worked at a few schools that were in need of teachers on the east coast.'

'And Resslick is currently the lucky school.' She smiled. 'Milk?'

'Thank you.'

She took the milk bottle out of the underground storage and brought it to the table. 'After Edinburgh, this area must seem extremely quiet.'

'That's what I wanted.'

'Me too, after London and York.'

'That is where you are from?'

'York, yes, but I live in London now.'

'I like London immensely, so much to see and do. Are you north or south of the Thames?'

'North, in Mayfair.'

His eyes widened and he quickly looked at the doorway as Finlay entered, carrying a handful of heather and ferns.

'They are pretty.' Cece gave Finlay's shoulder a squeeze.

'They are for you.' He put the bouquet on the table. 'I'm sorry I ran off.'

'I understand. Mr Evans this is Finlay,' Cece introduced them. 'Finlay, Mr Evans is Resslick's school teacher.'

Finlay nodded his head to Mr Evans and with a worried look at Cece fled from the kitchen.

'Well, I'm pleased I didn't have that reaction from you.' Evans laughed, accepting the teacup from her.

Through the window Cece saw Finlay run into the barn. He wasn't having a good day today. The normal happy young fellow was struggling with his memories it seemed.

She sat at the table and gave her attention to Mr Evans.

'So, what brings you to this out of the way place?' Evans asked, forking a piece of tart. 'London has to be much more preferable than here.'

'My grandmama bought me this cottage. I thought I should come and see it. I've never been to Scotland before and it gave me the opportunity to see some of the country.'

'And your husband? Will he be joining you?'

'I don't think so. He is remaining in London.'
Cece tucked a strand of hair behind her ear. She hated
lying to people. The web of deceit was becoming
wider.

'You must find it difficult being apart from each
other?'

Cece glanced down at her piece of tart. 'No, not
really. He is often away on business. I'm used to
being on my own.'

'Well, Mrs Marsh, I hope that while you are here
you will regard me as a friend, and not be lonely?'

She smiled at him. 'Thank you. One can never
have enough friends.' She glanced at the headlines of
the newspaper he'd put on the table. 'Prime Minister
Bonar Law resigns due to ill health. How terribly sad
for the poor man.'

'Yes, he's extremely sick, apparently. The word is
that Stanley Baldwin will replace him, he probably
has done by now. This newspaper is a few days old,
but I've not had the chance to read it yet. I thought I
would sit by the loch and finally get to it, but it's old
news. I shall go into Fort William and buy a more up-
to-date newspaper on Monday.'

'Do you catch a lift with someone or have your
own motor car? Resslick is so far away from
anywhere and the village has no shops at all. After
living in York and London and having everything at
my fingertips, I'm struggling being so isolated.'

'I agree. Thankfully, I have my own little car, an
Argyll Flying Fifteen. She's old, built in nineteen
fourteen but I bought her cheap last year and have not
regretted it for a moment.'

'I simply must do something similar. I need
transport out here and I can drive.'

'You can?' he asked in astonishment.

'Oh yes. I learnt a couple of years ago.'

'That's incredible. I insist you borrow my little car any time you choose.'

'I couldn't.'

'Of course, you can. I really do insist!' He sat on the edge of his chair, his eyes imploring. 'Do you fancy a drive tomorrow afternoon?'

She blinked in surprise and was flattered that he'd offered such an invitation. 'Yes, I don't see why not? Thank you.'

'Excellent. I do hope we become good friends, Mrs Marsh. I find it rather lonely out here. The village people are nice, but they are not English, if you know my meaning? Some haven't ever left the village. Imagine? Whereas you and I can talk about all manner of things, can't we?'

A knock on the front door drew Cece up from the chair. 'Excuse me.' She hurried to the front room and opened the door. 'Oh, Mr Cameron.'

'I thought you were going to call me Ross from now on?' He grinned. 'I've brought a basket of things that Isla claimed you needed.'

'How kind, do come in.' Flustered at having two male guests, Cece felt her face grow hot as Ross's step faltered on seeing Mr Evans sitting at the table.

'Mr Cameron.' Evans reclined back as though he was very much at home. The smile he wore a little smug.

Ross gave him a steady look. 'Mr Evans. I wasn't aware you were a friend of Mrs Marsh.'

'We are becoming better acquainted each time we meet, aren't we, Mrs Marsh?'

'Indeed. I am most fortunate to have met such good people so quickly.'

'Isla sends her regards.' Ross placed the basket on the floor. 'I shan't hold you up.'

'You're not,' Cece said, wanting him to stay. 'Please sit, have some tea.'

Ross seemed to weigh up the invite and decided to accept. 'How's young Finlay?'

'He's awfully busy. The chickens laid two eggs today, and he was excited by it.' She fetched another teacup and poured him some tea.

'The hens must be happy in their environment then, otherwise they wouldn't lay.'

'Wouldn't they?' Cece had no idea. 'That's good then. They must like the home he's made for them.'

'I'll go and see him in a moment.'

'Would you like a piece of tart?'

'No, thank you, though Isla informs me that you were a star pupil.'

'Pupil?' Mr Evans sat forward. 'What are you studying, Mrs Marsh?'

'Nothing intellectual, I can assure you. I am not a cook, Mr Evans, and Isla has kindly offered to teach me the basics until I hire a woman to help me.'

'I shall keep an ear to the ground for you about a cook. We can't have you slaving over a range like a common skivvy, can we?' Evans's stare was a little too intense.

Sipping her tea, Cece dropped her gaze. 'I can't say it's something I want to do all day every day, but I did enjoy my lessons with Isla.' She turned to Ross. 'What is in the basket?'

'No idea.' He shook his head with a smile. 'By the time my sister is finished I believe all the items in my entire house will be in this cottage!'

Cece laughed. 'I am sorry.'

Evans lifted the teapot to pour more tea into Cece's cup. 'What else do you require, Mrs Marsh? Can I be of any assistance?'

'Thank you, Mr Evans, but I do trust that I'm on top of things. Naturally, I'd like the front room to be more comfortable, but that will come in time.'

'I could take you to Inverness to find some more furniture, if you wish it?' Ross said.

'That would be lovely, thank you.'

Evans finished the last of his tart. 'That was delicious, truly. Well done, you. I'd never would have imagined you hadn't done this before by the taste of it. Yet, I can see you are not meant for the drudgery of the kitchen. You, Mrs Marsh should be doing nothing more strenuous than sipping tea and attending balls and dinner parties.'

Cece reddened, not used to compliments. 'Thank you. I have attended a great many.'

'Do you enjoy dancing?'

'Yes, I do. My sisters and I used to go to balls a lot in York, before they both married.'

'Then we should visit Fort William when they hold their next town ball. Why do we not invite your sisters to attend, too?'

Cece laughed. 'Millie lives in Northern France now. She is far too busy being a mother of two little boys and a wife to a chateau owner.'

'A chateau?' Evans's eyebrows shot up. 'Your sister married a Frenchman?'

'No. She married Sir Jeremy Remington, an Englishman with French ancestry. It's a long story. It's more impressive that Chateau Dumont's champagne is sold all around the world now. Millie wouldn't come to Scotland. She had far too much to do.'

'And your other sister?' Evans drank more tea.

'Prue? She is also extremely busy. She works for a lady's magazine in London owned by her sister-in-law, Lady Mayton-Walsh.'

'How industrious your family are!' Evans exclaimed.

'Unlike me.' Cece glanced at Ross and then back to her tea.

'Nonsense. You are finding your own talents by the day from what I can see,' Ross said quietly.

Evans stood. 'Thank you for your hospitality, Mrs Marsh. Your egg tart was delicious. I shall expect great things from you now when I call for a visit. I'm so pleased you've come to live here. Resslick suffers from a serious lack of beautiful gentlewomen such as yourself.' Evans gazed around. 'However, I do consider a woman such as yourself should be living in a palace and not a cottage.'

'Perhaps not a palace,' Cece laughed, 'but yes, this is not what I am used to.'

'But you're coping well enough?' Ross prompted.

'Indeed, I am managing quite well.'

'I really should be heading off.' Evans smiled, donning his hat. 'Thank you for the tea and tart. I shall collect you about two o'clock tomorrow?'

'Yes, that is suitable.' Cece walked out with him. 'I look forward to it.'

'Not as much as I am.' Evans kissed her hand, dipped his hat and walked down the drive.

Back in the kitchen, Cece felt a little shy being alone with Ross. She'd thought a lot about him in the last two days, which surprised and confused her.

'You're going on a trip with Evans?'

'Yes, a drive somewhere. He has a motor car. We were talking about transport, and my need to purchase some type of transport myself. He's offered me the use of his motor car.' She began to clear away the plates.

Ross stood, his gaze not leaving her. 'Be careful with Evans.'

She stilled and looked at him. 'Oh? Why?'

'He's a bit sketchy about his past. He's been here a year, and no one knows anything about him, only that he likes the ladies.'

'Likes the ladies?' Cece's eyebrows rose.

'Yes, anyone he takes a fancy to seems to be his for the taking, married or not, high or low born. Strangely enough most of the local women find him delightful. It must be his English accent?'

'He is handsome, I suppose.'

Ross's expression became stony. 'Apparently so.'

'Well, it is only a drive in his motor car, Ross. I'm sure I'll be safe enough,' she said it as a joke, but it fell flat.

'I'd best be going.'

'I thought you were going out to Finlay? He'd like to see you.'

'Another day.' He nodded his head in farewell and strode from the cottage.

Cece remained where she was, trying not to feel upset by his abruptness. Ross was just like Monty. Too eager to walk away from her.

Chapter Eleven

Cece wore one of her better dresses of apple green linen, her green cloche hat and soft brown coat and gloves. She'd worked tirelessly on curling her hair, so it sat exactly right under her hat. Lastly, she applied some light make-up.

She wasn't sure why she was making such an effort for Mr Evans, but she could count on one hand the amount of times handsome young men had asked her to spend time with them in any capacity. She'd been too shy and too overshadowed by Prue and Millie to grab the attention of male friends when they were growing up.

This giddiness was what Prue must constantly feel. It wasn't as if she was deeply attracted to Mr Evans, not like she was to Monty... and a small part of her brain suddenly added Ross to the list, still, she felt light-headed at the fact that Mr Evans had wanted to spend time with her. He was seeking her out, just her, no one else. She liked the feeling.

'Cece, he's here,' Finlay called from downstairs.

Collecting her bag, Cece took a deep breath, went down and said goodbye to Finlay and walked out to meet Mr Evans.

His car was shiny red and black. He leaned against the bonnet wearing a light brown suit and hat. She couldn't deny he was rather dashing.

'Where shall we go?' he asked once they'd left the cottage behind.

'I have no idea.' She smiled. 'I don't know this area at all.'

'I've brought a picnic. We can stop once we find a nice spot.'

'How wonderful.' It pleased her that he'd been so thoughtful. 'It is perfect weather for a picnic.'

He sped the car up and gave her a wide grin. 'It's a perfect day indeed.'

Half an hour later they pulled to a stop beside the loch and taking a blanket and the food basket out of the motor car, they found a grassy spot in the sun beside the still water.

Cece settled herself on the blanket as Mr Evans poured them a cup of cider. 'Have you been here before?'

'A couple of times, yes. It's pleasant when the weather is kind. I try to make the most of the fine weather. I've spent one winter here, and it was dreadfully cold for so long. I couldn't wait for the warm days to arrive.' He leaned back on his elbows. 'Will you be here for the winter?'

'No, I don't think so.' She stared out over the water. When she thought of winter, she thought of the baby and she avoided that at all costs for that meant making life-changing decisions.

'Was this the life you imagined to be living?' Evans suddenly asked.

Cece relaxed, enjoying the warmth on her stocking clad legs. 'No. I thought I would be happily married with a few children by now.'

'*Happily* married?'

Realising her mistake, Cece sat up straighter, ready to dart away. What a fool she'd been, when for weeks she'd been so vigilant with what she said.

Evans placed his hand on her arm. 'You're not happy with your husband?'

'I'd rather talk about something else.'

'What are you running away from? Him? Do you not love him?'

'I'm not running away at all,' she lied.

'You can trust me. I'm not an idiot. No one comes alone to a remote cottage in the Scottish Highlands for fun.'

'I have.'

He watched her carefully. 'You are lying.'

'That's rude. You don't know me.'

'You're not wearing a wedding ring.' He picked up her hand and his thumb rubbed her finger where a wedding band should be.

She shivered at his touch.

His voice softened. 'Are you divorced? Running away from the scandal of it?'

'Something like that,' she murmured, liking his gentle touch, his kindness, the whisper of his voice.

'Let me be a comfort to you then. Two lonely people in the middle of nowhere.'

Cece shook her head and pulled away. 'Ross said you were a ladies' man, and he was right,' she said it with a smile, not accusingly.

Evans shrugged. 'I like women. I like being with them. I see no harm in having a mutual understanding. Two people are allowed to find comfort in one another as long as they don't cause hurt. Wouldn't you agree?'

'I'm not sure.' She thought of Monty and the comfort they gave to each other that one night. She had enjoyed every touch and kiss Monty gave her. They hadn't hurt anyone in their actions. The only consequence had been her getting pregnant.

Evans poured out a glass of wine for them both. 'Ross Cameron doesn't like me because I tried to get close to his sister. He stopped anything from happening between us.'

'Were you serious about Isla?'

He stared out over the water, sipping his wine. 'I could have been, yes. I'd like a home, a family. Every day I see other families, children, and I long for that environment. Instead I return home to an empty cottage.'

Cece stared at his profile, hearing the sadness in his voice. 'I've always wanted a family, too.'

'You will have that.'

'I doubt it. I've made mistakes.'

'We all make mistakes.' He took her hand and held it before gazing back out over the water.

She liked the closeness. A simple touch of their hands. A connection. She wasn't alone.

He kissed the back of her hand. 'You are unbelievably beautiful. Too beautiful to be sad.'

She turned to him and he took her in his arms and kissed her. Their kiss wasn't like the passionate desperate heated kisses she shared with Monty. It was a kiss of two people displaced and lonely, seeking closeness.

Evans laid her back on the blanket and kissed her some more. 'I've wanted to kiss you from the very first moment I saw you.'

Cece sighed in delight as his mouth kissed her neck. Desire built. She gripped his shoulders, as his lips sought hers again. He made her feel wanted, desirable, but when his hand touched her stomach, she jolted upright and away from him.

'I'm sorry.' He frowned.

'No, it was me. I shouldn't have kissed you.' She scrambled up.

Standing beside her, he took her hands. 'Do you feel as though you're betraying your husband?'

Cece closed her eyes. Lord, she couldn't go on with the lies. It was against her nature to be so deceitful. 'I'm with child.'

'Oh.'

'Yes. Oh.' She couldn't look at him.

'Does this make you happy or sad?'

'I feel nothing. It is only an inconvenience.'

'Does your husband know?'

'No.'

'Why?'

Cece couldn't answer.

'Is the child not his?' He prodded gently.

Suddenly Cece felt as though the weight of the world was on her shoulders. 'I'm not *Mrs* Marsh, but *Miss* Marsh.'

'I see.' There was no censure in his voice, just acceptance. 'I am rather pleased there is no Mr Marsh.'

Tears gathered hot behind her eyes. 'You were right. I am running away. I am just lucky enough that I have the money to do that. I dread to think what would have happened if I didn't have the cottage.'

'We are all running from something, but don't worry, you have me as well as your cottage.'

'You?'

'Is that a distasteful thought to you?'

'You hardly know me.'

'I know enough. I know you're good and kind and beautiful and smart. I know that I want to take care of you. Can I do that, Cece?'

'I don't know…'

'You don't have to decide right this minute.' His arms came around her and she buried her head into his shoulder, grateful for his embrace.

~ ~ ~ ~

As May slipped into June, the warm weather continued, surprising everyone in the Highlands. Cece and Finlay transformed the cottage, painting the front room a cheery yellow with white trims. The kitchen also received a painting of white to brighten the room. Finlay worked hard in the vegetable garden. Neat rows of soil were sprouting seedlings of various vegetables and the fruit trees were beginning to show their immature fruit. Cece bought more chickens and a small goat, which was tethered in front of the cottage to keep the grass low. The garden beds below the cottage windows were planted with more roses and Cece added pansies and hollyhocks.

One a sunny day in the middle of June, Cece was hanging out the last of the washing. With her back breaking at the laborious task, she had new-found respect for laundry women the world over. She had no idea how labour-intensive and arduous washing clothes was until she began washing her own clothes. She hated the job! She really needed to find a woman to do all the gruelling work before her hands were ruined beyond salvage.

However, finding women out here in the middle of the highlands who didn't already have positions or their own homes to manage was proving difficult. Evans mentioned putting an advertisement in the Fort William newspaper, and she had it on her list to do the next time she visited Fort William.

Her thoughts turned to her family. She needed to write letters to them all, but it was difficult to tell them her activities when they were expecting her to mention travelling and seeing the sites of Scotland. Instead all she did was work at making the cottage a home for her and Finlay. She could write of her frequent trips out with Christopher Evans, and his growing attentions, but that would create more questions.

She couldn't tell them of Finlay, or her friendship with Isla, and how Isla was teaching her so much about cooking and running a home without staff. Nor could she mention Ross, who was never far from her mind even though she barely saw him, and she felt as though she was betraying Christopher each time she did. Isla said Ross was busy moving the flocks of sheep to different hillside pastures or visiting relatives in other parts of the area. Finlay had stopped asking when he'd come to see them.

Instead, she wrote of other things. Previously, she'd written about the village and the characters in it. She spoke of Alf and Murray, old Mrs Durie from whom Cece bought her milk. She wrote of Fort William, the weather and her plans to travel and see more of Scotland, which of course she had no intention of doing. Neither did she mention the children Evans taught, and who Cece now played the piano for every Friday afternoon at Evans request. It was becoming harder to fill a letter, so she wrote less frequently.

Of the child she carried she gave no thought or tried not to. Her little round stomach was noticeable when she was naked, but thankfully she wore loose blouses and dresses which hid her shape, at least for the time being. Apart from the few times she was out with Evans, or at the school on Fridays, she remained at the cottage.

The clip clop of hooves and the rumble of wheels alerted her to someone coming down the road. She walked down the side of the cottage and smiled a welcome at Isla who drove up the drive.

'How lovely to see you. I thought you weren't coming until Thursday?'

'I had to go into the village. Mr Hingis has had a wee fall, and I took him some fresh bread and a pot of stew. He used to be one of our shepherds.' Isla climbed down from the buggy. 'I'm glad you're home.'

'Why wouldn't I be?'

'Well, you seem to spend all your time with Mr Evans from what I hear, so I wasn't sure.'

Cece frowned. 'I don't spend all my time with Mr Evans.'

'That's not the talk going around the village.'

'It's not true. We are friends and have gone out on a few excursions…'

'Alf was telling me just now that Mr Evans was in the pub last night, awfully drunk and mouthing off how delectable you are and was his for the taking.'

'I beg your pardon?' Cece's blood ran cold. Had Evans spilled her secret to the village?

'Words to that effect, for sure. I've come to warn you. He's a wee slimy eel if you ask me but you're a grown woman who can choose her own friends.'

Cece couldn't believe he would do that. Since the picnic he'd been so solicitous and respectful. He'd played the perfect gentleman and every time she saw him, he offered her nothing but friendship and comfort and understanding. She liked him more each time she was in his company. 'You're not keen on him, are you?'

'You *what*?'

'I know that Mr Evans once tried to have a friendship with you. If you wish for me to stop seeing him because you want him—'

'Now wait just a wee minute!' Isla's anger was clear on her face. 'I've been nothing but a good friend to you and I'll not stand here and be insulted.'

'Insulted? How am I insulting you? I don't mean to suggest...' Cece put her hand out in apology. 'What I mean is—'

'What you mean is I want Evans for myself. Well, I can tell you now, that's not my intention at all. I don't *like* the wee man. He's secretive and eyes up women like they're goods on sale at a wee market.'

'I'm sorry. I didn't mean to offend you, Isla. Christopher has been kind to me, but we are only friends, no more than that.'

'Christopher, is it now?' Isla climbed back onto the buggy's seat. 'I came here in good faith. Evans has talked treacle to every wee woman in the village and a few in Fort William, too. I thought you should know.'

'Thank you, but we are *only* friends.'

'If you say so.' Isla shrugged. 'I'm having a wee party next Tuesday for Ross's birthday. I wondered if you and Finlay would like to join us?'

'Yes, that would be lovely, thank you.'

'I'll send one of the men down to collect you.' With a click of her tongue, Isla turned the horse around and drove away.

Feeling disheartened, Cece walked inside the cottage and sat on the sofa. She replayed the conversation in her head. Had Evans talked about her in the pub, and for what purpose? She had promised him nothing. It upset her that he had done such a thing. She'd begun to think she could trust him. He said he was her friend.

'Cece, I've brought in some more water,' Finlay called from the kitchen. He came into the front room. 'I thought to have a bath tonight.'

'Another one? Without my prompting? Very good.'

'Are you all right?'

'Yes.' Though she didn't sound it.

'Are we having the rabbit this evening?' He was pleased as punch having caught a rabbit yesterday in his snare set behind the barn.

Cece nodded. 'It's been cooking slowly all day in the pot. Mrs Beeton's book says the longer the better. However, the onions have disintegrated. I hope that is meant to happen.' She stood and then felt a weird feeling in her stomach and gasped.

'What is it?' Finlay was instantly beside her, looking worried. 'Are you sick?'

'I...' The feeling came again, like a butterfly trapped in her stomach. Then it dawned on her. The baby was moving, and all her world shifted.

'What's the matter?'

155

His anxious expression made Cece want to cry. This boy relied on her, as did this baby. Yet, it was too much responsibility. This wasn't how her life was meant to be. She'd always dreamed of having an adoring husband, a pretty house in York, beautiful children and a dazzling social life.

Instead, she was unmarried, carrying an illegitimate baby she didn't want and had a thirteen-year-old boy depending on her to give him a home. She was out of her depth. She wanted her mama, and Millie, even her grandmama's wise words would be welcomed right now...

'Cece?' Finlay's thin voice reached her.

She smiled reassuringly. 'I'm all right.'

'You can't get sick and die. I like living here,' he said worriedly.

Her heart softened, and she brushed away his over long hair from his face. 'I'm not sick or going to die.'

'Truly?'

'Truly, and next time I go to Fort William, you are coming with me and getting your hair cut at the barbers.'

He screwed up his face at the thought and heaved a long sigh. 'If you say so.'

'I do.'

The sound of an engine came through the open windows. Cece opened the door, her eyebrows raised in surprise as Ross turned off the lorry's engine and climbed down from the cabin. She quickly put a hand to her hair and patted the unruly mess into place. Glancing down, she muttered under her breath as she had her oldest skirt and blouse on, which she wore when working about the cottage.

'Mr Cameron!' Finlay darted out of the house and ran to his side.

Ross ruffled Finlay's hair and spoke quietly to him and Finlay nodded before dashing to the back of the lorry.

'Good morning,' Ross said, coming closer to Cece.

'Good morning. This is a pleasant surprise.' Cece smiled a welcome as Finlay walked back towards them.

'Look, Cece! Mr Cameron has given us a puppy.'

'He has?' Cece stared at the scrap of black and white fur. Good heavens, the last thing she wanted was a dog!

'He's the runt of the litter and the mother has another ten to cope with. This little one wasn't getting the attention it deserved, and I thought young Finlay here might like the job of taking care of him?' Ross gave Cece a tender look. 'That's if it's all right with you?'

'I can hardly say no, now can I?' Cece shook her head as Finlay rubbed his cheek against the puppy who licked his face.

'Can I keep him, Cece, please?' Finlay's voice was full of longing.

'It's a big responsibility.'

'I'll look after him properly, I promise.'

'He's been weaned,' Ross said. 'But he's undersized. You can feed him milk with bread soaked into it each morning, and at night bits of meat will do him fine.'

Cece wiped a hand over her face, this was just another fly in the ointment of her plans.

'He'll be our guard dog when he's bigger.' Finlay gazed adoringly at the puppy.

'We don't need a guard dog,' Cece murmured. In truth the puppy was a little darling, and she'd always wanted a dog of her own, one who would be her devoted companion. Yet, the timing was not ideal at all.

'If Mrs Marsh says no, then you'll be a man and accept her decision,' Ross warned.

Cece gave him a quelling glare for making her the potential bad person. 'You can keep him, Finlay, but,' she put up a cautionary finger, 'he's yours to care for and if you grow bored with him, then he's to be returned to Mr Cameron.'

'Yes, Cece, but I won't grow bored. I've never had a dog before. I'll look after him, I promise.'

'Finlay go make a bed for the little scrap,' Ross said.

'Yes, Mr Cameron!' Finlay walked away, crooning to the little pup.

Ross watched him go. 'I thought the pup would give the boy some companionship. Isla said you're not staying here, and I thought that if the boy was back out on the streets at least he'd have the dog to keep him company.'

'I wouldn't put Finlay out on the streets,' she snapped. 'Do you assume I would be so cruel?'

'Then what do you plan to do with him when you leave? He's too young to stay on here by himself and take care of the place.'

'I know that.' Feeling under attack, she took a calming breath.

'He's settled well here, and the boy has taken a shine to you.'

Cece gritted her teeth. Why did Ross always put her on the back foot? 'And I him. So, I'd always want the best for him.'

'Isla and I thought we could always take him on.'

'Thank you. I had hoped…'

'Why can't you stay?' Hope shone from Ross's eyes.

'I'll come back…' Another lie.

'Aren't you happy here? Or do you miss London too much, or your family?'

'My family live their own lives, as I must do.'

'Is it your husband? Does he want you to go home?'

Ashamed, she couldn't look at him. 'It's complicated.'

'It doesn't have to be. If you have no strong reason to return down south, then stay here where you have friends.'

'I cannot. At least, I must go away for a while, then I'll return.'

'With or without the baby?'

Cece gasped. She stared at him, her mind working overtime. 'How… What…' She felt faint. So, Evans had told everybody.

'Calm down. I guessed.'

'You guessed… How?' The sun was hot on her face, she was going to be sick.

'Come inside.' Ross gently man-handled her into the front room and onto the sofa. 'I'll get you some water.'

He returned quickly, and she took the glass and drank deeply, fighting the urge to faint or be sick, she didn't know which.

'Cece, may I call you, Cece?'

She nodded. The kindness of his voice, the concern in his eyes, made her want to cry.

'Listen to me, I've been a farmer all my life and detecting pregnancy in animals is a large part of what I do.'

'I'm not an animal,' she said, subdued and humiliated. For some reason Ross finding out her disgraceful secret made everything worse.

He grinned. 'No, but anyone who really looked at you on a regular basis, would see the small amount of weight you are gaining around your waist. Sometimes, when you aren't even aware of it yourself, you touch your stomach in that way expectant mothers do.'

Did she really do that? She wanted to die from the shame. 'I thought I was being so careful.'

'Not always. You aren't married either, or you?'

'No.'

'I thought not. You aren't wearing a wedding ring. You never mention your husband unless forced to, you never speak of him in conversation. That's not the way a woman behaves. When she is in love with her man, the world can see it. So, I assumed you weren't married. Finally, why would you bury yourself here in this cottage when it's obvious you come from a far more privileged background? You speak of your family with love and devotion to Isla, and she isn't stupid, she soon realised that you're hiding something. Why else would a lady of means hide in the Highlands unless there was a secret to be hidden?'

Silence stretched between them for a moment.

'You've worked it all out, haven't you?' she said sarcastically.

'No, but I would hope that you trust me and Isla enough to share whatever it is that troubles you, and that we can help.'

'You cannot help me.'

'Are you sure about that?'

'When all the people in the village know that I am having a child and I'm unmarried, I will be scorned, driven out. That's why I made up this stupid marriage lie. So, when I was large with child, people would believe it was my husband's.'

'A husband who is in London. Where *you* would be if you were married. No married pregnant woman would come way out here alone to a cottage unfurnished with no help. It made no sense to me or to Isla.'

'What must you think of me?' She couldn't look at him.

'I don't judge you, if that's what you are wondering.'

'Thank you, but you should. I'm a fallen woman. A pariah.'

'Mistakes happen. Others might understand too if they were to know the truth, but they don't need to know, do they? Isla and I will keep your secret. Your friend Mr Evans might keep his distance perhaps, once he is aware of your condition. His fantasy that you are his for the taking might come undone when he sees a large stomach.'

'He already knows.'

Ross took a step back in shock. 'He does? Why would you tell him?'

'He got me at a weak moment.' She gave a condescending snort. 'It seems being weak is something I'm rather good at. I suppose I needed to talk to someone about it. I've been bottling it up inside me for months. He was there…'

'Is there something between the two of you?' A harshness crept into his tone.

'No! No, not really.' She rubbed her forehead. 'I don't know, really. That is the last thing I need right now, but he cares, and that means something to me.'

A muscle worked in Ross's jaw. 'He isn't to be trusted.'

'So, you say, but to me he has been a gentleman, a kind and considerate friend. God knows I need as many of those as I can get. Christopher cares for me and that feels wonderful.'

Ross knelt in front of her where she sat. 'Cece, listen to me...'

'Cece, come look,' Finlay called for her as he came into the kitchen.

Ross straightened and Cece stood, together they went into the kitchen to admire the small crate filled with straw that was now the puppy's bed.

Five minutes later, Ross left, and Cece sighed deeply. Her lies were unravelling, as was her life.

Chapter Twelve

In the comfortable sitting room of his family's ancient farmhouse, Ross smiled and shook hands with guests who'd come to attend his birthday party. Although he'd told Isla many times, that he didn't want a party, she'd ignored him as usual and gone about the task with her driving personality and enthusiasm.

Yet, now he was surrounded by good friends and loving family, a drink of whisky in his hands, and the presence of Cece in his home, he considered himself lucky indeed.

'Thirty-five, you old git.' His cousin Donald slapped him on the back. 'You'll be investing in a funeral pension soon.' He roared with laughter, nudging another cousin, Fraser, who stood beside him.

'Nay,' Fraser shook his head, 'the man's not married, he'll live to be a hundred or more!'

'Aye, you're right, course you are!' Donald chuckled.

Fraser threw back the last of his dram. 'Lucky bastard. Marriage takes years off a man, I'll tell you no lie.'

'Only if they are married to your missus!'

Ross grinned as they laughed again. Joking amongst the cousins was a lifelong habit.

He took their empty glasses to fill with more whisky. Beneath the smile he wore was the knowledge that his cousins were right about one thing. He was the last of the male cousins to marry. Being single had never worried him. No woman had come along to make him pledge love and loyalty. In the past he'd had flings with many a bonnie lass, but building up the farm, keeping the money coming into the family was his main concern. After leaving the army after the Great War ended, he'd wanted nothing more than to be on the farm and live an easy life. He'd been doing that for five years now and with the farm and his other investments going well, it was time to look for someone. Only, the one woman he wanted was a red-haired English rose, swelling with another man's child and who had no room in her life for further complications.

Filling the glasses from the small whisky barrel on the table, he glanced around for Cece. She stood near the door leading into the hallway, wearing a pretty cream linen and lace loose fitting dress that hid her bump. A delicate blush coloured her pale face as she chatted to one of his aunts. Beside Cece, Finlay stood eating cake from a plate. He was dressed in a clean blue shirt and grey trousers, his hair neatly combed. The boy had grown inches since arriving at the cottage. Ross liked him and wanted to see him do well. If Cece did leave, then he'd take the boy on to work on the farm.

He took a long drink of whisky, hating the thought of Cece leaving. He had to make her stay, but how he didn't know. He needed to gain her trust, show her that she could depend on him.

'Ross.' James, his best friend since childhood, and an Inverness policeman, came to his side. 'When you've got a wee spare minute, I can tell you the information I've managed to find out.'

Ross nodded with a sharp intake of breath. 'Come this way.'

Slipping away from the guests, Ross stepped outside with James. 'Well?'

'It took some digging. Your wee friend is a slippery character.'

'What did you find out?'

'Christopher Evans is a schoolteacher, that much is true. I had to call in some favours from over the border, but it was worth it. The man is wanted for questioning by Manchester police for a robbery enquiry.'

'Robbery?'

'Apparently, Mr Evans likes to select ladies of a certain class, usually widows left with a sizeable amount of money from their dear departed husbands.'

'I knew it.'

'One woman has filed a complaint saying Evans wooed her until she was ready to commit to him and then he persuaded her to transfer some of her money into his account so he could buy them a house in a new area for a fresh start for the widow and himself. Only, of course, he scarpered with the money the minute it was transferred.'

Anger filled Ross until he wanted to smash Evans's teeth down his throat. 'I knew there was something untrustworthy about him. Why would an

Englishman come here to teach in a tiny school unless he was hiding from something?'

James raised his eyebrows. 'Why indeed?'

'Thank you for doing that for me.' Ross patted James on the shoulder.

'I hope she is worth it, my friend.'

'She is.'

'Well, the English lady is pretty enough but what are your plans? They say she's married.'

'She's putting her trust in Evans, for now I simply need to stop him from making a fool out of her.'

'I hope you're successful.'

'Will the police be doing anything about him?'

'The lot down in Manchester only want to question him. It's only that woman's word so far. She might be a spurned woman making trouble for all we know? At this moment he's not broken the law, so he's not high on their priority list and they can't do anything on this side of the border. The case will need to be transferred to us, and again with all the paperwork he won't be a priority.'

Ross rubbed his chin. 'That's what he is banking on.'

'Naturally. If he's of a criminal mind, he'll know how to get around the law.'

They turned and walked back inside, and Ross entered the kitchen to tell Isla what James had told him.

'Cece likes him, Ross,' Isla said, slicing more fruit cake. 'She confronted him about his drunken night at the pub, and he said he didn't tell anyone about her secret. She believes him. They remain friends, good friends. He is always at the cottage. If Cece wants him, they that is none of our business.'

'But he's no good. How could she want him?'

'We aren't her keepers to tell her what to do.'

'No, but we can warn her,' Ross argued.

Isla shrugged and passed the plate of cake to their cousin Hilda to take out to the guests. 'Why are you so bothered, anyway? She's a grown woman and one who is leaving at the end of the summer and will probably never return. She has enough problems to deal with without us interfering in her life.'

Ross glared at her, knowing she was upset that her friendship with Cece was built on lies and would be cut short. 'Do you want Evans to hurt her? He's wanted for questioning in Manchester regarding a robbery. Do you want Cece caught up in all that?'

'No, of course I don't.' Isla puffed a wayward strand of dark hair out of her eyes. 'Go and mingle with our guests and we'll talk about it later.'

Ross left the kitchen to find Cece. She was now talking to an elderly uncle. His chest tightened as she turned and smiled at him. 'Do you need anything?'

'No, thank you. Finlay has just gone to the kitchen to ask for a cup of tea for me and your uncle Bob.'

'She's not bad for a wee English woman, ain't she, Ross?' Uncle Bob spoke too loudly due to his hearing loss.

'Better than most I would say.' Ross grinned as Finlay joined them with two cups of tea.

'How's the puppy getting on?' Ross asked him.

Cece huffed. 'Oh, the pup is doing simply fine, we on the other hand are struggling.'

'How so?'

Cece sipped her tea before answering him. 'It cries all night. The first night Finlay was up and down the stairs a dozen times. The second night was just as bad. When I went down in the morning, I found

Finlay sleeping beside the puppy on the floor in front of the range.'

Ross groaned. 'Sorry, lad. I didn't think he'd be such a nuisance.'

The boy shrugged. 'I don't mind.'

Cece gave him an indulgent look. 'No, you don't now because on the third night I woke to a snuffling noise and I go into Finlay's bedroom and there is the puppy on his bed!'

'It was the only way to settle him,' Finlay explained.

'You'll spoil him. You have to be stronger if you're going to train him properly,' Ross tried to be stern. 'Have you thought of a name?'

'Yes, nuisance!' Cece laughed.

Finlay chuckled. 'I was thinking of King. As he's the boss of us!'

'And we run to do his bidding,' Cece added, smiling.

'That's a grand name.' Ross nodded. 'I like it. You'll turn him into an obedient dog.'

Finlay swelled with pride at the praise.

Ross glanced at Cece and found her looking at him with a softness he'd not seen before, and his heart did a silly flip. Christ, he was falling for her quick and hard. What the hell was he going to do about it and that slimy scoundrel Evans?

~ ~ ~ ~

The afternoon faded into early evening, and feeling a little tired, Cece said her goodbyes, dragging Finlay away from a game of dominoes he was playing with Ross's younger cousins.

'I'll take you back down the mountain, Mrs Marsh,' James said. 'I've a journey back to Inverness and I'd like to make some of it in daylight.'

'Thank you that is kind.' Cece climbed into his little motor car with Finlay for the bumpy ride back to the cottage. She liked Ross's friend. Tall and with an air of authority, but also a sense of humour, James had chatted to her about Inverness and some of the incidents he'd encountered as a policeman.

'So, young Finlay, will you'll become a policeman?' James asked as they traversed the dirt road.

'No, sir, I'm going to be a farmer like Ross. I want my own place one day.'

'And why wouldn't you? It's a noble ambition.'

'When I'm older and with my own farm, I'll be able to take care of Cece as she's taken care of me.'

Cece hugged him to her. 'That is the most loveliest thing anyone has ever said to me.'

Embarrassed, Finlay squirmed. ''Tis true.'

When James turned his little car into the drive at Willow Cottage, Cece was surprised to see Mr Evans leaning against the bonnet of his car.

'You have a visitor,' James said.

'I wasn't expecting anyone so late.' Cece wondered why Christopher waited for her.

After thanking James and waving him on his way, Cece walked to Christopher. After confronting him a few days ago about his drunken night at the pub and his assurance he'd not told a soul about her secret, Evans had called every day since. He was doing his best to win her trust again and brought her little gifts of wild flowers or jars of sweets he'd bought in Fort William.

'This is a surprise,' she said, walking towards him. 'It's late.'

Finlay ran inside to see the puppy not giving Christopher a glance. Cece needed to talk to him for the boy was barely civil to him.

Christopher gave her a warm smile and touched her arm. 'I didn't realise you weren't at home. I thought you might have gone for a walk and decided to wait for your return. I wanted to see you. My days don't feel whole unless I see you at least once.' He kissed her cheek.

Looking into his eyes she saw only kindness and amazingly desire. 'I enjoy seeing you, too.' It was true. When Christopher was around, she felt wanted, treasured.

'Who were you with just now?'

'Oh, that was James. He's Ross Cameron's friend. He gave me a lift home from Ross's birthday party.'

'Yes, I heard there was a party up at the farm. Most of the village is up there. I wasn't invited, but that is to be expected.' His tone spoke that he didn't care but his expression told a different story.

'Care for a cup of tea?' Cece asked, going inside.

In the kitchen there was no sign of Finlay or the puppy. Cece shook the kettle to check for water in it and placed it on the hob. She added more newspaper and kindling to the small fire which was nearly out.

'Did you have an enjoyable time with the Camerons?' he asked, leaning against the door jamb.

'Yes, it was very pleasant. Ross has a large family, and it was nice to meet new people.'

'Is that wise?'

'Pardon?' She turned from closing the oven door.

'Well, they might ask too many questions.' He came closer to her and held her arms gently. 'I've been thinking.'

'Oh?'

'I believe I am in love with you, Cece.' His smile was sincere.

'Gosh.' She didn't know what to say. No one had ever said that to her before. As much as she longed to hear it, she never thought it would happen.

'Now, don't answer me immediately, but I feel you and I can make a good go of it together. I know the truth about your past, and I'm happy to accept this baby,' he placed a hand on the small swell of her stomach, an intimate gesture that touched her heart, 'but I'll also accept your decision and fully support you should you want to put the baby up for adoption. Whatever you decide, if you want me, I know we can be happy. We can travel somewhere new; America, Australia, or New Zealand. Anywhere you want. I can get work as a teacher just about anywhere so I can support you.'

'You don't need to worry about supporting me. I have enough money to support my needs.'

'As my wife, I'd like to take care of you,' his tone was gentle. 'Let me look after you, Cece.'

'You really want to marry me?' She couldn't trust his words. A handsome, clever man wanted to love and take care of her, finally. It seemed unreal.

'I'll go and leave you to think about it.' He kissed her tenderly, his gaze full of love. 'I'll come and see you on Saturday.' He kissed her again as the back door opened.

They drew apart and with another look of longing, Christopher walked out of the cottage.

'What did he want?' Finlay asked, holding the puppy.

'Nothing, just dropped by to see how we are. Are you hungry?'

'No.' Finlay sat at the table, putting the puppy on the floor to play. 'I don't like him.'

'I know that. You make yourself noticeably clear on that subject. May I ask why?'

Finlay shrugged.

'I've told you that you don't have to go to his school.' Cece poured the hot water into a jug to take upstairs so she could have a wash. 'You don't have to go to any school if you don't want to. I hardly think the authorities will be coming out here to see if you're attending school or not. I doubt you've ever been listed on any record ever apart from the orphanage.'

'I don't need school. I can read and write. I'm old enough to work,' he defended.

'I agree, if that's what you want. So, I don't understand the animosity towards Mr Evans.'

He was about to answer when the puppy ran out of the open back door and Finlay chased after him.

From the step, Cece watched Finlay run with the puppy to the barn.

She yawned, tired and worn out from a day of socialising and making sure she didn't give her condition away.

She took the jug upstairs into her bedroom and sat on her bed.

What was she to do about Christopher's proposal? Did she want to marry him? Becoming Mrs Evans would solve a lot of her problems. She didn't love him as she had Monty and that might help her, too, for she'd not get hurt like before...

She thought of Monty for the first time in weeks. He was no longer on her mind constantly. Instead, he'd been replaced by Ross. The quiet handsome Highland farmer who enjoyed his own company amongst his sheep and the heather. The one who made her heart skip a beat and who, *sometimes*, gave her narrowed looks of desire, or did she imagine that?

Yet Ross hadn't asked her to marry him and so she had to put him from her mind. He wanted her as a friend and that was all. Why would he want her as a wife when she carried another man's baby, and especially when he could have his pick of Highland women?

She stared down at the bump. Christopher said he'd take the child or support her if she gave it up for adoption as she planned to do. She gently rubbed her stomach, feeling the fluttery movements. This baby hadn't been asked to be born. That was hers and Monty's mistake. Did it deserve to be with a mother who didn't love it? Wouldn't it be fairer to give it to a loving couple who desperately wanted a baby? People who would cherish its every breath?

If she kept the baby and married Christopher would she forever look upon the child and see Monty? Would Christopher? Would he grow to hate the child that wasn't his?

Marrying Christopher gave her the option to move away, go to a new country and start again. Finlay would stay with Ross, she was sure of that.

Her stomach flipped at the thought of saying goodbye to Ross. How had she let it happen again? Why did she fall for men who didn't want her in return?

She had to get away from here, from Ross. She couldn't take another heartbreak.

Marrying gave her respectability. She could hold her head up high again, reunite with her family. She'd not be lonely, forgotten, unwanted. In time she could love Christopher, how could she not when he treated her so wonderfully? She had so much love to give, so why not give it to him?

Chapter Thirteen

In the days and weeks after Ross's party, Finlay grew more distant, the more Christopher was around. A surly thirteen-year-old and the tiredness of the pregnancy made Cece irritable and snappy. She soon lost interest in the cottage and the work Finlay was doing and waited impatiently for Christopher to come and take her somewhere in his motor car. Usually they went into Fort William and had tea and went shopping. Cece spent money without thought, buying things for Finlay, clothes, books, tin toy soldiers for him to paint, a globe so they could talk about different countries in the world. She was keen to continue what rudimentary education he received at the orphanage.

She also bought pretty things for Isla, despite Isla begging her not to, and she bought Christopher items such as ties and a new hat and binoculars for when they went walking around the loch. She still hadn't made a decision on whether to marry him, but time was running out and she knew something would have to be decided soon.

Christopher had found a young girl, Nell, an older sister of one of his pupils, who, for a small wage, came each day to do the manual work around the cottage of cleaning, cooking and washing, leaving Cece to spend more time reading, sewing, walking along the loch and generally being bored. With no society to belong to or charity work to do, time weighed heavy on her hands, giving her too much time to worry and ponder her life.

'Are you ready for this trip then?' Christopher asked, as they travelled the winding road alongside Loch Ness on a blowy rainy day in late July.

'Yes, I am, despite the weather!' Cece laughed. 'I've been wanting to visit Inverness since I arrived in the Highlands.'

'Well, I have a surprise for you,' he said over the noise of the engine and rain.

'A surprise? What is it?'

'That would spoil it, wouldn't it?'

'No, go on, tell me!' She gripped his arm, excited. The best thing about Christopher was he made her laugh and he never failed to lift her spirits.

'All right. Now, I have done some investigating and there is a place that sells sporty little motor cars, and I thought that one of them might be perfect for you?'

'For me? A motor car?'

'Yes, what do you think?'

'I can't believe it. That's wonderful!' she breathed. 'I've always wanted one.'

'I know, you've told me a dozen times.' He grinned. 'Naturally, I wanted to buy it for you as a surprise for your birthday tomorrow, but then I thought you might want to pick it.' He slowed to corner a bend.

'How thoughtful of you.' She reached over and kissed his cheek. 'But such an expensive present is too much. I couldn't accept you paying for it.'

'How can it be a present if you pay for it?'

'Christopher, please. I don't want to embarrass either of us, but you know I have more money than you do. I'd feel guilty if you bought me such an expensive present.'

'I don't want you to feel anything but happiness, sweetheart. So, if that's your wish, I'll agree to it.' He gave her a glance but had to concentrate on the road as the windscreen wipers were not working properly and reduced visibility.

'I do insist.' Excitement made her clap her hands. 'A motor car of my own! Christopher this will be a fantastic day!'

He reached for her gloved hand and kissed it. 'You owning a better car than me means we can enjoy more journeys of a longer distance, rather than taking our luck in this old piece of garbage.'

'Yes, this motor is becoming unreliable.' She nodded, remembering last weekend when his motor car had broken down as they travelled to Fort William, and the week before that he'd walked to the cottage as the car wouldn't start at all.

'It also means,' he paused to change gear, 'that if we got married, then we'd have a decent car to travel down south to meet your grandmama in London. I don't think this old banger would make it.' He grimaced. 'Though of course with a lovely new car you can travel wherever you wish to with or without me.'

Cece

Cece stared out the rain-splattered windscreen. Lately, she'd been missing her family more each day. Their letters were becoming sparse with her lack of responses. She must write to them, but the shame of her condition stopped her each time. The last letter she received from Grandmama mentioned she'd been unwell, and Cece had worried for days about her grandmama's age and how some minor health problem could easily turn into something more serious.

It was time she wrote more often and perhaps she should mention Christopher. Was it also time to give him the answer he wanted?

Yet, whenever she thought she would tell Christopher that she'd marry him, she stopped short of uttering the words. There was no one to speak to about it, as Finlay refused to discuss anything concerning Christopher, and Isla and Ross had been away for weeks as an elderly aunt was on her deathbed in another part of the Highlands, and somewhere else a cousin was getting married, so they were going between the two places helping out as much as they could.

Still, with them gone, and their critical opinion of Christopher removed, Cece was able to focus on whether she wanted a life with Christopher. And weeks later, she still didn't have a concrete answer.

They stopped to take a peek at Urquhart Castle on the shores of Loch Ness, but the miserable weather kept them in the car, and they continued to Inverness.

Gale force winds heralded them into the grey old town and Christopher was exhausted from driving in such terrible conditions.

'Shall we go for a cup of tea somewhere?' Cece asked, peering through the car window at the passing streets and wet grey buildings.

'Sounds perfect.' He traversed the main thoroughfares, filled with people wanting to get out of the foul weather.

'Heavens, it's like going back in time. There are so many horses and carts.' Cece was staggered by the amount of horse-drawn vehicles and the lack of motor cars.

'Modern ways have yet to reach this place it seems,' Christopher grunted.

'Is the place that sells the cars close by?'

'Not far. The fellow's letter said he was along Friar's Street, near the river. He's only got a few motor cars, you see, and doesn't need a big forecourt.' Christopher navigated along Church Street until he found a small café between shops. 'This will do.'

The wind and rain battered them as they stepped from the car. Cece nearly lost her headscarf as Christopher ushered her inside.

'What weather,' he muttered, then smiled at a young waitress who came to show them to a little table by the window. The café was entirely empty.

'Ye brave commin oot in't this gale,' she said, her accent thick.

Christopher scanned the chalkboard on the wall. 'Soup and tea?' he asked Cece.

'Yes, excellent.'

With the order taken, they made themselves comfortable while outside people dashed past holding onto coats and hats.

'I didn't pick a particularly good day for us to come to Inverness, did I?'

Cece chuckled. 'Never mind.'

'If you don't see a car you like, then we'll come back another day. There isn't a great hurry, is there?'

'No, but now we are here I'm hoping to find a suitable one.'

'If you do see a car you like but you don't want to drive it home in this weather, then we can leave it and return next week to collect it.'

Cece thought about it for a moment. 'Sounds sensible, but to be honest if I find a car I want, then I'll take the risk to drive it home, for if this weather continues it'll be handy to have transport instead of walking.'

'There is that, yes.'

Their soup and tea arrived, and they ate hungrily. When they finished, there was a slight lull in the wind and the rain lightened to a drizzle.

'Want to venture out into it?'

'Might as well, as we've come this far.'

Christopher paid the bill and then helped her back into the car. He drove a short distance until they were in Friar's Street and found the address.

Cece glanced about, noting the old houses nestled on either side of the street, there was a vacant plot of land and beside that a small house with an open back area where three cars were parked.

Immediately Cece was drawn to a green car, that even in the awful weather was shiny with its black convertible top.

Christopher guided her to the cars with his hand under her elbow. 'What do you think?'

'I like this green one.' Cece walked around it just as a man came out of the house wearing a long over coat.

'Good day to you, both. I'm Ron McDougall.' He shook Christopher's hand and then Cece's. 'I wondered if you might give it a wee miss since the weather is so unkind.'

As though his words commuted to the heavens, the rain fell a little faster.

'What does the fine lady wish for?'

'This one seems nice.' She ignored the other two black cars, which were big and heavy.

'Ah, the Galloway 10/20. I only just bought it from the factory at Tongland right here in Scotland. It's built under the Arrol-Johnston banner. Come, sit in it. Shall we take it for a little ride?'

'Can we?' Cece eagerly climbed in and out of the rain, while Christopher sat in the back.

While Mr McDougall drove slowly down the surrounding streets, he gave a running commentary about the delights of the motor car. 'It was built in a wee factory run by a woman, and her workers are wee women.'

'Is that true?' Cece was amazed and loved the car even more.

''Tis a wee phenomenon to the whole world and of course something us Scots should be proud of. I'm all for women earning a living. However, they are struggling to keep the factory going and are looking at closure, which is regrettable.'

Cece knew she wanted the car. It was built by women struggling to keep their business open. Her papa had forbidden her to be a suffragette but now she could do her little bit for women workers.

Mr McDougall carried on talking about the handbrake being placed near the driver's seat instead of under the dashboard, and the seat raised for better viewing for women drivers. In general, the motor car was lighter and was more spacious than any other on the market in the country.

'How much is it?' Christopher asked as they pulled to a stop back at McDougall's house.

'Four hundred and ninety pounds. A wee bargain.'

Cece caressed the wooden dashboard. 'I'll take it.'

'Wait a moment, Cece.' Christopher opened the door for her and helped her out. He leaned closer. 'We can't appear too eager. I'm sure I can get the price down.'

'You want to bargain with him?' Cece had never bargained in her life.

'Sweetheart, I don't mean to be condescending, but I might, as a man, be able to get him down on the price.'

'Well, yes, if you think you can.'

Christopher squeezed her hand and winked. 'Right, this is what we are going to do. We're going to tell him we'll go away and discuss it. We'll go away for a few hours and then I'll come back and bargain him down. Do you have your chequebook?'

'Yes, in my bag. I carry it everywhere I go.'

'Good. Now, try not to look too eager,' he joked.

Excited to be playing the game, Cece straightened her shoulders and lifted her chin in the manner her mama adopted when she was addressing the staff. 'Thank you, McDougall. You have been most informative.'

The salesman bowed.

Christopher stepped forward. 'We have some thinking to do, but if we decide to go ahead, then we shall return in an hour or so.'

'Very good, sir.'

As Christopher drove them away and back into the main streets of the town, Cece's mind buzzed with the joyous anticipation of having her own transport at last. 'It's brand new, Christopher, it would make the journey to London easily, wouldn't it? I could travel anywhere in safety and with peace of mind.'

'Very easily.'

'I must buy it.' Joy filled her. She'd be free to come and go as she pleased.

'Not for the full price you won't.'

She laughed at him. 'What shall we do for an hour?'

'Do you fancy a bit of shopping?'

'Yes, good idea.'

Christopher parked the car along High Street and they spent the next hour shopping. Cece bought a new tablecloth, more socks for Finlay for the boy went through them at a rapid rate and no matter how much she darned them, a new hole appeared within a few days.

Pausing beside a haberdashery shop, she peered into the window, noticing a white maternity blouse on a stand in the window display. A little of the joy left her. She needed to buy such clothes for she was becoming bigger now.

Christopher returned from a tobacconist where he went to buy cigarettes. His smoking habit was becoming more pronounced.

She turned to him as a chilly wind whistled down the street, ripping her headscarf from her head and sending it up into the air and over the river. 'Damn!'

Christopher ushered her inside the shop. 'Look, the weather is getting worse. I'll go back to McDougall on my own, shall I? You can stay in the shops where it's warm.'

'Are you sure?'

He cupped her cheek in his hand and kissed her softly on the lips making her blush.

'We are in public,' she gently admonished.

'I don't care. I like kissing you.' His intent gaze held hers for a moment.

The warmth of the shop was indeed pleasant for the owner had a large fire blazing in the corner. Cece felt a little depressed at the thought of buying larger clothes, but she'd rather do it without Christopher watching. She didn't like reminding anyone that she was pregnant.

'May I help ye?' the owner asked with a smile as she tidied some shelves nearby.

'Yes, I'll be just a moment.' Cece took out a pen and her chequebook from her bag and signed her signature at the bottom of the cheque and gave it to Christopher. 'Go and buy my motor car.' She grinned.

'Are you certain you can afford the full price if I can't get him down?'

'Yes. I just want that motor.' She laughed lightly, again feeling excited about it. 'It is perfect for me. I can't wait to show it to Finlay.'

Christopher squeezed her hand affectionately. 'He'll be excited for sure. I'll get the best price I can for it. I'll have McDougall drive your car here. Then we can set off straight way for home with you following me. Are you up for driving that far?'

Despite being a little tired, Cece nodded eagerly. 'I can do it.'

Christopher kissed her forehead, his gaze tender and loving. 'Stay here where it's warm.'

Once he'd left the shop, Cece strolled around the displays, selecting a box of different sized needles to add to the ones she had at the cottage. She took her time choosing reels of coloured cotton, then she ventured to the back of the premises where pre-made clothes were hung on rails.

'Do ye need any help, madam?' asked the shopkeeper, a small round woman with salt and pepper hair.

'Yes, I need some blouses, and skirts...'

'I can measure ye and make them to size if ye prefer?'

Cece plucked one of the white cotton and lace blouses from the rail. 'These are for pregnant women?'

'They are, madam. Some of my customers aren't sewers. I provide a variety of articles readymade.'

'And you have skirts?'

'Aye, and day dresses, too. If ye wanting evening wear, I make that to order.'

'No, day wear is fine.' Cece spent half an hour with the woman, deciding on four blouses in white, cream, yellow and blue, as well as three skirts, in brown, navy and black. She also bought two pairs of tights and ribbon for her hair, which was becoming rather long, but she didn't know where she could get it cut and styled.

With all her purchases paid for, Cece had been in the shop for over an hour.

'May I wait here?' she asked the older woman as rain lashed the street outside.

'Yes, yer very welcome. It's not fit for body or beasts out there.' The woman brought out a chair for Cece and placed it near the fire.

Grateful to be sitting down, Cece, pored over her purchases, happy with what she had bought.

She glanced at the clock above the fireplace. She felt a little hungry, the soup and tea were consumed over three hours ago now.

'He's taking his sweet time, ye husband, ain't' he?' the woman said.

Cece smiled. 'Men!'

The woman shook her head. 'Shall I make us a cup of tea? This weather is keeping people from shopping unless they have to.'

'That would be lovely, thank you. I don't know what's keeping him.' Cece wondered if perhaps Mr McDougall was a keen negotiator and wasn't prepared to budge on the price. The motor car was new and no doubt he could sell it quite easily.

Another hour passed by. Cece finished her cup of tea and two pieces of shortbread brought to her by the shop owner.

When the bell above the door rang, Cece jerked from the chair, but disappointedly regained her seat when a woman and a small child entered.

Cece watched the customer, her child on her hip, as she deftly grabbed a bolt of gingham and asked for a couple of yards of it. She bought cotton and a small reel of narrow lace and paid for it all with one hand as she held the little girl. Cece was in awe of how easily she went about her business unobstructed by the weight of the child.

When the shop was quiet again, Cece stood and walked to the window. The rain was easing again, but there was no sign of Christopher. She was beginning to worry that something had happened to him.

The shop owner came to her side to stare out of the window as well. 'Are ye sure he said to stay here? Perhaps he's going all over town looking for ye?'

'I hope not. He said to remain here where it is warm.'

'Well, madam, I don't mean to be rude, but I'll be closing at four.'

Cece glanced at the clock. It was now ten past three. 'I shall go and have a walk around since the rain has stopped. Can I leave my packages here, please?'

'Aye, course ye can.'

'I'll be back before you close.' Cece left the shop and walked down High Street towards the river. There was no shiny green motor car in any direction she looked. She couldn't even see Christopher's motor car. Maybe his motor car had broken down? It was always causing problems lately.

Making the decision to walk to Friar's Street, Cece crossed the road and headed down Church Street.

With the freezing wind at her back, she grew more annoyed as she reached Friar's Street and continued along it. Where was Christopher?

At McDougall's house she walked down to the back area where the motor cars were, only she stopped and frowned. The three motor cars were gone. She stopped in front of the house and banged on the door, which set off a barking dog further up the street.

She waited a few moments and banged again. The silence told her no one was at home. After ten minutes of waiting, she returned the way she'd come.

Fed up and tired she once more went into the haberdashery shop.

'Ah, ye back. Did ye find him?'

Cece sighed. 'No. He's not been here?'

'No, madam.'

'I don't know where he could have got to.' Cece took her packages from the woman and thanked her for her kindness.

Leaving the shop, she had no alternative but to walk the streets, searching for Christopher. The dark grey clouds hovered lower over the rooftops, making it feel more like a winter's day than a summer one and Cece silently begged them not to send down another deluge.

For two hours she walked the streets, her arms ached, and her feet throbbed. She didn't understand what had happened unless Christopher had been in some kind of accident. Wearily, she stopped a man passing by and asked where the police station was.

'Castle Wynd, lass, down by the castle.'

'Thank you.' Each step felt as though her shoes were made of lead, but the thought that Christopher had become hurt drove her on.

Inside the stone building of the police station, Cece waited her turn to go to the desk. In front of her was a crying woman and behind her was a furious-looking man.

'Mrs Marsh?'

Cece swivelled, surprised at hearing her name. 'James!' She could have cried at seeing a friendly face.

'What are you doing here?' James, wearing full police uniform, took her elbow and drew her to a bench seat by the wall.

'A friend of mine has gone missing.'

'Tell me everything.'

Several minutes later, Cece had told James all she knew up to that moment.

'Oh dear.' James shook his head sadly. 'It's not looking good.'

'What do you mean? Is he hurt? Do you know something?'

'I thought Ross would have told you by now.'

'Told me what? I've not seen Ross for weeks.'

'I told Ross at his birthday party that Resslick's schoolteacher, Christopher Evans was wanted for questioning by Manchester Police.'

'Wanted by Manchester Police?' Cece gasped in horror. 'Why?'

'An allegation was made against him by his former lover that he'd stolen from her.'

'No!' Cece stared at him, not wanting to credit such a claim. 'Is it definitely the same man?'

'Yes, I believe so. He matches the right description. Has the correct credentials and background details.'

'Then why haven't you arrested him yet?'

'He's only wanted for questioning. We have been to Resslick to talk to him, but each time we go, he's not home. We've passed the details onto the Fort William constabulary now. They might have better luck finding him at home.'

She slumped back against the wall. 'He's truly been accused of robbery by some woman?'

'Yes, and you've signed a blank cheque and have willingly given it to him in front of a witness.'

She swallowed, feeling stupid, betrayed and deeply hurt. 'It might not be as we are making it out to be?' she said hopefully. 'There could be another reason he can't find me?'

'Perhaps. I'll go to Friar's Street and see what I can find out. Stay here. I'll be back shortly.'

Cece watched James talk with another officer and the two of them left the building.

Cece

Wretched, she sat on the bench, her parcels at her feet and wondered if all this was just a bad dream.

Chapter Fourteen

Under the dripping willows, Ross rode his horse through the gates of Willow Cottage. He'd returned from his aunt's funeral the evening before, noting the wild weather and some of the damaged it had caused about the farm. Setting his men to fix the slipped slates on the roofs and chop down any broken branches or fallen trees, he'd saddled Bailey, his father's horse, and ridden to check on his flocks and see if any damage had been done elsewhere on the property.

The narrow river that crossed his land was flowing fast, but he'd not found anything to cause him alarm and carried on into Resslick to check whether the village folk had also escaped the storm without damage. Luckily most had only minor damages.

Finally, his duty done, he reined Bailey towards Willow Cottage, hoping that Cece and Finlay were fine too.

Dismounting at the cottage, he jumped as the front door was flung open and Finlay ran to him.

191

'Is Cece with you?' the boy cried, his tussled hair and shadows under his eyes showed his torment.

'With me? No.' Ross steadied the boy with a hand on his shoulder. 'What's happened?'

'She didn't come home yesterday.'

'Didn't come home?' A cold hand of fear clutched Ross's innards. 'Where did she go?'

'Out with Mr Evans yesterday morning, early, in his car, but it's been breaking down a lot and they haven't come back! I asked Nell if she'd heard anything in the village, but she doesn't know anything, stupid girl.'

'All right, calm down.'

'Has Cece gone for good? Have I sent her away because I don't like Mr Evans?'

'No, no, it won't be that at all.' Ross tried to reassure the lad, but his own mind was working ten to the dozen. 'Are you certain that she said she'd be back yesterday?'

'Yes, she said she would be back before dark and I was to do my jobs and keep the fire in the range going because she'd made a stew and it was on the hob. Nell had washing to do and was to clean the front windows.'

'So, she planned to come home, which means Evans might have had a problem with his car…'

'Maybe they've had an accident?' The lad's chin wobbled.

'Let us not get carried away just yet.' Ross patted Finlay's shoulder. 'I'll go home and get the lorry. I'll take a drive towards Fort William and see what I can find out. You stay here. Where's Nell?'

'In the kitchen crying because she'll lose her job if Cece doesn't come back.'

'She'll be back.' Ross took Bailey's reins, wishing he was already in the lorry. Had Evans kept Cece out all night? Had she willingly wanted to take that step with the cad? Jealousy and anger mixed in his veins. How could she do this? To frighten the boy in such a way?

Astride, he turned Bailey about and looked back at Finlay. 'I'll be back as soon as I can.'

'Look!' Finlay rushed forward as a small white motor car came through the gates and under the willows.

'It's James.' Ross frowned, quickly dismounting.

'And Cece!' Finlay cried, running to hug her as she climbed from the car.

'I'm sorry you were worried.' She kissed the boy's head and hugged him to her. She gave Ross a nod as she passed him and shuffled into the cottage. He stared after her. She looked distraught.

'What's happened?' Ross asked James.

'Christopher Evans strikes again.'

Rage burned in Ross. 'What did he do to her?'

'Stolen her money and left her high and dry in Inverness.'

'Bastard.'

'Come inside and I'll tell you the story, but Ross,' James held him back, 'she's been through it and has had no sleep. Be gentle.'

He swallowed down his anger as they entered the cottage and stepped into the kitchen, where Nell was making cups of tea and Finlay was stoking up the fire. Cece sat on a chair, pale, quiet and with a look in her eyes that was hard for him to see.

James sat at the table and told the story of Evans and his cunning plan. 'So, you see, McDougall was in on it, too, it seems, for he's scarpered as well. We've sent bulletins to all the stations but there's an incredibly good chance both Evans and McDougall have left Scotland, probably changed their names as well.'

'But he's a schoolteacher,' Nell said, cutting up slices of ginger cake. 'How could he be so bad?'

'Teaching wasn't enough for him, it seems.' James ate some cake. 'His real intentions are to have relationships with wealthy independent women, who,' James smiled sadly at Cece, 'who are gullible to his attentions and flattery.'

Cece's head dropped.

'He gains their trust and then takes off with their money and, or, possessions,' James added.

'How much money has he taken?' Ross asked quietly.

James sipped his tea. 'Until we hear from the bank, we won't know. A wire has been sent to Cece's bank offices in York and London.'

'Did he know how much money you had?' Ross murmured to Cece, not wanting to upset her.

'He knows I was comfortable,' she answered without looking up from her teacup.

James sighed. 'Whatever figure he's written on the cheque will be a guess. He can't go too high as the bank might reject it when he cashes it in and then he's blown his chance. I doubt, if he's clever, he'll go higher than the price of the motor car Cece wanted to buy for he knew she was going to write a cheque for that amount, and it would be honoured.'

Ross swore under his breath, wanting to kill the bastard.

'I'd best go.' James drained his cup. 'I'm on duty the evening. Finlay, there are Cece's parcels in the back of my motor, will you fetch them for her, please?'

Finlay left the room, the puppy bounding after him.

Cece rose slowly as though she was a very old woman and Ross's heart broke at the haunted look in her eyes. She turned to James and kissed both his cheeks. 'Thank you for everything. I don't know what I would have done without you.'

'I'll be in touch with any news. Write to your bank manager again, give them full details of everything and close down the account. Better still, go into Fort William and make use of a telephone and speak to the manager directly, or travel to York. Take care of yourself, get some rest.' James shook Ross's hand and left the cottage as Finlay came back, his arms loaded.

'Where shall I put them, Cece?'

'Anywhere,' she said, not caring.

Ross stepped forward, but she shrank from him, her fierce glare took him by surprise.

'I want you to leave,' she snarled.

'Cece, I...'

'I blame you. You knew what Evans was like, what he'd been accused of, James told you at your birthday. Yet you didn't think to tell me!' Her blue eyes were like chips of ice and full of loathing.

'It wasn't the right time then.'

'Would there ever have been a right time?' she snapped.

'You wouldn't have listened! James told me Evans hadn't broken the law and was only wanted for questioning. Whenever I spoke about Evans you defended him! Would you have listened to me if I'd mentioned it? I hardly think so! You thought the sun shone from his backside! I warned you from the start that Evans was no good and so did Isla and you accused us of being biased against him.'

'You still could have tried to tell me after James confided in you.'

'I wanted to, many times, but Isla said you were too keen on Evans to take any notice of what we said. Then we've been away, and I've been tearing myself inside out wondering if you had agreed to marry him or not.'

'What do you care about any of that?' she snapped. 'Just go. You are no longer welcome here.' She left the room and he could hear her footsteps going upstairs.

Deflated, offended and annoyed at her accusations, he gave a brief nod to a bewildered Finlay and strode out of the house.

He mounted Bailey in one swift movement and urged him down the drive. He cursed himself for not telling her what he knew about Evans. He just hoped that in time she would forgive him.

~ ~ ~ ~

A fierce and energy-sapping cold descended on Cece the day after she returned from Inverness. She kept to her bed for the whole of the following day, wallowing in self-pity, which she knew her grandmama would utterly disapprove of, but she couldn't help it.

What Evans had done to her made her feel a mixture of emotions, mostly self-loathing that she had been so quick to trust him, so eager to seek another man's attention, so needy to believe that a man who is good-looking and smart would want her.

How many more times was she going to let herself get carried away seeking the good opinion and attentions of a man? Well, no more! She was done. Relationships with men gave her nothing but pain and humiliation. Enough was enough.

As she lay in bed the second day, mentally preparing to rise and dress, she heard a noise from downstairs and then voices. Whoever it was, Finlay would deal with them. There was no need for her to go down.

Her bedroom door was flung open and Isla marched in as though she was a sergeant-major on a drill. 'Finlay tells me you're sick.'

'I am. And do you ever knock?'

Isla slapped her hand against Cece's forehead. 'You're not too hot.'

'I was worse yesterday.' In truth she'd done so much sleeping she barely remembered the day at all.

'The wee lad is upset.'

'He'll be fine,' Cece argued, though she noticed Finlay had been quiet on the few times he came up with a tea tray.

'You need to speak to Ross.'

'No, I don't.' She blew her nose on a handkerchief.

'Yes, you do, for my brother is losing his wee mind over you, and I'll not stand by another minute and let that happen.'

'I have nothing to say to Ross.' She'd pushed Ross, just like the baby, to the darkest part of her mind. On no account would she think about either of them, it was too much.

'I'm so mad at you I could slap you into next week!' Isla puffed.

'At me?'

'Yes, you!'

'Whatever for?'

'For encouraging that twerp Evans, for falling for his smooth talk, for picking him over Ross.'

'Over Ross?' Cece stared at her. 'There was no Ross in the equation to pick over.'

'He likes you. A lot.'

Cece stared at her, ignoring the flip of her heart. 'Does he? He has a funny way of showing it.'

'Och, that's because your wee head was turned by that smarmy git, Evans.'

'Yes, well I've paid the price, haven't I?'

'And it's not Ross's fault.'

'He knew about Evans.' She sniffed, feeling her temperature rising again.

'So, did I!' Isla yelled.

Cece felt another wave of betrayal. 'Yes, Ross told me.'

Isla sat on the edge of the bed and took Cece's hand. 'We didn't tell you because you wouldn't have listened.'

'You don't know that.'

'Nonsense, whenever we said anything about him, you sprang to his defence. I'm speaking the truth, aren't I? You thought I was jealous, didn't you?'

Cece stared out of the window at the blue sky. 'Even if I hadn't listened at first, it would have planted a seed of doubt in my mind for later.'

'Perhaps it would. We'll never know now, but to blame Ross is wrong and I'll not have it. My brother thinks the world of you.'

Her stupid heart did another little skip at Isla's words, but was it really true? Ross didn't give her any clues as to what he felt. He didn't flirt or go out of his way to spend time with her. He didn't offer to take her on picnics or walks along the loch. 'You are exaggerating, Isla, not that it matters because I'm leaving.'

'When?'

'As soon as I'm over this cold. I'll ask Finlay what he wants to do, either stay with you and Ross, which Ross said he could, or come with me.'

'Where will you go?'

'I don't know. New York, maybe.'

'I'd rather you stayed here.'

'It's impossible. My condition will soon be noticeable.'

'Who cares?'

'Don't be naïve. You know everyone will care, they will make it their business to shun me. The scarlet woman who dared to come to their village and taint it with her wanton ways.'

'They'll come around, people do.'

'Not always and I'm not taking that risk. I'm giving the child away.'

Isla was quiet for a while then she squeezed Cece's hand. 'I'll take it.'

'What?' Nothing else Isla could have said would have surprised her more at that moment.

'I'd like a child to love. I don't see myself marrying, but that doesn't mean I have to miss out on being a mother.'

'Isla...'

'Think about it. If you give it to me, then you'll know it is loved and cared for, you will know where it's living and the kind of life it'll have. You'd get none of that with an adoption agency, would you?'

The idea rocked Cece to the core. She couldn't think straight.

'When is it due?'

'Um… November.'

Isla stood by the bed. 'It's late July now, so you have three and bit months to think about it.'

'What will people say when they see me with a large stomach and then the next minute you have a baby?'

'Who gives a toss?' Isla shrugged. 'I'll tell them you've gone away for your health. Ross and I will raise the baby. He loves children.'

'He'll agree to this madness?'

'Course he will. He's my brother, and he loves me.'

'I don't know…'

'As I said, think it over, but just don't leave until you've weighed all the options carefully.' Isla walked to the door. 'I've left some fresh bread with Finlay and brought you a potato and kidney pie.'

Left alone with the crazy idea of giving her baby to Isla, Cece climbed out of bed and paced the room. Could she? Should she? There were many reasons to do it. The child would be loved by people Cece knew. She could return to London and start again knowing the baby would be happy at the farm. She'd never have to wonder if the people who had the baby really wanted it, for it was obvious Isla wanted the baby.

It gave her a strange feeling to think of Ross raising her child. He would be a good father, she knew, for he was kind and understanding to Finlay and his cousin's offspring's that were at the party.

She dressed in a skirt and flowing blouse to hide her stomach and went downstairs to find Finlay. He wasn't in the kitchen, so she ventured outside and up to the barn. The barn was empty and quiet.

She skirted around to the chicken coop, but the hens were out roaming the yard. She saw Nell up in the far field picking wildflowers, but Finlay wasn't with her.

Shielding her eyes against the sun, she searched the trees for him or the puppy that was his constant companion. Nothing.

Walking down the side of the cottage, she saw the goat tied to the stake its long rope allowing it to graze the grass under the willow trees lining the road. Bending down beside the lopsided gate, Finlay worked, the puppy rolling in the grass beside him.

'What are you doing?' Cece asked, reaching him.

'Mending the gate. I know you hate that it's broken.'

Cece's chest swelled with emotion at his consideration. 'Thank you, but it is too big a task for you to do alone.'

Finlay shrugged. 'I'll manage.'

'The gate is too heavy, and the hinge is broken.' She blew her nose, wishing this cold would hurry up and go away. 'Nell should have offered to help you.'

'Nell is stupid. I've got another hinge from the barn. I took it off one of the old horse stable doors.'

'And how are you going to attach the gate once the hinge is on? You can't hold the gate and screw the hinge at the same time, can you?'

'I'll prop the gate up somehow. I just need to get the hinge on first.' He started hammering nails securing the hinge to the wooden post. He worked furiously, as though in a great hurry.

'Slow down, or you'll—'

Finlay hammered straight onto his finger and yelled in pain.

'hurt yourself,' Cece finished lamely, going to him to examine the damage.

'I'm all right,' Finlay protested but his eyes welled with tears.

Cece cupped his cheek. 'It hurts, it's bound too.'

'I'm fine.' He turned away. 'I've… got to… finish…'

She took his arm and turned him back to face her. 'No, you don't. It's just a gate.'

'But you hate that it's broken and if I fix it…' He shrugged her hands off him and picked up the hammer again.

'If you fix it then what?' She knelt beside him forcing him to look at her. 'What is it?'

'Nothing.' He wouldn't make eye contact.

'Finlay!'

He swallowed and sucked his finger.

'Finlay!'

'If I fix it, then it'll be another thing done, another thing you won't hate anymore, and you might stay…'

She gently took the hammer from him. 'Look at me.' When he did, she brushed back a lock of brown hair from his eyes. 'I have many decisions to make, and, as it happens, you have two decisions to make, as well.'

'Me?'

'Yes. You can either stay here with Ross and work up at his farm, or you can come with me.'

'With you?'

She nodded with a smile. 'I won't influence you in either way and will accept whatever you decide to do.'

He looked uncertain. 'You won't want me to come with you.'

'Why wouldn't I?'

'Because I also knew about Evans being wanted by the police and I didn't tell you.'

She frowned, her head hot. 'You did? How?'

'I heard Mr Ross and his policeman friend at the party talking about it.'

'Why didn't you tell me?'

'Because you wouldn't have believed me. You knew I didn't like him.'

'That's understandable. You have better instincts than I do.'

'I never liked Evans. He looked shifty, he reminded me of some of the nuns who hated having the orphanage as part of their duties. They were mean and cruel, you could see it in their faces, and that's how he would stare at me sometimes when you weren't looking. I thought he'd make me go to school, or just send me away.'

'You should have told me all of this.'

'I thought you'd get rid of me. That's what he wanted.'

'I would never have sent you away. Evans is a bad man. I'm sorry I didn't see it sooner or learn the truth about him before he caused such misery, but he's gone now, and will never come back.'

'Good riddance.' Finlay pulled a long stem of grass. 'Why do we have to leave here though? I can make the cottage look pretty for you.'

Her heart melted at his sweetness. 'I know you can, but I'm having a baby.'

'A baby!' His eyes widened, and his smile spread wide.

'Did you not notice?'

'No, I didn't. That's the best news though, isn't it? A baby.'

'No, it's not, not really.'

'Why? Will your husband come here now? Or will you go to him?' Sadness changed his face, and, in his eyes, she saw the bleakness return.

'No, he won't be coming here. There is no husband. I made him up.'

'You made him up?' he quizzed, confused.

'I'm not married, Finlay, and unmarried mothers aren't accepted in society, they are scorned, and ridiculed and shunned by family and friends and strangers.'

'So, you pretended to be married?'

'Yes.'

'Then keep pretending.'

He made it sound so simple. 'I can't. People will find out, ask questions. I'm either going to have to go away and give the baby up for adoption, or—'

'No!' He grabbed her hands. 'No, don't put it in an orphanage. They are no good. My sister died there. It's horrible. You can't do it.'

His desperation made her wince. 'All right, calm down.'

'There has to be another way.'

'Miss Cameron said she would take the baby, and, if she does, I can't stay here. I'll return to London and you can come with me.'

'Without the baby?'

She swallowed, this was becoming unbelievably difficult. 'Without the baby.'

'Can't we just take the baby to London, the three of us?'

She shook her head sadly and wiped her nose. 'No. My family will not understand, there will be a scandal, and...' She thought of Monty and his reaction should he ever find out. 'No, the baby stays in Scotland.'

He nodded bleakly.

She stood, shaking her feet as pins and needles throbbed through them. She smiled, sniffling, wanting to change the subject. 'Let us finish this gate. Then we can close it and lock out the world.'

Chapter Fifteen

Despite her best intentions to keep the world out, it wasn't practical. However, Cece felt she and Finlay had a few weeks where it was mainly just the two of them, working about the cottage, with Nell turning up whenever it pleased her. Of course, Isla was never far away, and would often spend at least one day a week at the cottage, chatting to Cece about the farm, her relatives and village gossip. Thankfully Isla didn't mention Ross, and Cece was grateful for he wasn't a topic she wanted to discuss.

From her bank manager in London, she received a letter that a thousand pounds had been withdrawn. She wrote to James and told him. He said the case was continuing but there had been so sign of Evans. She didn't care much about the money, but the deceit, the lies and the planning Evans went to made her angry and sick. Even now, weeks later, she still felt ashamed she had trusted him so completely. Why had she been so gullible? Prue nor Millie would not have fallen under such charms so quickly.

On a bright August afternoon, while Finlay was hoeing in the vegetable garden, Cece sat on a chair in the sun. Nell had failed to show up today, the girl was totally unreliable, and Cece had spent the morning ironing. The postman had delivered post that morning, but she was only just now getting around to opening the letters.

Mama's letter was short, mentioning a trip she had done with Jacques to Marseilles and soon she'd been visiting Millie, Jeremy and the boys for a week while Jacques travelled on a business trip to New York. Mama also hoped Cece had a nice birthday. It was the first time Mama had not been with her on her birthday. She spoke of the awful temperature of summer in Paris and was relieved that Millie's chateau was a much cooler house to live in during such extreme heat.

Cece folded the letter away and thought of the pleasant warm days here at the cottage, but also wished she could see Millie and Mama. She'd write to them tonight. It had been a few weeks since her last letters were posted.

She next opened Prue's parcel. She withdrew a letter, a magazine and a shimmering pale pink silk scarf.

Dear Cece,

Although you rarely write to me, I do hope you are well and enjoying Scotland. What keeps you up there for so long I cannot imagine.

I hope you like the scarf. I bought it in New York on my last trip there. I know I'm late in sending it to you for your birthday, but I hope you had a most

*happy birthday doing whatever it is you are doing up
there.*

*When will you come back to London? It must be
over six months since I last saw you!*

*The magazine is doing well. Naturally, all new
businesses go through a settling period. But Alice is a
power house and works until the small hours to make
sure the magazine begins as we mean to go on. I've
enclosed the latest edition. The selection of outfits on
page three and four are all my doing. I handpicked
each of the evening dresses and accessories. I was
most happy with the outcome. The magazine is
becoming noticed in all the correct social circles,
which is our market. Our competition is* Vogue
'Brogue'*, but I consider we will be better than that
production.*

*Tell me your thoughts about the magazine. I am
interested to know your opinion, as will Alice.*

*Brandon is well. He's been in Yorkshire for the
last couple of weeks. His parents are getting rather
on in years and are relying on him more to be around
to oversee the estate.*

*Perhaps you could come down to Yorkshire and
I'd travel up and we can spend a week together?*

Much love,
Prue
*P.S. How is your little cottage? Have you put it
into shape yet? How remiss of Grandmama to buy
you a ruin!*
XX
London,
14th August 1923.

'How remiss indeed,' Cece murmured, but although she had hated the cottage at first, she now adored it. Cleaned, painted, tidied and filled with furniture and people, the cottage sat basking in the sun, overlooking the dazzling loch and at that moment Cece didn't want to be anywhere else.

The baby suddenly kicked her, and she winced as it moved against her ribs. She was becoming bigger each week and her bump could no longer be hidden by wearing loose clothes. As much as she didn't want to contemplate the future, time was eroding fast and soon she'd have to make a final decision about the baby.

To distract herself, she flipped through the magazine Prue had sent her. The colours were bold and bright, and she liked most of what the models were wearing. She felt it missed something though, perhaps a personal touch of some kind, she wasn't sure. She'd have a think about it and let Prue know her thoughts. It pleased her immensely that Prue had asked for her opinion. Prue never asked her for anything.

Putting the magazine to one side, she touched the delicate silk of the pink scarf. It was beautiful and Prue had excellent taste. It wasn't often that she missed Prue, for out of the three sisters, she and Prue fought the most, but right now she wished her sister was here. Prue had a sense of humour that could lighten a dreary day, she could make you laugh when you didn't even want to smile, and she missed Prue's no-nonsense ways. What Prue would have to say about the baby she didn't really know, but she guessed that out of all her family, Prue would be the one to perhaps not censure her as harshly as the others.

Opening the next letter, she frowned at the writing she didn't recognise.

Dear Cece,

Forgive me. I never meant to cause you hurt or embarrassment. I genuinely thought the world of you.
I am not the kind to live simply, there is a streak in me that is always looking for the next horizon. However, on reflection, I trust I could have been happy with you if it was in me to live a normal life.
I beg of you not to judge yourself too harshly. You are not to blame for any of this. I took advantage. Forgive me. I am what I am.
I will not contact you again.
Christopher.

For several moments, Cece stared at the note, her mind blank. Then a great tearing rage built within her chest.

She jerked up from the chair, nearly overbalancing in her haste, and sending her post onto the grass. She read the note again, seething, pacing the yard.

'I should not think too harshly of myself?' she yelled. 'The arrogant, evil, selfish guttersnipe!'

It took all her control not to rip the letter into shreds, but James would want to see it. Hurrying back to her chair, she picked up the envelope from the ground and searched it for clues as to where it was posted from. All it had was a London postmark from two days ago.

'Cece?' Finlay stood at the end of the vegetable garden. 'What's wrong?'

'Nothing.' She lifted her head at the sound of an engine. The loudness of it could only mean it was a lorry, and the only person she knew who had one was Ross.

'Mr Cameron has come!' Finlay dropped his hoe and ran around to the front of the cottage, King, the lanky puppy, loping after him.

Cece stayed where she was and took a calming breath. She wasn't ready to face Ross.

The sight of Ross walking with his hand on Finlay's shoulder, bending down to listen to the boy made Cece's chest tighten.

Ross stopped and gave a hint of a smile. 'Good afternoon, Cece.'

'Good afternoon, Ross.'

'I was passing by and I thought I'd check in on the puppy.'

'As you can see, King is growing well.' She indicated to the furry pup as it rolled onto its back to receive scratches from Finlay.

'Is he any trouble?'

She shook her head. 'No, as long as he sleeps with Finlay at night, he's happy. He's chewed his crate, but he was growing too big for it, anyway. He has an old horse blanket now in the kitchen to sit on when we are inside.'

'Watch this, Mr Cameron.' Finlay stood straight and serious. 'King, sit.'

The puppy sat, his head tilted in enquiry.

'King, paw.'

The pup lifted a paw for Finlay to shake.

'Well done, lad.' Ross was impressed.

'Go give King a treat, Finlay. There's some of Nell's bread in the larder. We'll not eat it.'

'King isn't too fond of it either!' Finlay ran off with the pup.

'Nell is not too good at bread making I take it?' Ross laughed.

She smiled. 'No. She's worse than me.'

'Isla said you are doing well at cooking now.'

'She lies to bolster my confidence.' Cece collected up her post.

'I know you said I wasn't welcome here, and I do respect that, but I thought the lad might think I didn't care about him if I didn't show my face once in a while.'

Cece blushed. 'I was too harsh with what I said that day. I was taking my humiliation out on you, and that wasn't fair. I apologise.'

'You have nothing to be sorry for. Your reaction was natural, and you were right. I should have told you. I've been thinking over my past actions and there are many things I should have done differently.'

She handed Evans's note to Ross. 'Read that. It came today.'

Ross read the note. 'Evans is clever. He'll hide low in a busy populated place like London and when the time is right, he'll move on to another victim.'

'Yes, and I pity whoever it is.'

'We can only hope he is caught.' Ross passed the note back to her. 'How do you feel about what he's written?'

'I don't feel anything except anger at my own foolishness.'

His gaze became tender, but she turned away from it and walked inside the cottage.

'Would you like some tea or lemon cordial?' she threw over her shoulder.

'Lemon cordial would be grand, thank you.' He stood inside the doorway.

Finlay brought out of the larder a bunch of carrots and a round lettuce. 'Look at our bounty, Mr Cameron. We've been harvesting loads of things for the last few weeks, haven't we, Cece?'

'We have, and all thanks to you. I couldn't have done it by myself.' She handed a glass of lemon cordial to Ross and one to Finlay.

'You should be proud of your achievements, lad, you've done amazingly well.'

Finlay grinned. 'I'd best get back to it. You'll come say goodbye before you go?'

'I will.' Ross moved aside so boy and dog could run past.

'He never walks anywhere.' Cece shook her head fondly.

'How are you keeping?' Ross leaned against the door jamb.

'I'm fine.'

'You look well.'

Cece's hand hovered over her round stomach. Ross hadn't seen her for some weeks, and would no doubt notice her bigger size.

Ross drank some more of his drink and then took a deep breath. 'I came to see you because I wanted to talk to you about Isla's suggestion.'

'About wanting the baby?' Cece stiffened instinctively.

'Yes. I want you to know that I support her offer. My sister has always wanted to be a mother. Her chance died when her fiancé did. No other man has caught her interest since. If, by taking in your baby, if offers her a chance to be a mother and for you to be happy…'

'Happiness is something I doubt I will ever fully achieve.' Cece fiddled with the wildflowers Nell had placed in a jam jar on the table.

'I can't imagine having to face the decision you must face, but I want you to know that if you give the baby to Isla, I will help her raise the child. It will be loved.'

Tears swelled her throat.

'There is another option,' he said, coming closer to where she stood by the table.

She raised her eyebrows at him, unable to speak.

He placed his glass on the table. 'You could marry me, and I would give the child my name.'

Cece gasped and stared at him. Marry Ross? He made it sound like a business transaction. She swallowed the lump in her throat and took a step back. 'Thank you, but no,' she whispered, dying inside.

'I told Isla you wouldn't agree,' he murmured, the light dying from his grey eyes.

'Thank you for asking, but it's not possible. I hope you understand.'

'No, not really, but I respect your decision.' He gently touched her arm. 'I needed to ask.'

'Thank you.'

'I'll say goodbye to Finlay.' He turned, hesitated for a moment, then walked out of the door.

Cece went into the front room and sat on the sofa. Could she feel any more wretched? As much as she liked and admired Ross she couldn't tie him to another man's child. An inner voice whispered that Ross had never said anything about loving her, and that was what she needed to hear. Monty didn't love her. Evans didn't love her. Obviously, Ross didn't either.

Was she so unlovable?

Didn't she have the traits of Millie or Prue, which would allow just one man to fall for her?

She sat back and closed her eyes denying the tears that gathered. The baby kicked against her and she felt an insane urge to rip it out of her stomach. Why did she have to be the one to fall pregnant after only one time! She wished with all her heart that she'd never gone back to Monty's apartment that night. She didn't want to be in this situation.

The rumble of cartwheels had her sitting up and wiping the tears from her eyes. She craned her head to see out of the window and past Ross's lorry.

George was coming up the drive, pipe in mouth, and beside him sat—

Cece clambered up off the old sofa and strode to the window. 'No…'

She couldn't believe it. A shiver tingled down her spine and the baby kicked again.

In stunned disbelief, she watched George halt the cart and climb down to assist his passenger. The small woman, dressed in a beautiful lilac dress with inches of lace ruffle at her neck and sleeves, stood and stared about her.

Each step Cece took felt like she was walking to the gallows. Slowly, wishing with her every fibre she could lock the door and hide, she edged open the front door.

'Cece!'

'Grandmama.'

'Here you are, madam.' George placed her grandmama's luggage on the grass.

'Excellent. Thank you. I'd be more grateful if you took them inside though. Do you expect me to carry them?' Grandmama opened her bag to pay him. 'Unless you have a man, Cece?'

'No, I don't.' Cece squashed the urge to laugh hysterically. A man meant a butler or footman. She had neither. She had a *Finlay*.

George huffed and puffed carrying the small trunk and a large suitcase into the front room.

Cece hid her body behind the door. She didn't need George spreading her condition as gossip.

Grandmama paid George. 'Though in truth I expect *you* should pay *me* for having to concentrate so hard to decipher your accent.' She nodded farewell to him and then sailed into the front room. 'Why are you hiding behind the door, Cece? Is that any way to greet your grandmama who has travelled many miles to see you?'

Gathering her courage, Cece gingerly stepped out from behind the door and waited for her grandmama's reaction on seeing her round stomach.

There was a long silence.

Grandmama sat on the edge of the sofa. 'Well, I don't need to ask what you've been doing up here.'

'Grandmama—'

'Cece, Mr Cameron says—' Finlay came racing in only to jolt to a stop on seeing the older woman in the room. Ross came to stand behind him.

Grandmama's eyebrows rose. 'Someone needs to pour me a gin and tonic. I think I'm going to need it.'

'I don't have any gin or tonic, sorry.'

The glare Grandmama gave her made Cece flinch.

Chapter Sixteen

Cece closed the door on Ross, after he'd been introduced to Grandmama and then politely made his excuses to leave.

'So, Finlay, do you live close by?' Grandmama asked the boy, hovering beside Cece.

'I live here, madam. My room is upstairs, opposite Cece's.'

'I see.' Grandmama's raised eyebrow showed her displeasure.

'Go put the kettle on to boil for a cup of tea, please, Finlay,' Cece instructed.

'He is a kitchen boy?' Grandmama asked.

'No.' Cece felt light-headed. How could she explain Finlay to Grandmama?

'There are many things I do not understand.'

Cece hung her head. 'I beg your forgiveness, Grandmama.'

'Which bit am I to forgive, child?' Grandmama tilted her head in question. 'The lack of communication, the haphazard state of affairs here, or my inevitable great-grandchild you're expecting?'

Cece remained silent, not knowing how to answer.

'How far along are you?'

'Six months,' she whispered.

'So, it's not the handsome Scot's that just left?'

'No.'

'I take it is Monty's then?'

Cece's head shot up. 'How did you guess it was him?'

'Because I'm not stupid, dear girl. You've mooned over him for two years or so, then you have an evening out with him that ends extremely late and six months later you're swollen with child. It doesn't take a genius to work it out.'

'I'm sorry.'

'Sorry won't undo what has been done.' Grandmama sighed tiredly. 'I knew something wasn't right. I just couldn't understand what was keeping you here for so long. You've never been this long away from family. Your letters, when you bothered to write, were not the sort one would receive from another who is having a wonderful time exploring the country. Instead your notes, for that is what they were, contained details of the landscape, the people in the village and the weather. Not one thing that remotely interested me. I wanted to know what *you* were doing, *your* experiences.'

Tears built behind Cece's eyes. 'How could I have told you the truth?'

'How could you not!' The hurt was clear in Grandmama's voice.

'I was ashamed. I still am ashamed. I didn't want anyone to know. I didn't know what to do. I came here to think, but it's all such a mess. I never expected the cottage to be as it is…'

'We'll get to the cottage in a minute. Firstly, what are your plans? To stay secluded in this backwater for the rest of your life and bring the child up away from your family?'

'I thought to give the baby up for adoption.'

'A sensible idea. Give the child to a family who will love it, then you can return to London and continue with your life. Little blips like these happen in most families. It's unfortunate, but it's not the end of the world if handled properly. I will help you.'

'Thank you, but you don't need to. I have it all sorted out.'

'Well done. May I ask what you have arranged?'

'Ross Cameron, who you just met, and his sister, Isla, will take the child. They are good, well-respected people.'

'Excellent. I liked the look of him.' Grandmama paused. 'Have you told Monty?'

'No!'

'Good. Don't. Monty knowing will only confuse the matter. If he wanted you, he would have said so by now and since he's engaged to be married, then we can safely assume he doesn't want you.'

Cece winced at her grandmama's bluntness.

Grandmama reached out and pulled Cece down to sit beside her. 'Does anyone else know?'

'No.'

'Let us keep it that way. Your mama would never understand.'

'Agreed.'

'I once thought I'd have this problem with Prue, when we were in India. Never did I think it would be you that would be in this situation.'

'Prue?' Cece didn't believe she heard correctly.

'Yes, well, that's Prue's story to tell, *or not*, as she wishes. I'll say nothing more.'

Cece's mind whirled. Prue had *relations* with someone in India? Cece burned with questions but knew Grandmama wouldn't say another word about it.

'So, as much as this is a shock,' Grandmama paused, as if carefully choosing her next words, 'we must be pragmatic about the situation. The child will be born in November at some point you say, but it is beyond that we must consider. You will return to London and live with me, unless you want to go to Paris to your mama?'

'No, I'd rather not go to Paris.'

'I consider it wise for you to sell this cottage.'

'Sell it?' It was Cece's turn to be surprised. 'Why?'

'You do not need an excuse to keep coming back here. You'll use this place as somewhere to spy on the child. That is not healthy for you. The cottage needs to go, and you are not to return to Scotland. The whole incident of the child has to be erased from your mind for you to gain a normal and happy life with someone else.'

She dragged in a ragged breath. 'You make it sound so easy.'

'Not at all. It'll be the hardest decision you'll ever make. That's why you can't have this cottage to use as a crutch. Returning here will prolong the damage, or the healing, whichever way you wish to see it. A clean break is needed in every way.'

Cece wanted to argue but what would be the point. Grandmama was right. Coming back to the cottage would hold memories, but she would carry them with her anyway.

'I suggest you go to Lesley in America afterwards for a few months.'

'America?'

'Yes. Absolutely.' Grandmama nodded as though it was a done deal. 'Time and distance will be what you'll require.'

'I can't begin to plan that far in advance. I can't think past having the child, if I have to think about it at all.'

'Which is why I am here. I can do that for you. I'll write to Lesley and tell her you'll be arriving in America by early December.'

'But to spend Christmas with strangers…' Cece hated the thought of it.

'It'll be for the best. New experiences, new people, and all that.'

'I'd rather be with my family. Perhaps with Millie and the boys…'

'And be reminded of what you have just given up?' Grandmama snapped. 'Don't be so foolish, girl.'

'Of course…'

'Cece, I have your best interests at heart, I assure you. A clean break, my dear, it's the only way. Trust me.' Grandmama glanced around and huffed. 'Now, this cottage. I'm ashamed that I was done a raw deal with this place. If I had known, I'd never had given you the deeds. The agent assured me that it was a small manor, pretty and cared for, but I was a gullible fool and didn't check for myself. I'm sorry.'

Cece's throat worked back the emotion. Grandmama never apologised. She considered it to be a weakness. 'We can all be gullible at times, even the most strongest among us. But I confess, I hated this cottage when I arrived.'

'I can totally understand. Look at it.' Grandmama sniffed with disgust. 'You should have gone elsewhere and rented something much more suitable and sold the place.'

'But now I kind of love it here.'

'You do?' Grandmama's blue eyes widened in disbelief. 'How can you possibly?'

'Because it's my home now. It has provided me a place where I can lick my wounds, hide from life. Just as you mentioned the day at the savoy when you told me about it.'

'None of this was what I had in mind. It's no more than a crofter's hut.'

Cece chuckled. 'Hardly that, and you should have seen it when I first arrived, if it hadn't been for Finlay—'

'Ah, yes, the boy. What is his story?'

'He's an orphan, walking the roads looking for work. I took him in, and his help and companionship has repaid me tenfold. He has become part of my family.' She smiled fondly.

'Is that wise?'

'He goes where I go,' Cece said determinedly.

'Are you certain about that?'

'He has no one but me, and for the last six months I've had no one either.'

'Don't be so dramatic. You have a family. You simply chose to hide from us.'

'What would you have me do otherwise, flaunt my large stomach to all of London society?'

'No, of course not.'

'Exactly.'

'A discreet holiday would have been sufficient. Now you are stuck with an adolescent boy.'

'I'm not stuck with him. I choose to have him in my life as more than just a servant.'

Grandmama waved her hand tiredly. 'I'm exhausted. I cannot continue this argument at this moment. Is there somewhere I can lie down for a few minutes?'

'Yes, my bedroom.'

After Cece had shown Grandmama to her bedroom, she went down to the kitchen and weary herself sat at the kitchen table.

Finlay came in carrying logs for the range. 'I didn't make the tea.'

'It's fine. Grandmama has gone to lie down for a little while. I'll make her one when she wakes up.'

'Will she take you back to London?'

'No, I need to stay here and have the baby.'

'Then what is she doing here?'

'She has come to see if I am all right.'

'How long will she stay?'

'Not long I shouldn't think.' At least Cece hoped so. As much as she wanted family with her, having Grandmama here would only cause problems. She couldn't keep Grandmama in the style she was accustomed to.

~ ~ ~ ~

That Grandmama was still at the cottage four weeks later, surprised Cece enormously. September was heralded in by high winds and cooler nights, but the days remained warm as the trees began to change colour and beautifully frame the dark waters of the loch.

'Cece, when is Mr Cameron arriving?' Grandmama asked, finishing her breakfast at the table.

She stiffened at the mention of Ross. 'I'm not sure. It is you who arranged the outing.'

'We might as well make the most of the fine weather. It is Scotland, after all. Why are you so sniffy about the excursion?'

'I'm not.' Cece rose to rinse the breakfast dishes, wondering why Nell hadn't arrived as she was meant to. Seriously that girl needed to be let go. She didn't turn up each day as expected and when she did arrive her excuses were lame.

'You are. Him and his sister are decent people. I like them. Is it because of the situation?'

Cece kept her back to the table. How could she tell her grandmama that each time she saw Ross she only thought of his offer of marriage, something that she hadn't told Grandmama.

For the last four weeks while Grandmama had been at the cottage, Ross and Isla had visited and the little party had got along ever so well. Yet, underneath the smiles and chatter, Cece struggled to make sense of her feelings.

Although both Isla and Ross didn't mention the baby, Cece was fully aware that it was an unspoken presence in the room. Beyond that, she saw Ross in a different light since his offer of marriage. The man was well-respected, not only in the village but throughout the entire area and by his clan. He was an important man, someone who people turned to in their hour of need. He'd fought in the Great War and he worshipped his sister. He could have any woman he wanted. Isla often mentioned the lasses that turned to watch him walk past them, their love-struck faces should he bid them good day. So, if he could have any woman in the Highlands, why on earth had he offered for her; a woman brought low by another man's bastard?

She didn't understand it. Could it be that he had feelings for her? Yet, why would he? She was definitely nothing special. This confusion manifested every time she saw him.

'Mr Cameron is here!' Finlay ran in from outside, King jumping up at his heels.

'I feel ashamed we do not have much to contribute to this picnic.' Grandmama left the table to pin on her hat. 'We should have champagne.'

Cece helped her with her shawl of blue to match her dress. 'We have added plenty. Besides, Isla will have enough food to feed an army.'

'That's not the point.' Grandmama pulled on her white lace gloves. 'Finlay, take the basket out to Mr Cameron.'

Cece checked herself in the mirror in the front room. She was wearing a pretty sky-blue dress with white printed flowers on it, an impulse purchase she'd made the last time she was shopping in Fort William. It was a day that Ross had taken her and Grandmama in the lorry, with much laughter and alarm of Grandmama's to be riding in a rough and loud lorry. Yet again, Cece had witnessed Ross's kindness as he assisted Grandmama around Fort William catering to her needs. Cece had enjoyed the day, of Grandmama spoiling her with presents of perfume and face creams, things Cece had long stopped using as she worked about the cottage. What use was there for such things when she never attended anywhere special or exciting, and when her main visitor was Isla?

Looking at her reflection now, she tried to look at herself as Ross did, as a man. She saw nothing to entice him. Her face was slightly rounder since becoming large with the baby. Her maternity dress fanned out over her stomach and she felt the size of an elephant and as attractive. She pulled her straw hat down low over her hair, which since becoming pregnant had darkened to a deeper, richer red, the only thing she'd seen as a benefit to her current condition.

'Good morning, ladies.' Ross stood in the doorway. His smile was warm and directed at Cece.

She returned it, a shiver of delight tripping her heart.

'Where shall we go?' Grandmama asked as Ross helped her up onto the seat of the wagon.

They'd decided previously that the lorry wasn't suitable and so it was back to horse and cart. Grandmama sat up on the seat with Ross, while Isla had made a cushioned bed for Cece in the back of the cart with her and Finlay.

'We'll find a nice sunny spot along the loch,' Ross said, his hands about Cece's waist as he lifted her up onto the back of the wagon.

Cece imagined that his hands lingered on her a little longer than was necessary but then would he, with her waist so large? How could that be attractive to him?

Ross hoisted himself into the driver's seat. 'Unless you all have a preference for somewhere else?'

'How should I know? You're the Highlander,' Grandmama replied with a grin.

'That I am, Mrs Fordham. I should show you the Glenfinnan Monument then.'

'What is the monument for?

'The Highlanders who fought for Bonnie Prince Charlie.' Ross declared with a cheeky smile.

'Jacobites?'

'Does it shock you that my ancestors fought against the British for centuries, that's when we weren't fighting other clans?'

'You're Scottish I'd expect nothing less. Hot-blooded the lot of you.'

'We are Clan Cameron, fighting for what we want is in our blood.' As Ross spoke of his ancestors' battles and history, Cece listened with interest and was impressed by his knowledge.

'And your family managed to keep hold of your land when the Highland clearances happened?' Grandmama asked.

'Our immediate family lost some land. I have relatives scattered throughout Canada because of the clearances of land last century. However, my great-grandfather was able to hold on to his land and pass it to his sons, who worked and struggled to build enough wealth so that more land was bought, thousands of acres across the Highlands, and never would we be at the mercy of lords and their clearances again.'

'It sounds as though the Cameron men were an intelligent lot.'

'Sense is knocked into us at an early age, madam,' he said proudly.

'Cece tells me you attended university.'

'I did.'

'And that you are the eldest of your family and therefore in charge of your cousins.'

'Not in charge...' Ross flicked the reins. 'I'm simply the eldest of all the cousins born from my grandfather and therefore I am the one who they turn to should they need help or advice.'

'A noble position.' Grandmama nodded approvingly.

They made the rest of the journey in companionable silence, broken by the odd comment about the loch as they followed its shoreline, or the landscape around them as they travelled further west.

Finally, they left Loch Eil behind and travelled between green rolling hills until Ross turned left and they trundled down a dirt track towards the top end of Loch Sheil. Mountains rose on either side of the loch, and despite them coming here to see the monument, it was the beauty of the loch and the scenery that took Cece's breath away.

'Isn't it beautiful?' Cece gazed in wonder.

'Aye, it's bonny right enough,' Isla replied, setting out a blanket and picnic baskets, while Ross opened the folding chairs.

'The viaduct it up that way.' Isla pointed behind them. 'It's a fair walk though, to get to it.'

'I don't have it in me.' Cece laughed.

Finlay bounded off with King to climb the stone wall at the base of the monument. The round stone tower was so tall Cece had to crane her neck to look up to the kilted Highlander at the top.

'If Prue was here, she'd be taking photographs,' Grandmama said, coming to stand beside Cece. 'You should buy a camera.'

'Perhaps I will.'

After watering the horse, Ross joined Finlay at the monument while Isla sliced the bread.

'Oh, Cece, I meant to tell you about your wee Nell,' Isla said.

'She's not my Nell. The girl never turns up.' Cece walked around the blanket, after sitting for so long, she felt a bit stiff. 'It's a shame though for when she *is* at the cottage, she works hard. She cooks and cleans and is an enormous help, but days can go by without seeing her and when I ask, she simply says she was needed at home.'

Isla opened the wax paper-wrapped slices of roast beef. 'Aye, well I suspect she enjoys the freedom of being away from home, but she is sorely needed there.'

'What do you mean?'

'I found out a few things. I've never really known her family that well. They keep to themselves and having the name of MacMartin, well, they were long enemies of the Camerons, and people don't forget. Anyway, I asked about and it seems wee Nell's father is dead, and her mam is a drunk. The eldest sister married a few months ago and has taken the wee bairns off the mam. She looks after them herself, but Nell helps her as well. I understand there are nine bairns younger than Nell. That's why she's not been at the cottage, for when she's not helping her sister, she's taking care of her mam who's in her cups all day and night.'

'How tragic,' Cece murmured, feeling sorry for the young slip of a girl who always had a smile on her face when she was at the cottage.

Isla opened a jar of pickles. 'I thought you should know.'

'Yes, I'm glad I do. Thank you.'

'You should get her to live in, Cece,' Grandmama added to the conversation. 'It might be what she needs, a chance to escape. Living with a drunk would be extremely difficult.'

229

'I'll ask her. I didn't before because she mentioned she helps her mother.'

Isla poured out glasses of lemon cordial. 'Not now the sister has taken the bairns, and I'd think the money would be needed if Nell worked more.'

'I'll talk to her and ask if she wants to live in, but the girl is utterly unreliable.'

Cece wandered down to the edge of the loch. Further along a man was fishing, and further along again another man was walking with his dog. In the distance was a large impressive house with a tower.

'You're not feeling too tired, are you?' Ross asked, coming to stand beside her.

'No, not at all.' She smiled then glanced away. The sun shimmered on the dark water, but clouds were lightly scattered on the mountain tops.

'Are your thoughts still the same about the baby?'

Her hand went automatically to her stomach. 'Yes. Why? Has Isla changed her mind?'

'No, not at all.'

They walked together a little way.

Ross bent down and selected a stone, which he threw and watched as it skipped along the surface of the water. 'I think you are brave.'

'Really? I see only foolishness in all my actions leading up to this point in my life.'

He smiled. 'We all make mistakes.'

'Perhaps, but mine seem to be gigantic.'

'I always thought the same, especially when I enlisted in the war, but I realise now that it was just me rushing through life. It's only been in the last few years that I've decided to slow down a little, make the years count. I needed to stop being in a rush.'

'I feel the opposite. For me it's as though nothing has happened in my life until the last seven months. I felt that life was passing me by, that I was a bystander watching everyone else live.'

'And now?'

She snorted. 'Now I feel out of control.'

'What do you want from life?' He continued to skip stones across the water.

'A home, a family of my own.'

'You have that already.'

She frowned. 'No, I don't.'

'You have the cottage, you've made it a home, and you have Finlay, you are his family.'

She stared out across the loch, digesting his words. He was right in some ways but not in others. She wanted a man to love her. It's all she'd ever wanted.

Isla called for them.

Ross turned. 'You could have much more, Cece.'

She watched him walk away. She understood his meaning. He was telling her she could have him and all that he had, but what of love and desire? Did he feel that, or did he simply want a wife to be mistress of his home, a body in his bed?

Chapter Seventeen

With a sharp knock at the door, Cece stepped back and waited. About her she noticed the neglect of the little crofter's cottage. Its thatched roof was dark with age, a wisp of smoke came from a lopsided chimney. The one window at the front was half boarded over with pieces of wood. Weeds grew up beside the white-washed walls that hadn't seen a lick of paint for many a year.

Cece knocked again.

A moment later the thick wooden door opened a crack. A woman's eye showed, blood-shot and squinting. 'Aye?'

'Are you Nell's mother?' Cece asked.

'What she done?' she grumbled.

'She hasn't shown up for work again. I wanted to know if she was either sick or perhaps not coming back?'

The door squeaked open further. 'Nell!' the woman yelled.

Cece jumped.

'Yer'd best come in.' The woman dragged the door open another inch, but it jammed on the uneven earthen floor.

Cece squeezed inside, the room in near darkness. A pitiful fire smoked, and a small iron bed had been pushed up close to it. The woman crawled onto it and pulled dirty grey blankets over her.

A door opened from the far wall, and Nell came in carrying a bucket of water. 'Mrs Marsh? What yer doing here?'

'I came to see you as you've not been to the cottage for several days.'

'Aye, I've been busy with me mam.' Nell put down the bucket and came to stand at the end of the bed. 'Yer not right are yer, mam?'

'Go away!' Nell's mother waved a dirty hand at her. 'Go earn something. I need me medicine.'

'Medicine?' Cece questioned Nell. 'Your mother needs medicine?'

'Ignore her.' Nell added another sod of peat to the fire and more smoke billowed into the room making Cece cough.

'Nell, here take this.' Cece took her money purse out of her bag. 'Go and buy her the medicine she needs.'

'She don't need any—'

'Shut yer mouth!' Nell's mother reared up out of the bed and snatched the several pounds Cece held.

'Mam, give it back!' Nell made a grab for the money, but the woman who Cece thought was on her death bed, ran from the cottage as quickly as a naughty child and was gone.

'I'm sorry, Mrs Marsh.' Nell hung her head in shame.

'I don't understand.'

'Me mam's medicine is drink. She's taken yer money and gone to Alf's to buy gin, and with the amount of money she's got, I doubt I'll see her for many days.' Nell sighed resignedly. 'Do yer want to report her to the police?'

'Police?' Cece's eyes were watering from the smoke.

'Aye, she stole it from yer.'

'No. It... it doesn't matter.'

Nell pushed away a strand of lank greasy hair from her face. 'I'd best come back with yer and earn it off. Me sister will go mad. I'm meant to be watching the bairns while she sits with her mam-in-law, who's properly poorly, not like our mam.'

'No, Nell. You go to your sister's house, that's more important than coming back with me.'

'But what about the money?'

'Forget about it for now.' With a last look around the decrepit cottage that stank of damp, Cece hurried outside for some sorely needed fresh air.

'I'll be over at yours tomorrow, Mrs Marsh.'

Cece, seeing Nell in her own environment couldn't help but feel sorry for the girl. Nell needed a bath, a good scrubbing, and new clothes. The limp dress she wore might once have been a shade of royal blue but was now a milky sky colour from all the washing and wearing. Nell wore no socks or stockings and her shoes no longer held claim to any shape as they flapped on her feet.

Cece had no more money in her bag to give her. 'Come in the morning for breakfast. You'll need something to eat before you start working.'

'Thank you.'

Walking back down the lane, which was on the far side of the village, Cece thought to sort through her meagre supply of clothes and find something decent for the girl. A day in Fort William might be in order too, the girl needed a haircut and new shoes.

Strolling down the main street of the village, she noticed a young man organising the children inside the school fence. A wide hat covered the man's face, not that Cece cared who was teaching there as long as Evans didn't return.

'Ho there, hen.' Murray waved to her from the bench outside of the inn. 'Care to rest yer bones for a minute?'

Nodding with a smile, Cece sat beside the old man. 'How are you, Murray?'

'Och, grand, hen, grand. There's no use complaining is there? As nobody will listen.'

Alf came out wearing his white apron that stretched over his ample girth. 'A lovely day to you, Mrs Marsh.'

'And to you, Alf.'

'Yon lad seems to be getting those bairns in order.' Murray nodded towards the man ushering the children inside the schoolhouse.

'Who is he?'

'Forget his name,' Murray said dismissively. 'A young chap sent from Inverness until the new teacher starts.'

Cece changed the subject. 'Tell me, has Nell MacMartin's mother been in here a short time ago?'

'Aye.' Alf folded his hands over his round stomach. 'Flushed she was. Where she got that much money I dread to imagine. Bought two bottles of gin.'

'Laughing like a loon she was,' Murray added. 'Yer'll not see her sober for days now.'

'Could you not have served her? Her family suffer enough,' Cece asked.

'Now, Mrs Marsh, it's not for me to tell her what to do. She had the money. I'm not her husband or father.'

'But you must have a duty of care, surely?'

'Huh?' Murray squinted at her in the sunshine. 'Duty of what?'

Alf shook his head. 'I only stop people drinking if they're going to destroy my premises. I run a business, hen. I'm not a priest to save their souls.'

'It is tragic though, you must agree?'

Murray lit his pipe. 'Mrs MacMartin has been a drunkard for years. She married into a family notorious for drinking. Her husband was a rum sod and all.'

'They all are, those lot,' Alf said. 'I'm glad a good many of them emigrated to America.'

'But her children…'

'They'll grow up like their mother and father.' Alf waved to a man driving by in his cart. 'Nell works for you, doesn't she?'

'Yes. When she turns up.'

Murray pointed his pipe stem at her. 'Watch yer valuables. I wouldn't trust any of that clan.'

Cece chuckled. 'I have nothing to steal.'

Murray's eyes narrowed. 'A MacMartin would steal the breath from yer lungs, if they could.'

'Speaking of no good folk. You've heard nothing from that no-good waster Evans?' Alf asked.

Cece stiffened. 'No.'

'He'll not show his face around here again,' Murray advised. 'He has debts from Fort William to Inverness I've been told.'

Alf snorted angrily. 'Aye, he left a hefty one behind my bar, so he did.'

Standing, Cece didn't want to talk about Evans. 'I'd best be on my way.'

'Your grandmother has come to stay, hasn't she?' Murray asked.

Cece nodded. Nothing got past Murray. 'Yes, she has.'

'A widow from London?'

'Yes.'

Murray stretched out his legs. 'Never been to London.'

'You both must come and have a drink,' Alf invited. 'I've a nice little ladies' room out the back.'

Having seen the state of Alf's back room when she first arrived, Cece knew Grandmama would rather walk on hot coals than drink in an inn like a local. 'I'll ask Grandmama and see what she says.'

'Grand.'

~ ~ ~ ~

Cece sat on the sofa before the fire darning a patch in the knee of Finlay's trousers. Night had fallen, and a sharpness was in the air.

'That fire needs more wood,' Grandmama said from the chair opposite where she was reading her mail.

Finlay, lying on the rug before the fire, got up and added another log to the blaze.

Cece recounted the story of meeting Nell's mother and sitting with Murray and Alf. She passed along Alf's invitation.

Grandmama watched Finlay tend to the fire. 'In the past I've had a few occasions where I've stayed in a country inn. Once in Ireland, I had a wonderful time when a local folk singer and her brothers played for all who was in the taproom. A lot of whisky was drunk that night.'

'Was that when you were in Dublin?'

'Yes,' Grandmama said wistfully. 'I met an Irishman, lovely he was. He showed me the sights.'

'I bet he did.' Cece laughed. 'This was before meeting Grandpapa?'

'Yes, before I met your grandpapa and fell in love properly. Until Edward, all other men were merely entertainments. Do you understand what I mean?'

Cece nodded. She did know. She had finally freed herself from the infatuation over Monty. She thought she had loved him, and perhaps she had in a certain way, but she hadn't loved Evans. He'd simply been a man who showered her with attention and made her feel wanted. That had all been superficial.

Ross on the other hand, her feelings for him were harder to rationalise. He was in her head all the time. She wanted his good opinion, his respect. Yet she deserved none of it.

Grandmama folded a letter and sighed deeply. 'I've decided to go home, Cece.'

Cece paused in her darning. 'You have?'

'Yes. I've some things that need my attention in London, and your mama writes that she is visiting next week. I should be home for her arrival and then I can reassure her you are well. Otherwise, I fear she may travel up here.'

'She cannot!' Cece dropped the needle. 'Mama can't see me!'

'Calm down. If I'm in London, I can persuade her that you'll be returning soon and stop her from travelling here.'

'Yes.' Cece's stomach churned at the thought of her mama coming to the cottage.

'Also, you should be sleeping in your large comfortable bed, not stuck on Finlay's single bed in his room, and the lad works hard, he shouldn't be sleeping on this sofa. He needs a decent bed and a good night's sleep for his labours.' Grandmama smiled fondly at the boy. The two of them had grown close.

'I was wondering if you'd stay until the birth,' Cece murmured, hopefully.

'I'd have liked to, but it's not required. Miss Cameron is a good friend and will be a support to you. Finlay knows to run for Mrs Gallan, the village midwife when your pains start.'

Cece knew she had to put a brave face on it but her first impressions of Mrs Gallan when Isla had taken her to see the older woman last week had been of an abrupt and no-nonsense character who often slipped into Gaelic and Cece hardly understood her.

'I'll leave in the morning.' Grandmama stacked her letters together.

'In the morning? So soon?' Cece swallowed a whine.

'It's Thursday tomorrow, that cart man, George, will be passing by. He can take me to Fort William train station. Finlay can watch the road for him in the morning.'

'But it's not a comfortable way to travel to Fort William in George's cart. Why not wait until Ross can take you?'

'Mr Cameron mentioned he was off to the sale yards in Inverness this week and would be staying over. No, my mind is made up.' Grandmama rose then bent so Cece could kiss her cheek. 'Goodnight, my dear.'

Cece

Cece gripped her grandmama's hand. 'I wish you were staying. I'm scared.'

'Dearest, you are stronger than you know. You'll do fine, and remember, when it's all over come straight to me in London. I'll be there waiting for you. Then you can start your life again.'

Cece nodded but feared such a thing was impossible.

Finlay, as he did every night, took the lamp and led the way upstairs so Grandmama could see where she was going.

Staring into the flames, Cece shifted as the baby kicked. Another four or so weeks and she'd no longer feel those movements. Was it a boy or a girl? No, she couldn't ponder on those thoughts!

She pushed herself off the sofa, tidied up her sewing and placed it into the basket and then banked down the fire.

'I'll put the guard up.' Finlay came back into the room and placed the steel mesh guard on the hearth. 'I'll miss Mrs Fordham. She's truly kind.'

'Me, too.' Cece smoothed down his hair.

'Mrs Fordham said that when we get to London, she'll find an apprenticeship for me in anything I want to do.'

'Are you sure you don't want to stay with the Camerons?'

'No, I want to be with you.'

She hugged him to her. 'I'd like that, too. Tell me what apprenticeship you would like to do?'

'Farming, like Mr Cameron.'

'There isn't much call for farming in the heart of London. You'll have to go away to do that.'

'Leave you?'

'Yes, but you can come back and see us.'

He turned away. 'I'll think about the apprenticeship then.'

'You don't have to make a decision for a while.' Cece squeezed his shoulder. He was growing taller all the time. 'Let King go outside to do his business then get some sleep. Good night.'

'Oh, Cece? Mrs Fordham said I could be a gentleman, and if I wanted, I could go to university one day, but I don't want to do that. The nuns taught me to read and write and that was bad enough. I don't fancy getting caned every day again.'

'No one will hit you ever again, Finlay.'

He collected his bedding from behind a chair. 'No, they won't and that's why I'm not going to go to any university even if I want to be like Mr Cameron.'

'You just concentrate on being your own person, all right? There's time enough to decide.'

'I just want to stay with you.'

She kissed his forehead. 'That's what I want too. Goodnight.'

~ ~ ~ ~

The cottage seemed noticeably quiet in the weeks after Grandmama left. Cece cleaned and cooked as the days became shorter and the nights colder as October drew to an end.

Cece wondered if her stomach could grow any larger, she seemed huge and the prospect of giving birth gave her nightmares. She was tired all the time, snappy and never comfortable. She no longer left the cottage but knew through Nell's chatter that the village was rife with gossip about her. Where was her husband they asked, why was she all alone? What was her involvement with Evans, why had he gone off never to be seen again?

The village school received a new permanent teacher, a woman named Miss Spencer, in her late forties, and she was unlike Evans in every way. She was stern, unfriendly, strict with her students and demanded excellence from them. She didn't chat with the parents unless it was about their education. She attended church twice on a Sunday and was tee-total, an unheard-of phenomenon in the Highlands.

'Miss Spencer is a right tartar, so they say,' Nell told them as she scrubbed the kitchen table.

Cece, washing the last of the carrots that Finlay had dug up, let her talk. She had no opinion of Miss Spencer.

'Apparently, old Murray Higgins gave her a wink when she walked past him, and she gave him a right bawling.'

Cece smiled, imagining Murray sitting on the bench outside of the pub doing exactly that. 'Enough of Miss Spencer, Nell, I want to know if you considered my proposal the other day.'

Nell sighed heavily. 'I dinnae know, Mrs Marsh. Me sister needs me help, and me mam is poorly. I dinnae know if I could stay here full time.'

'That's fine. I simply thought the money would come in handy for you. At the moment you are barely here two days a week, you aren't earning much at all.'

'Aye, it's hard, I'll not lie.'

'Well, we'll not speak of it again. I shan't be here much longer myself, possibly another month or so then I'll be returning to London. You'll have to find another position soon anyway.'

'I hate the thought of yer going. Yer've been really good to me, understanding about me mam and all that.'

'You're lucky the cottage is so small. If it had been bigger, I'd have to have replaced you weeks ago, but as it is, Finlay and I can cope.'

'He's a lucky lad to be going to London with yer.' Nell opened the back door and threw the bucket of dirty water over the grass. 'Och, it's clouding over for rain.'

Cece felt the chill of the cold air from the open door as she put the carrots to one side and started on the potatoes. 'You could have come with us to London and worked in my grandmama's house, but I know you don't want to leave your family.'

Nell returned inside, rubbing her arms. 'Och no, Mrs Marsh, I cannae live in London, I'd be scared to. All that traffic and noise and people. I dinnae even like going into Fort William!'

Cee grinned. 'Then perhaps it's best you stay in Resslick.'

The door opened and Finlay came in, carrying a bucket of water and looking worn out. By his side, King stared up at him.

'Is it very cold outside?'

'Don't know.'

'Are you done for a while?' Cece asked him with a frown at his surly tone. 'I'll heat some water for a wash, shall I?'

Finlay sat at the table, his hands grubby, his pale face sweating and streaked with dirt. He coughed into his fist.

'What's wrong with yer then?' Nell jabbed him playfully.

'Nothing. Go away.'

Cece, used to their petty arguments, ignored them as she cut the potatoes and put them in the pan. She had some leftover lamb, a gift from Ross, ready for a pie. 'I'll need some more rosemary, Finlay, if we have some.'

'Aye.' He dragged himself up from the chair.

Cece paused. 'What's wrong?'

'I think I'm getting a cold. I feel all achy.'

'Leave the rosemary, I'll go and get it in a minute. Sit down.' Cece poured him a glass of water. She stroked his head, finding him hot to touch. 'You're definitely coming down with something.' She turned to Nell. 'Fill a bowl with warm water and take it up to his bedroom so he can have a wash.'

'I'm not finished outside,' Finlay mildly protested.

'It can wait.' Cece pulled him up from the chair. 'Come, Finlay, upstairs. You need to rest.'

He slowly stepped through to the front room. 'The chickens…'

'They'll be fine. Get washed and lie down for an hour,' Cece called after him.

When Nell returned from taking up the washing bowl to Finlay, she came to Cece, who was basting the meat. 'He looks peaky, he really does.'

'He must be coming down with a cold.' Cece closed the oven door. 'Can you put the chickens in the coop for me please? Take them some breadcrumbs and those vegetable scraps, they'll follow you in and then just shut the door behind them and lock it.'

'Aye. I'll see to them.'

Cece finished cooking the pie while Nell ironed clothes. Rain fell steadily, bringing the night in early. Autumn weather had replaced the sunshine of summer.

'I'll be away then, Mrs Marsh,' Nell said, folding the last of Cece's clothes.

'Right you are.' Cece divided up the hot pie and placed a generous portion in a bowl and put it in the basket along with a small loaf of bread. 'Take that home for you and your mother.'

'Ta, yer kind.' Nell shrugged on her coat, with its holes in the elbows and a button missing, but at least the skirt she wore was relatively new being one of Cece's last purchases before her stomach became too big to wear it.

'You'll be in tomorrow?' Cece asked hopefully.

'Aye, should think so.'

With Nell gone, Cece took the ironed clothes up to her room and put them away in the drawers before adding wood to the small fire in the corner of the room. Her bedroom needed a fire each night now to starve off the chill and damp.

Crossing to Finlay's bedroom, she peeked in on him and found him awake. 'How are you feeling?'

'Terrible, but I'll be fine by morning,' he croaked and then coughed.

'I doubt that. A day in bed is what you need.' She touched his forehead, and he was still hot. Dampening a cloth in the bowl of water, she laid it on his forehead. 'You've developed a nasty cold it seems. I'll heat up some water and fill the water bottle for your feet.'

'Aye.' He stroked King who lay beside him on the bed. 'Are the chickens locked up?'

'Yes, Nell did it.'

'Did she do it properly?'

'I'll go and check, shall I?' She smiled. 'I'll bring you up some tea shortly. Are you hungry?'

'No.' He coughed again.

'Stay in bed. I'll be back soon.'

Cece ventured out into the dismal rain and checked on the chickens and the unhappy goat, who was huddled under a tree. She ate some of the pie and then banking down the fires, she took a tray of tea up to Finlay and thought to read to him.

'What book is it?' He asked between coughs.

'*Robinson Crusoe.*'

He closed his eyes, shivering under the blankets. He nodded off and on as she read, restless, hot and then cold, always coughing, but never complaining.

She read to him for two hours, until her throat was sore, and she grew tired. Outside the rain still fell in the darkness.

'Cece?'

'Yes?' She leaned over him, her back aching for sitting in one position for so long.

'My bones hurt.'

'I know, my sweet. You'll be better soon.' She hated seeing him so unwell.

'Can I have some water, please?'

'Of course.' She helped him to sip at the glass, feeling the heat radiating off him like a furnace.

Limply he fell back against the pillow and closed his eyes.

Cece watched him for a moment, not liking the waxy colour of his face, the shadows beneath his eyes. She went into her bedroom and grabbed a pillow and blanket off her bed and returned to Finlay's room.

'I'll stay here for a bit longer,' she told him, making herself as comfortable as she possibly could on a hard-wooden chair.

Throughout the night she was woken many times by Finlay's moans and coughing. She stripped him of his nightshirt and blankets when he burned with the fever, then covered him with as many blankets as she could when he shivered as though caught in a blizzard. His cough grew worse, and now when he coughed, he spat up globs of mucus.

King sat at the bottom of the bed, watching.

When dawn broke, Cece's back felt as though there were knives sticking into it. She could barely straighten when she tended to Finlay as he laboured for breath. Catching only minutes at a time of sleep, she wiped the grittiness from her eyes and tried to get Finlay to sip more water.

He was unresponsive, delirious.

Pacing the small bedroom, she wrung her hands, frightened.

'Cece…' Finlay's weak murmur had her clutching his hand.

'Yes, dearest. What do you need?'

'I don't want to die…'

She jerked back as if slapped. 'Die! No, don't be silly, you aren't going to die.'

'My sister…'

Recalling his tale of how his sister had died in the orphanage, Cece squeezed his hand. 'No, you'll be fine. You're strong and brave.'

He didn't answer her, and another coughing fit overtook him.

As the morning wore on, Finlay became less responsive, he no longer shook or shivered, instead as his body burned, he lay still not opening his eyes.

'Finlay.' Cece shook him, holding a glass of water. 'Finlay, have a drink.'

When he gave no response, fear clutched her throat. She shook his shoulder harder, and he flopped like a rag doll.

Smothering a cry, she put the glass down and bent close to his ear. 'I'm going to get help. I'll be back.'

She turned away reluctantly, not wanting to leave him, but Finlay was suffering more than just a cold and she needed a doctor's help. She rubbed King's neck. 'Watch over him, boy. I'll be back as soon as I can.'

Donning her coat and hat, she went downstairs and pulled on her yard boots. Rain still fell, only a wind now blew the tops of the trees. A storm was building.

As she left the cottage and the icy rain smacked her in the face, Cece cursed not having a motor car, and the thought made her think of Evans and she cursed again.

At the bottom of the drive she turned and headed for the village, though Resslick had no resident doctor. She could knock on Mrs Gallan's door? Would the midwife be of any help, or was it wiser to walk all the way to Ross's farm and get him to collect Finlay and drive them to Fort William? Was Finlay even strong enough for the journey?

She needed help, and Ross was her logical choice as she walked, head down against the wind and rain. Her back was bent against the pain that throbbed at the base of her spine. She'd never spend a night in a chair again.

Ten minutes later she saw the turning to the road that led up the mountain to Ross's farm. She hesitated. Take the mountain road or continue into the village? Was there anyone in the village who could help her? No one had a motor car. Alf at the inn might have a horse and cart, and some of the other smaller farms on the outskirts of the village had horses and carts, but would they be quicker? Ross's lorry would make the journey in half the time.

She made the decision and turned for the mountain road. The rain continued while the wind whipped itself into a frenzy. She winced with the pain in her back with every step she took. Little rivulets ran along the ruts in the dirt road. Cece cradled her stomach with one hand and the other she rubbed her back. The gradual incline of the road didn't ease her agony as rain dripped off her hat. Finally, at the top of the rise, she paused to catch her breath. The road meandered down into a shallow gully, which had a swollen stream at the bottom. Cece concentrated on getting to the bridge. She'd rest again at the bridge.

With that single thought in mind, she continued walking, an intense pain circled her back and stomach. Had she pulled a muscle sleeping in that stupid chair all night? The icy rain washed her face, seeping through her coat, making it heavier and uncomfortable.

At last she reached the bridge and shuffled across it. The swirling water rushed beneath, turned angry by the storm. Cece watched it for a moment, breathing heavily to deal with the pain. Ahead the road inclined slightly as it cut through a strand of trees.

She took a deep breath and walked on, every step agony. Once in the trees, the wind whistled like a banshee. Low grey clouds hugged the treetops. A sudden pain gripped her insides. She gasped, stumbled and fell to her knees. She stayed in that position for a few moments, wincing at the agony ebbing through her. It took a lot of effort to rise and keep walking, but she had to get to the farm.

She'd only taken three steps when water gushed between her legs.

Astonished, she instantly thought she'd wet herself. Ashamed, distraught, she hobbled to the nearest tree as pressure built up between her legs. Then it dawned on her. The baby was coming. She was in labour, it wasn't sleeping in a chair that had given her this pain.

As her brain clicked into gear, she slid down the tree trunk as another body-tearing pain ripped through her insides. She remembered Millie being in labour with her first baby, the one she'd lost. There had been so much blood. Cece drew her coat apart and looked down at her skirt. Blood would be a sign something was wrong. Her skirt was soddened but no blood. Relief made her sag against the tree.

She took deep breaths as another pain gathered strength. Why were they coming so quickly? Didn't it take hours for babies to be born? Mrs Gallan had said so. Millie had said so.

Panicking, she drew her knees up. The tautness in her stomach was torture.

She had to get up, get to the farm. Isla would help her. Ross would take her to Fort William. She cried out as she tried to stand. The effort caused her stomach to spasm.

She sat back down and leaned against the tree, panting. The rain continued unabated, the wind howling. She couldn't have the baby out in this, they'd both die, surely? She wanted a clean hospital bed, a doctor and nurses attending her. That had been her plan. Giving birth out in a storm wasn't a plan, it was barbaric.

'Come on, Cece,' she murmured between pains. She could do this. Grandmama said she was stronger than she knew. And Finlay needed her.

Taking a deep breath, she eased herself up against the tree trunk and then rested. Her legs were wide apart and suddenly she was afraid to move. The pressure was intense. Something wasn't right.

Awkwardly, she shuffled sideways, reaching for the next tree. A gust of wind blew her hat off, ripping it from the hairpins that secured it. Her coat flapped about her as she took another step.

She wiped the rain from her eyes, pushing her dripping hair from her face. Another step, then another. Just when she thought she could straighten a little, a pain stronger than the others sent her back to her knees. She screamed. Sharp stones struck at her knees, she rolled onto her back, breathing heavily.

'Help!' she called out, the wind whipping the sound away.

There was no one to help her. She would die out here and no one would know.

Dragging air into her lungs, Cece dragged herself backwards into the shelter of the trees. Again, something was happening between her legs. Shivering, she lifted her skirt and pulled down her stockings and knickers. With a cold, shaking hand she touched something round, damp between her legs.

Whimpering, she guessed it to be the baby's head. She glanced around, praying someone would come to help her. The only presence was a small flock of sheep taking shelter at the edge of the trees.

She sat for a moment, locked in a world of disbelief and shock. She was giving birth under a tree in wind and rain. How was this even happening?

Another pain broke through her daze. Suddenly, the urge to bear down and push was too much. Her body took over, blocking everything out. She grabbed her knees and strained with all she had. Movement between her legs gave her the courage to do it again as her body worked to expel the child.

251

Cece cried out, groaning as she pushed harder. She paused and rested for a moment, panting heavily. She was so frightened. Another wave of tightening and pain gathered. Cece gripped her knees and bent forward, gritting her teeth as she pushed.

She heard a noise, but the sudden flush of the baby slithering out of her body made her grunt at the abruptness. The noise grew louder in the distance.

Cece stared at the baby, blue and wet, with spots of blood and gunk covering its tiny body. It lay still, quiet on her skirt.

Cece's heart stopped. She whimpered.

Breathing rapidly, terrified, she lifted the baby up under its arms. It hung limp and lifeless in her hands.

'No, no, no!' She jiggled the baby gently, not knowing what to do.

It was dead. She screamed at the horror of it.

'Cece! Cece!' Ross skidded to his knees beside her.

She jumped at the suddenness of his arrival, then thrust the baby at him. 'It's dead!' she screeched at him. 'Help it!'

Ross ignored the baby and scrambled up and ran back to the lorry parked on the road. He quickly returned with a Swiss Army knife and cut the cord, releasing the baby's attachment to Cece. Hugging the baby to his chest, he ran back to the lorry.

Cece stared as Ross climbed into the cabin and wrapped the baby in a thick coat. In a daze, she watched him rub the baby's tiny body. His gentle voice coaxing the baby to breathe, to live.

Closing her eyes, feeling so cold that she couldn't function, Cece fell back and wanted to die with her baby.

She was roughly jerked awake by Ross shaking her shoulders. 'Cece! Come on. I've got to get you to the house. Get up! You're bleeding too much.'

'No. Leave me.' If she was bleeding, then something was wrong, she was dying like the child. It was her punishment, she acknowledged that without any emotion.

'I'm not leaving you. Cece!' He scooped her up into his arms and with a grunt got to his feet. He carried her to the lorry and hoisted her up onto the seat.

She felt as though she was falling and grabbed for the door. Ross stepped up on the small footstep and pushed her further into the cabin next to the coat-wrapped baby.

Cece turned away from it, not able to look at her dead baby. Aching and sore, cold and wet, she slumped against the seat, swaying with the motion of the lorry as Ross drove it hard up the mountain.

One handed, he rubbed the baby between changing gears. Cece closed her eyes, hating herself for hating the baby. She had killed it. Her lack of care, of love, had killed that baby. What had she done!

Ross tooted the horn a half dozen times before jumping out of the cabin.

Cece was aware of yelling, raised voices, the passenger side door being opened, and she was in Ross's arms again. He placed a kiss on her forehead, and she liked it. She was so tired…

She woke as she was laid on a bed. Her mind foggy, she had something to say, but what?

Where was she?

Was this her bed?

No?

Finlay's?

Finlay!

Cece jerked up and grabbed Ross's arm. 'Finlay!'

Ross knelt beside the bed. 'It's all right. I'll go and tell him you're here.'

'He's sick!' A terrible thought filled her brain. 'He's dying, too! We are all dying.'

'No one is dying, my darling. Lie back, rest. I'm going for the doctor.'

'For Finlay…' Strength drained from her. Her head swam, her vision became hazy and blurred. 'Finlay…'

Chapter Eighteen

So exhausted that he could barely concentrate, Ross pulled the lorry to a stop and turned off the engine. Lights shone from most of the windows in the farmhouse. He sat for a moment, not wanting to go inside, but a nudge from King made him pat the dog and move himself.

No matter what was waiting for him, he'd have to face it. After bringing Cece and the baby to the house, he'd yelled instructions to Isla, who'd sprang into action with Fi, and he'd left Cece and the cold, blue baby with them and immediately left again to find Mrs Gallan and bring her to the farm. After that, he'd turned the lorry around again and gone to Willow Cottage.

He'd not believed Cece when she spoke gibberish about them all dying, but he thought he should check in on Finlay and let him know what had happened to Cece. The shock of scouring the outbuildings and not finding the boy, worried him enough to run inside and search upstairs. Seeing Finlay in bed, looking no better than a corpse, took the wind from him. He'd

carried the boy downstairs and drove straight to Fort
William and the small hospital there.

Now it was past midnight, Finlay was under the
care of a doctor and nurses and Ross had driven home
to find out whether Cece or her baby were still
breathing.

With King at his heels, he slowly opened the
kitchen door and walked into the warmth and comfort
he'd always known in this house. Isla sat before the
fire in their mother's old rocking chair. In her arms
was the baby.

Isla glanced up at him with a small smile. 'She's
so bonny.'

Relief made his knees buckle. He sank beside his
sister and peered at the tiny little face peeking out of
the soft blanket. 'She's alive?'

'Aye. She's a fighter. It was touch and go for
hours, but Mrs Gallan was brilliant. This little one has
even had an ounce of milk. It was only watered-down
cow's milk, as that is all we have, but Mrs Gallan said
it's better than nothing until Cece can feed her or we
can get to the shops and buy some of that baby milk
formula.'

'And Cece?' he asked hopefully, swallowing the
lump in his throat.

'She's weak. Mrs Gallan delivered the afterbirth
and stopped the bleeding; the end of the bed is
propped up to help with that. Cece won't be getting
up any time soon, that's for certain. Mrs Gallan is
sitting with her now while she sleeps.'

'Thank God she is all right.' He yawned, fatigued
with worry.

Isla stood. 'Sit down and hold this one for a
moment while I make some tea and get you some
food.'

Gently, as though he'd break her, Ross sat in the rocking chair and held the baby in his arms. She was as light as a feather, but all he could think about was the dreadful moment he found them on the side of the road.

'How's Finlay? Was he shocked when you told him about Cece?' Isla put the frying pan on the stove to heat and added strips of bacon.

'I haven't told him anything. When I got to the cottage, I found him in bed, terribly ill.'

'Ill?' Isla stared at him as she sliced the bread. 'Is that why Cece was out in the storm, to come here and get help?'

'It has to be the reason.'

'And she went into labour. She must have been so frightened, I can't imagine.'

'Yes. I took Finlay to Fort William.'

Isla stopped slicing again. 'Fort William? He's that bad?'

'I thought he was dead, Isla, truly I did.' He rubbed his forehead, still alarmed by the day's events.

'Dear God.'

'The whole way to Fort William I couldn't stop thinking that perhaps today three people would die.' Emotion caught in his voice and he looked away.

Isla came to him and hugged him. 'You have saved them, all three of them.'

Ross cleared his throat. 'The doctor believes Finlay has pneumonia, poor lad. They don't know if he'll make it.'

'He will,' Isla said determinedly, going back to the table. 'He's at the hospital, the best place for him.'

Ross gazed down at the tiny little sleeping face. She was perfect. He willed her to not die, to be strong and tough like her mother.

257

'You need to eat.' Isla mashed the tea in the pot and set the table for him. 'Fi is making up the trundle bed for Mrs Gallan, she'll have to stay the night, for you're not going out again until morning.'

'The rain has stopped, but the stream is lapping at the bridge.'

'It'll be down by morning if we don't have any more rain.'

'Yes. We've got King, too. I doubt he's eaten.' He nodded towards the dog and yawned again. Sitting in front of the fire, warm and thankful to be home, Ross fought sleep.

Isla came and took the baby from him. 'Eat.'

'I'm not hungry, only tired.'

'You can go to bed once you've eaten.'

They turned as Mrs Gallan entered the kitchen. 'Could I get a cuppa?'

'Of course. Come sit down. I'm making Ross some bacon sandwiches. Do you want one?'

'Och, who ever says no to a bacon sandwich?' Mrs Gallan took the baby off Isla and sat in the rocking chair. 'She's colouring up well. This one has got better colour than her mam, that's the truth.'

Ross swallowed. 'Can I go in to see Cece?'

'Aye, she's asleep though, so don't wake her,' Mrs Gallan advised as the baby murmured.

Ross left the kitchen and crossed the hall. Lighted lamps on the hall table and on the first half-landing bathed the staircase in golden light. Another lamp lit the way along the bedrooms' corridor. In his mad rush earlier, he'd carried Cece up to the first bedroom off the landing, a spare room used when the cousins were staying. He entered it now and smiled at Fi, who was adding logs to the small fireplace in the corner of the room. 'How is she?'

'Sleeping, Mister Ross.'

'I'll sit with her a while.'

'Aye then.' Fi left the room and Ross sat in the padded chair by the tilted bed.

He took Cece's hand in his and held it gently. She looked so pale. Her hair had dried, and the vibrant redness of it was in stark contrast to the whiteness of the pillow her head laid on. Shadows bruised under her eyes. She lay so still, the creaminess of her cheeks bleached away. He wanted to take away all her pain, all her worries, but she wouldn't let him. She had no trust in men now, nor did she have any self-worth, and that hurt him more.

Her eyes flickered open. She had beautiful blue eyes.

'Ross.'

He smiled and squeezed her hand. 'You're all right. Everything is all right.'

'Finlay?'

'He's at the hospital in Fort William. The doctor is a good man and they are looking after him.'

'Thank you.'

'Do you want a drink or something to eat?'

She shook her head.

'Or do you want Mrs Gallan?'

She frowned. 'Mrs Gallan?' Then her hand went to her stomach, still swollen but not as large as it was. 'The baby?'

'She's alive.'

'Alive?' She struggled to sit up.

'Yes, lie still. You're weak and are not to get out of bed.'

A dazed look came into her eyes. 'I thought it was dead.'

'She's like you, stronger than she looks.'

Cece turned her head away. 'I thought I had killed it...'

'You didn't. Cece, listen to me. I can—'

'No. Please, I'm tired...' She closed her eyes and turned away.

He had no choice but to leave the room.

Back downstairs, Ross entered the library-come-study and poured himself a glass of whisky and stared out into the black night. How was he going to convince Cece that he wanted to take care of her and the baby?

Isla found him a few moments later. 'Your sandwiches are cold, and your tea.' She came to his side. 'Is she still sleeping?'

'She woke up. I told her about Finlay and the baby. She thought she had killed her, that she was dead.'

'But she didn't, and it might have scared her enough for her to change her mind and keep the baby.'

Ross turned to her. 'Is that what worries you? That you can't have the child?'

Isla gave a small smile and shook her head. 'I only said about me, *us*, raising the child to stop Cece from moving to some filthy city and giving the baby away to a terrible orphanage.'

'Really?' He was confused. 'She doesn't want it.'

'No, she *didn't*, but now the baby is *here*, and Cece faced nearly losing her. I believe she'll think differently now.'

He stared at his sister, wondering how she could think that way. 'And what if she *doesn't*? Do *you* want the baby?'

'Aye, I'll take her in.'

Ross threw back the rest of his whisky. 'I want to marry Cece.'

'Aye, I know. Why do you think I've been making these plans?'

'She doesn't want me.'

Isla gave him a queer look that she often did when she thought he talked nonsense. 'Cece doesn't know what she wants, but she will, trust me.'

~ ~ ~ ~

Cece winced with soreness as she swung her legs over the edge of the tilted bed. A rooster crowing woke her, but she'd heard the baby's cries during the night and hardly slept. She plucked at the nightgown she wore, obviously one of Isla's. She needed her own clothes so she could go to Fort William to see Finlay.

The door opened and Isla came in, smiling and cheery, carrying a breakfast tray. She placed the tray on the bed next to Cece. 'Morning. How are you feeling? Did you get much sleep?'

'A little. I was uncomfortable, my body feels weird.'

'Do you need the pot? You shouldn't be getting up.'

'I need to see Finlay.'

'Finlay? In Fort William? No, that's not a clever idea. You just had a baby yesterday. You need to stay in bed.'

'Finlay will want me to be with him.'

'Finlay is thirteen. He'll be fine. Whereas your little one needs her mam.'

Cece shuddered. 'No.'

'No? What do you mean? She needs feeding. She had us all up most of the night. Mrs Gallan says she's hungry and she's not taking the bottle Mrs Gallan gave her. She needs your milk.'

'No! I'm not keeping her so why would I put her to my breast? That's a ridiculous thing to say. I'm going home.' Cece wobbled a little as she stood, and Isla grabbed her arm.

'You're not sturdy enough to leave this room, never mind go to your wee cottage. Sit down and be sensible.'

Cece gingerly sat back on the bed, feeling a wetness between her legs. 'I need to change. I'm leaking. Lord, this is so ghastly.' She wanted to give in and cry but knew that was weak.

'I'll go get Mrs Gallan to have a look at you before Ross takes her home. Stay there. I'll be back.'

After an examination by Mrs Gallan, who declared Cece was bleeding normally and not excessive enough to cause alarm, Isla bundled Cece back into bed and ordered her not to get up. Mrs Gallan also mumbled under her breath about Cece not wanting to feed the baby, calling it unnatural. The comment hurt Cece but what could she do? To look or touch the baby would bring her undone. She had to pretend it wasn't hers.

The baby's cries were heard every time someone opened Cece's bedroom door, and she flinched at the sound. She didn't want to acknowledge the baby's existence. She fought hard to put the whole episode of the birth and the thought that the baby was dead from her mind. The whole appalling incident had terrified her. She wanted to be in her cottage, recovering, and have Finlay home and well, then they could leave for London and start again.

The day passed slowly and frustratingly. Cece wanted to visit Finlay but Isla promised her that Ross would go and report back. She'd let Finlay down. He'd be expecting her.

As the sun was setting on a long and emotional day, Ross knocked and entered the bedroom, in the background the baby was crying again. Cece cringed at the sound.

He held a cup of tea in his hand. 'Isla sent me up with this.'

'Thank you.' A little embarrassed to have him tending to her, she took the cup off him and placed it on the bedside table next to her. 'Did you visit Finlay?'

'I did. He is responding to the doctor and nurses. The doctor said he's out of the woods now. Still ill, obviously, but the danger period has passed. They want to keep him for a few days until he is no longer so weak.'

'Thank you!' Cece reached out and grasped his hands. 'I'm so relieved. I was so worried. I took too long to get help for him.'

'That wasn't your fault, was it?' He smiled softly, his eyes full of tenderness. 'I spoke to Finlay briefly and filled him in on all that has happened. He was happy you and the baby are well.'

Cece lowered her gaze and withdrew her hands. 'You've been exceedingly kind to both Finlay and I, and I cannot thank you enough for all that you've done.'

'I don't want your thanks, Cece.'

'You saved us all.' Tears built hot behind her eyes. 'Would you take me back to the cottage, please?'

'Is that wise? You haven't regained your strength yet.'

'I have and I will, but I need to leave here, Ross. To be in this house with the cries…'

'You're not well enough to live by yourself.'

'I'll ask Nell to stay a few days with me.'

'Cece—'

'Please? I beg you to take me. I simply cannot stay here.'

He sighed, his expression showing his lack of enthusiasm. 'Isla will string me up for taking you.'

Cece gave a little smile. 'Isla will be too busy. She's too used to getting her own way all the time. She forgets that I am also an independent woman.'

Minutes later and incensed Isla stood at the bottom of the bed. 'You're doing what?'

'I need to go back to the cottage,' Cece said.

Ross stood leaning against the wall with his arms crossed over his chest. 'I did explain it to her.'

'Well, you can't go. What are you thinking? Are you mad?'

'I'll have Nell.'

'Nell? The lass doesn't have a sensible thought in her wee head!'

'I'm not an invalid, Isla. I can move about. I'm quite able to sit on a chair in my own kitchen than I can here.'

'That's not the point. You need to rest.'

'And I will, in my own bed.'

'Do you think I'm soft in the head? You won't rest. You'll be packing to leave, I know you. The minute Finlay is out hospital you'll be gone.'

Cece blinked at the anger in Isla. 'You know that has been my plan all along.'

Isla stormed out of the room and moments later came charging back in carrying the baby, which she unceremoniously dumped in Cece's arms.

Shocked, Cece stiffened, not daring to look at the baby she held, which was squirming and making little squawks.

'Look at her!' Isla demanded. 'She is yours. She has survived being born beside the road. Look at her! She's starving. Look at her!' Isla leaned closer. 'You always said you wanted a wee family, well you have one. It might not be the wee sweet normal family you imagined, all done properly and neatly, but that's not her fault! *Look at her*!'

Ross stepped forward and dragged his sister away. 'That's enough!'

Cece closed her eyes, the tears trickling over her lashes. 'Take her.'

Ross hurriedly took the baby and crooned softly to her.

His tenderness made the tears fall faster.

'I thought you to be better than this, Cece,' Isla murmured, heartbrokenly.

'I need to get dressed.' Cece swallowed, dashing away her tears.

Ross, carrying the baby, and Isla left the room.

Slowly, Cece dressed in the clothes that had been washed and ironed for her. The maternity skirt and blouse were ugly to Cece, but it didn't matter. She just needed to go back to the cottage before her heart broke into a thousand pieces.

Ross was the only one in the kitchen when she hesitantly opened the door. King sat at his feet. Ross gave her his arm and escorted her out to the lorry and helped her up into the cabin. King jumped up beside her. Without speaking they drove away from the farm, away from her baby.

Cece gazed out of the window not seeing the sheep, the fields, the distant mountains, or the clouds in the orange sky as the sun descended. She saw nothing, felt nothing, and she hoped that was how she'd remain for an exceptionally long time.

At the cottage, Ross built a fire in the kitchen range and another one in the front room. He made her a pot of tea and placed a pan of cold stew on the range to reheat. In the dark, he fed the chickens and moved the goat to a new patch of grass. He brought in more water and then fed King.

'I'll be back in the morning to take you to Fort William to visit Finlay. Is there anything else you need me to do?'

She shook her head and swallowed the lump in her throat. He'd been so kind.

Coming closer, Ross took her hands. 'I can stay and sleep on the sofa if you don't want to be alone?'

Her heart begged her to say yes to him, but her head overruled. 'No, thank you.'

Gently, he pulled her into his chest and held her tight. 'You're not alone. While ever I have breath in my body, I am here for you. I am yours.'

Impulsively she reached up and touched his cheek. 'Thank you.'

She gazed into his grey eyes that showed such devotion and nearly changed her mind, but what good would that do? To stay here and be with Ross would mean claiming the baby, and she couldn't do that. It wasn't fair to ask Ross to bring up another man's child. And it would also mean confessing to her Mama, her sisters, family and friends what she had done. Then all of this upset she'd endured for the last nine months would have been for nothing.

No. Her plans had to stay as they were. She needed a fresh start, away from Scotland, away from the Camerons, the baby and the memories.

America was the answer. She'd take Finlay to New York to see the sights, to forget what they had been through. Then, later, she'd return to London, pick up the pieces of her life and start again.

At the kitchen table, she listened to the lorry's engine grow more distant as Ross drove away.

King licked her hand, and she patted his head.

Chapter Nineteen

After a restless night, where she'd suffered nightmares of screaming babies hidden in trees, Cece sat beside Finlay's narrow iron bed in the small hospital. Outside the dismal cheerless room, the grey sky matched her mood. Ross had collected her at ten o'clock and driven her to Fort William, in near silence. He'd not come in with her, but mentioned he had some appointments to attend to and he'd return in a couple of hours. Without doubt the tension between them was palpable, but Cece didn't know what to say to ease the situation.

Finlay woke and smiled on seeing Cece. 'I didn't think I'd see you for a while,' he croaked.

'Well, I couldn't leave it too long without annoying you,' she joked. 'You look better than the last time I saw you.'

A healthy colour glowed on his face now, not the flush of fever. His lips were dry and cracked, and his hair needed washing, and he was all skin and bones again but at least his eyes appeared clearer.

'When can I go home?'

'Soon, a few more days yet.'

'I don't like it here.'

'It's the best place for you at the moment.'

'I want to be at the cottage with you and King.'

'You will be soon. King slept on my bed last night. He misses you.'

'Where's the baby?'

Cece hesitated. 'With Isla.'

Finlay's eyes closed. 'Bring her home…'

Remaining silent, Cece glanced out of the window again as Finlay dozed. Her skirt was a little tight, and she stood to adjust the waist and stretch her legs. Apart from her breasts being sore and her clothes either too big or too tight, she felt well. She made sure she ate enough to regain her energy. Tonight, she'd start packing up the cottage ready to leave.

With Finlay asleep she slipped from the hospital and walked to the post office, there she posted a note to Grandmama informing her the baby was born, and she'd found a home for her, that Finlay was ill, and she'd be on the next train as soon as Finlay could leave.

Strolling back to the cottage, she noticed a shop window display of fine knitted baby clothes. Her heart twisted, and she hurried on.

Once back in Finlay's room, she found him awake, sitting up, looking better and sipping soup the nurse had brought. Ross sat on the chair beside the bed.

'Everything all right?' Ross asked, standing up to let Cece sit down.

'Yes. I had to visit the post office.'

'I could have done that for you.'

Cece flashed him a tight smile and sat by Finlay's bed. 'That soup looks good.'

'It's better than yours.' He grinned.

'Ha! Cheeky. You're obviously getting better.'

'I might be able to leave tomorrow. The doctor just said so, didn't he, Mr Cameron?'

Ross nodded. 'He did indeed.'

'That's wonderful news.' Cece glanced out the door. 'I'll go and speak to the doctor and confirm.'

She quickly found the doctor further down the short corridor and he declared that if Finlay had another good night, he should be able to go home to rest tomorrow.

Delighted, Cece went back into Finlay's room. 'Yes, it seems a possibility if you have a good night tonight.'

'I will.' Finlay nodded.

'Then I'll be back to collect you in the morning, young man,' Ross said.

'There's no need, Ross,' Cece cut in. 'The hospital will bring him to the cottage in the ambulance. The doctor said so.'

'I see.' He looked disappointed. 'Well, if you're ready, I need to get back to the farm.'

'Of course.' Cece kissed Finlay's forehead. 'I'll be waiting for you tomorrow.'

The long ride back to the cottage seemed to last forever as Cece sat silently beside Ross.

As he pulled the lorry to a stop in front of the cottage, he turned to her. 'The baby...'

She stiffened and didn't look at him.

'Cece the baby isn't thriving. She's not taking to the powdered milk, or anything. All she does is cry.'

Opening the door, she grabbed her bag.

Ross held her arm to stop her from climbing down. 'Cece, please.'

'What do you want me to do?' she snapped.

'Mrs Gallan came last night, and she's worried about the baby. She warned us that if she doesn't drink soon, she'll not make it. Isla is frantic.'

Her stomach clenched, but she fought back any feelings. 'Take the baby to the hospital then. Give it to them.'

'It? It?' Ross banged his hand on the steering wheel. 'It's a she! She's a girl, your daughter.'

'No, she isn't! I gave her to Isla! If Isla doesn't want her, then give her away!' Cece scrambled down and hurried inside the cottage and slammed the door. It was a while before Ross started up the engine and drove away.

Slumping onto the sofa, Cece let the sobs come, her chest hurt, she'd held them in for too long. She cried for herself, she cried for her baby and she cried because she didn't know what to do any more. She wanted to go home to Elm House in York, she wanted to return to the times when she was happy and surrounded by her family and friends, when her life was simple and easy. She feared it could never be that way again.

She cried until she was exhausted and wrung out like a used dishcloth. Slowly, like an old woman, she rose and shuffled into the kitchen. Adding more paper and kindling to the smouldering coals, she watched the flames for a long time until King nudged her with his nose.

'Are you hungry, boy?' she murmured tiredly. Emotionally drained, she fed King the scraps from the larder, wanting nothing more than her bed.

The front door was flung open, frightening Cece.

'Cece!' Isla rushed into the room carrying the baby who was wailing pitifully.

Cece

'What is it?' Cece shushed King who set up barking at the intrusion.

'The baby!' Isla thrust the whimpering child into Cece's arms.

'What?' Cece automatically held it, she had no choice.

'I think she's dying,' Isla wailed, setting King off barking again and the baby crying harder.

Heart thumping, Cece braced herself to glance at the baby wrapped in a soft warm blanket. Its little face was screwed up and red, its whole body convulsing with sobs.

'There now. There now.' Rocking the baby in her arms, Cece glared at Isla. 'Why did you bring her here? She isn't mine. She's yours.'

'I can't cope with her!' Isla defended. 'It's too much. She won't drink.'

Cece kept rocking the baby and suddenly her breasts tingled with a sharpness that made her gasp.

'What is it?' Isla was beside her in seconds.

'I don't know. My breasts. They hurt and feel like they are ready to burst.'

'It's your milk. It's come in.'

'It has?' Astonished, Cece tried to remember what Millie did when she breastfed her boys.

'Feed her, for God's sake, Cece, feed her, or she won't live. *You'll* have let her die!'

Instinct made Cece drop to a chair and unbutton her blouse and pushing aside her bra she was embarrassed to see the milk seeping out. 'Oh my gosh!'

Isla helped her to adjust the position of the crying baby so she could suck and within moments the baby had latched on to her nipple and was pulling gently. It felt strange.

Silence descended.

Cece stared down at the little downy head at her breast. Her closed eyes were red and swollen, but her tiny button nose was perfect.

The baby drank for what seemed hours to Cece, who sat stiffly on the wooden chair, but she felt relief from one breast at least.

'Swap her over to the other one,' Isla advised, making them a cup of tea.

Doing as she was instructed, Cece awkwardly swapped the baby to the other breast.

A few minutes later the baby fell asleep, a dribble of milk on her lips.

'Right, I'm off.' Isla stretched and yawned. Night had descended.

'You're going?' Cece hated the thought of being alone but handed the baby to Isla so she could re-arrange her clothing.

'I'll be back tomorrow.' Isla handed the baby back. 'There's a box of the baby's things in the cart. I'll go and get them.'

'What do you mean?'

Isla paused by the door. 'She stays with you tonight. I need a good night's sleep and she needs feeding.'

'I can't do that!' Cece walked after Isla.

'Yes, you can.' Isla fetched the box of baby things and then climbed up onto the cart, lit the lantern and turned the horse about. 'Goodnight. Oh, and give her a name!' she called, trundling away.

Stunned at being abandoned, Cece stood in the doorway holding the sleeping baby.

She returned to the kitchen not knowing what to do. Carefully, she placed the baby on the table, knowing it couldn't roll off. Millie's boys didn't roll until they were several months old. Secure in the knowledge that the baby would be safe, she hurriedly ran upstairs and made a fire in her bedroom. With that going, she raced back downstairs, checked the baby and then gulped down her cooling tea. She let King out to do his night-time business and then banked the range fire.

Pouring another fresh cup of tea, she quickly sliced some bread and buttered it. She took that and the tea up to her bedroom, then returned and fetched the baby. Her hands shook as she let King in, and they went up to the bedroom and she closed the door.

Cece stood staring at the sleeping baby placed on the bed. Carefully, she unwrapped it from the blanket and studied her tiny body wearing only a little white gown and a towel napkin. The baby had such little feet, with tiny toes. Her fingernails were so cute and when Cece put her finger into the baby's hand its fist closed around her finger and the tug of love flew straight to Cece's heart.

Blinking back her tears, Cece wrapped the baby up and cuddled her to her. 'I'm sorry.' More tears fell. 'I'm so so sorry.'

~ ~ ~ ~

Finlay returned from hospital mid-morning and was delighted that the baby was at the cottage. 'You are going to keep her, aren't you?' He asked from his position on the sofa in front of the fire.

'No, she belongs to Isla.'

'Then why is she here and not at the farm?'

'Because at the moment I am feeding her until she is stronger to take the bottle and the powdered milk. Apparently, she doesn't like the powdered milk.'

'She's very small.'

'Yes, but she'll grow.' Cece smiled and gazed at the baby in her arms. She'd just fed her again. The baby had slept for most of the night, only stirring a little just before dawn when sleepily Cece had fed her again.

'Will Miss Cameron come and get her soon?'

'Yes, at some point.' For an instant Cece didn't want Isla to come and take the baby, but she squashed that thought. She couldn't be selfish.

She forced a smile to her face. 'Now, do you want something to eat? I've collected the eggs this morning and the hens have been busy. We've got seven. So, I can make scrambled eggs and bacon? I know it's late for breakfast, but it's something light for you.'

Finlay nodded. 'Yes, please. I had porridge at the hospital early this morning, but I'm a little hungry.'

'Then that's what we'll have. I'm hungry too.' Cece laid the baby in the other corner of the sofa and Finlay watched her.

'She's got a tiny bit of red hair.'

Cece's step checked as she left the room. She glanced back over her shoulder at the baby. 'Yes... like me...'

When the sun had set and Isla still hadn't arrived to collect the baby, Cece began to worry. Having the baby, feeding her, changing her, washing the napkins, all took the time she needed to pack up the cottage. Besides that, she didn't want to grow used to having the baby for the saying goodbye would be hard enough.

Cece was helping Finlay to sit at the table for his evening meal when the back door opened, and Nell walked in.

'Ho there, Mrs Marsh and how are yer, Finlay?'

'Nell.' Cece stood with her hands on her hips. 'Where have you been? I needed you here three days ago.'

'I heard yer had the wee bairn.' Nell smiled as though it was all an everyday occurrence. 'And, lad, yer've been to hospital I hear.'

'And didn't you think I might have need of you?'

Nell shrugged. 'I'm sorry but me sister has had a bad toothache and I've had to mind the little 'un's. Me mam's been in bed and I've had to—'

'Yes, yes, all right.' Cece waved her away. Nell had no sense of priority, or maybe she did, and it was Cece who expected too much, she didn't know. 'Why are you here so late?'

'Oh, I thought to come and get me wages and see the wee scrap. I heard Mrs Gallan tell Alf that you had her on the side of the road!'

Cece closed her eyes at the thought of all the village knowing her business. 'Are you coming to work tomorrow? I'll pay you then.'

'I dinnae know.' Nell scratched her ear.

'Right well, I *want* you to be here to help me pack up the cottage.' Cece ladled out potatoes and carrots on Finlay's plate to go alongside the sausage.

'Pack?'

'Yes. Finlay and I are going to London in a few days.' Cece filled her own plate.

'In a few days? But what about me job?'

Cece raised her eyebrows. 'Really? Now you are worried about your position here? You've not cared about it all summer.'

'But yer know about me mam.'

'I do, yes, but I'll not pay you when you are hardly ever here.'

'All right, I'll come tomorrow,' Nell huffed.

'Don't do me any favours, will you?' Cece replied sarcastically. 'I'll see you tomorrow, Nell. I'm depending on you.'

'Aye, till tomorrow then.'

Finlay looked up from his plate when the door closed on Nell, he'd been silently eating throughout the whole exchanged. 'She ain't worth feeding, that one.'

Cece grinned at him and cut into her sausage.

'Are we really going to London in a few days?'

'Yes, as soon as you are a little more rested.'

'Are we taking the baby?'

'No. I told you, she belongs to Miss Cameron.'

'I want her to come with us.'

'She's better off here. I've explained this to you several times.'

'But you're her mam.'

Cece's heart contracted at his words. 'Eat your carrots.'

The following morning, Cece placed the baby on the bed after feeding her and started packing her trunk and a suitcase with her clothes.

'Cece!' Finlay's call from downstairs had her going to the landing and leaning over.

'Yes?'

'Mr Cameron is here.'

Her stomach clenched. She took a deep breath and tied her hair and left the bedroom.

Ross was in the kitchen scratching King's ears as she walked in. 'Good morning, Cece.'

'Good morning, Ross.' Her heart did a little skip in response to his warm smile. He looked handsome in a thick white Aran sweater and dark trousers, his jaw clean-shaven.

'How are you?' he asked.

'Fine, and you?'

'Grand.'

Cece's smile was fleeting. 'Isla not with you?'

He frowned. 'No. Should she be?'

'She said she'd come and take the baby yesterday.'

'She's gone away to our cousin's farm yon side of Ben Nevis.'

'Will she be gone long?' She tried not to sound desperate.

'I don't know. She didn't say.'

'I plan to leave for London on Thursday.'

The light died in his eyes. 'Right.'

'I want to know if you want to buy the cottage and land?'

'Aye, I'll buy it.'

'Good.' Her gaze flittered to Finlay who sat at the table folding washing. A task she'd set him that wouldn't exhaust him, and one that Nell should be doing but of course the girl hadn't turned up again.

'How is the baby?' Ross asked.

'Well.'

Finlay grunted. 'All she does is eat and sleep.'

'No screaming?' Ross jested.

'Nope. She's a bit boring, really.' Finlay folded another napkin.

'Are you here to take her?' Cece asked.

Ross frowned and shook his head. 'No, not at all.'

'But we are leaving in two days' time. Can you get word to Isla?'

'Not really, no. It would mean driving a few hours there and back.'

'Doesn't she want the baby?' Cece's voice rose.

'I don't know, Cece. I'm sorry. Isla didn't mention it before she left.'

'How inconsiderate!' Cece fumed. 'You cannot say you want a baby and then don't take it!'

'Can you delay your leaving?'

'I'm going to have to, aren't I? But that's not the point. I don't want to become attached to her...'

'Would that be such a terrible thing?'

'Yes! Yes, it would be. You know that!' Cece stormed from the room and back upstairs.

In her bedroom she stared at the sleeping baby, her mind in a whirl of confusion and her emotions out of control. None of this was going to plan.

If Isla didn't take her, then she'd have to go to Edinburgh or somewhere and leave the child at an orphanage. Was that an easy thing to do? Can you simply pass your baby to a stranger in a building and walk away? She didn't know. The thought filled her with dread. 'Damn you, Isla!'

A knock at the door sounded. 'Cece.'

'Come in, Ross.'

He came to stand beside her. 'I'm sorry.'

'It's not your fault though, is it?'

'Tell me what you want to do, and I'll help you.'

She sighed deeply and shrugged. 'I want to go back in time.'

'I can do many things, but I can't do that.' He gave a half grin. 'Besides, if you did that then you wouldn't have met me,' he joked.

'No...' Cece gripped her hands together to stop them reaching out and touching him.

'I don't want you to go,' he murmured.

'I must.'

Gently he pulled her closer until their foreheads were touching.

She closed her eyes. 'Please, don't...'

'Cece.' When his lips pressed against hers, she sighed at the simple wonder of it. She longed to give into the delicious sensual caress of his mouth and when his tongue lightly touched hers a thrill shot down her body. Long buried sensations coursed through her. She held onto him, feeling the strength of his body.

The baby woke, snuffling and whimpering. Cece jolted back into the world she'd made and out of the one she'd fantasised about.

Ross ran his hand through his hair. 'I'd best go. I'll call again tomorrow.'

She nodded, not looking at him as she picked the baby up.

After calming the baby, she went downstairs, thankful that Ross had left.

Finlay sat on the sofa reading *Robinson Crusoe*. 'The post has been delivered.'

Cece sorted through the letters from Millie, Mama and Cousin Agatha and two catalogues. She opened the letter from Millie first and sat down to read it.

Dear Cece,

How are you going in the wildest of the Highlands? We miss you terribly. Will you come and see us soon? The boys are growing so fast. You'll be shocked at the size of them when you do come here. Will you make it for Christmas? It was a shame you missed Charles's first birthday, but we understood that you were travelling.

I'm keen to hear of all your adventures during the summer. Mama was visiting us last week, and she says you barely write to her and she was most put out, but I suspect your lack of letters are due to your travels. You must be having a most wonderful time. Is it getting cold there now? Have you met some new or old friends?

I received a letter from Cousin Agatha only yesterday and she tells me she is with child. She's so happy. Isn't that simply marvellous?

Cece smothered a groan. Agatha pregnant? Next it will be Prue pregnant and they'll all have babies but her! Her baby will be somewhere else, never acknowledged, forever a secret. She burst into tears.

'Cece! What's wrong?' Finlay threw the blanket off his legs and hurried to her.

'It's nothing.'

'Hardly.'

How could she explain the pain she had in her chest about leaving the baby? A baby she had now held and fed at her own breast. A baby she had cuddled and changed, cleaned and soothed to sleep. All the things she didn't want to do so she could escape easier and now, thanks to Isla, she was broken, shattered into a million pieces at the thought of parting with her.

'We have to go.' She dashed away the tears on her cheeks.

'Go?'

'Tomorrow. It'll be Thursday. We'll stop George as he passes.' She jerked to her feet and paced the room. 'I'll leave Ross a note about buying the cottage. I'll start the process when I get to London. Go up and pack the small suitcase I left in your room.'

'What about the baby?'

'I'll have to take her with us, and I'll sort out her adoption in London.'

'No, Cece.'

'Don't censure me, Finlay. It's for the best.'

Subdued, he bent his head. 'What about King?'

Cece blinked, thinking. 'Er… he'll come with us.'

Finlay beamed. 'Thank you.'

In the kitchen, Cece pulled a box down from the top shelf in the larder and began packing the food that would spoil. She'd give it all to George.

The kitchen door opened and sheepishly Nell stepped in. 'I'm sorry I'm late.'

Cece didn't have the time or energy to chastise her. The girl looked unkempt, filthy and underfed. 'Go up to my room and pack all my clothes, please.'

'Yes, Mrs Marsh.'

Cece found a piece of paper in the dresser's drawer and sat at the table to write a note to Ross. Her pen hovered over the page as she tried to find the right words to say goodbye. Her chest tightened at the thought of never seeing him again, of never seeing his tender smile or the way his grey eyes lit up when she was near. She didn't deserve Ross Cameron, but it didn't stop her loving him, and she did love him, she knew that now.

Dear Ross,

We have left the cottage.

The chickens and goat are yours as are all the contents of the cottage and land.

In London I will make arrangements for the transfer of the cottage deeds into your name as a thank you for all the help and friendship you have given myself and Finlay since we arrived.

Please pass on to Isla my best wishes and that I hold no hard feelings towards her. I know she thought she was doing the right thing by giving me back the baby. However, I'll sort out an adoption once in London.

You are a dear man, and I will never forget you. If circumstances had been different, then I would have been proud and delighted to have been your wife.

Thank you for all you have done for me.
Cece Marsh

Chapter Twenty

Cece shut the cottage door and paused. That was that.

George had come up the drive after Finlay flagged him down, and with Finlay up on the seat beside George holding the baby, their few belongings and King in the back of the cart, Cece had put out the fires in the range and the front room and with a final glance around the cottage she once hated, but which bizarrely she was sad to leave, she stepped outside.

'Off for a day in Fort William is it, hen?' George asked as they rumbled along the road by the loch in the cold misty morning air.

'No. We need to go to the train station.'

'Going on a trip somewhere then?'

'London.'

'London. By, that's a long way.'

They waved to Murray who, with a fishing rod over his shoulder was out early to snag a catch. Cece glanced over her shoulder, watching him walk down to the water's edge. He'd been so kind when she first arrived. So many of the villagers had been kind and welcoming. What would she have done without the help of Alf, the innkeeper, giving her food and things to get her started? Or Isla and Ross's friendship? Mrs Gallan and even Nell, in her own unique way, had been a help and the poor girl had cried when Cece gave her the box of food to take to her sister's house when she left last night.

Her time in Resslick could have been a lot worse without those kind and generous people.

She deliberately squashed all thought of Christopher Evans.

Subdued the entire journey, she left the chatting to George and Finlay. The baby slept in her arms, well wrapped up against the cold.

At the train station, they took their goodbye of George and she left the baby with Finlay while she bought the tickets.

'The train will be leaving in a few minutes,' Cece said, over the hissing steam as she took the baby from Finlay. 'Let us find our seats.'

While the porter took their suitcases and trunk, Cece ushered Finlay onto the train with King. She took one last glance along the platform, not knowing why, but wishing perhaps Ross had arrived early at the cottage and seen her note.

Annoyed with herself for being so stupid, she boarded the train. She couldn't think about Ross.

The journey to London took all day with many stops and time waiting for other trains to pass. At York, they were told they had a thirty-minute wait, and so Cece sent Finlay to buy sandwiches and tea while she visited the ladies' rest room in the nearby hotel and fed the baby.

Being at York Station was difficult, as so many times in the past she'd been on those platforms with her family, making the journey to London to see Grandmama. Back then never in her wildest imagination did she think that one day she'd do it again, only this time carrying her illegitimate baby and accompanied by an orphan boy.

At last they were on their way again. Cece thought she should have perhaps telephoned Grandmama, but it was too late now, and she'd been so busy with the baby the thirty-minute standing time had flown by in a blink.

Tired, hungry, and not too clean from the soot in the air, Cece was glad when the train pulled into King's Cross. She hired a taxi to take them to Mayfair, and it began raining just as they pulled to a stop outside Grandmama's townhouse.

'Wow!' Finlay's eyes were wide with the wonder of London. He'd had his nose pressed to the window the entire trip from the station.

'Come on,' Cece urged him out of the taxi as the baby started to wail.

Kilburn, Grandmama's butler, opened the big black door and quickly hid his surprise. 'Miss Cece. Splendid.'

'Good to see you, Kilburn. Is Grandmama home?'

'Indeed, miss. She's in the drawing room.'

'Can you see to everything, please? Oh, and take King into the kitchens, he'll be hungry.'

'Certainly.' He was already reaching into his pocket to pay the taxi driver but took King's lead instead.

Cece jiggled the baby in her arms, her cries becoming louder.

The drawing room's double doors were opened and Cece stared in horror at her mama.

'Cece!' Mama rushed towards her, her smile faltering as she glanced at the crying baby. 'This is such a surprise and oh my, who is this little cherub?'

Beyond her mama, Cece saw Grandmama easing out of her chair and taking a deep breath as though ready to do battle.

Cece's knees buckled a little as Mama ushered her into the room. Finlay stuck to her side as though glued.

'Cece, darling?' Grandmama's tone was questioning.

'I'm sorry…' Cece's eyes filled with tears. 'I thought you'd be alone. I didn't know Mama was home from Paris.'

'Cece?' Mama stood on her other side, looking resplendent in peach silk as though she'd just returned from the opera. 'Whose baby is that, and who is this young man?'

Wondering if she might faint as she looked into her mama's surprised blue eyes so like her own, Cece stuttered. 'I-I…'

'Sit down,' Grandmama commanded.

Cece sat and Finlay sat beside her. She jiggled the baby again, crooning softly, praying she would quieten. 'She needs feeding…' Cece murmured.

'Shall we send one of the kitchen girls to come and take the baby?' Mama asked hopefully, perched on the edge of her chair.

'No. She'll not settle until she's fed.'

'Surely, they'll give it something.'

'It's not an *it*, Mama, she's a girl.'

Mama looked a little offended. 'Yes, well. Where does she belong, dearest? Why do you have her? I don't understand.'

Cece swallowed and took a deep breath. Straightening her shoulders, she stared at her mama. 'She's mine. My daughter. She was born last week.'

'Good God!' Mama rocked back as though struck. 'No! Not you!'

'Violet!' Grandmama snapped at her daughter. 'Stop acting like it's the end of the world.'

'It is the end of the world! How has this happened? Please tell me you are secretly married, Cece? I've guessed correctly, haven't I? You have married in secret. Is he not suitable? Is that why you've been so mysterious? I'll accept him, of course I will. Why wasn't I told?'

'Violet. Stop,' Grandmama ordered.

Cece lifted her chin. 'I'm not married, Mama.'

'Not…' Mama looked stricken. 'You mean…'

Grandmama sighed. 'Violet, calm down, for goodness' sake. Cece fell pregnant and travelled to Scotland to have the child.'

'You knew!' Mama accused. 'You knew of this catastrophe and didn't tell me?'

'No, I didn't know until recently, and you're correct I didn't tell you because it is Cece's business.'

'You visited Cece, and you never told me what was happening to my own daughter. How could you?' Mama reproached her mother.

'Because I knew you'd react just like this!' Grandmama snapped. 'And as far as I was aware Cece was giving the baby up. I'm as shocked as you are that she is here with the baby.' Grandmama shook her head and sighed. 'No, that is a lie. I had strong feelings that Cece wouldn't be able to give the child away. She is too soft-hearted.'

Mama had gone white. 'How will we face people? What will we tell them? Your sisters…'

'We tell them nothing,' Cece murmured as the baby finally stopped crying. 'I'm not keeping her. I do plan to find an adoption agency.'

'Oh, my…' Mama placed her hands over her face.

'That can be talked about later.' Grandmama waved her hand as though dismissing such difficulties. 'First, feed the child.' She smiled at Finlay. 'It's genuinely nice to see you again, dear boy. Are you hungry?'

Finlay nodded.

'Of course, you are.' Grandmama smiled. 'Come with me and we'll sort something out. Cece, go upstairs and see to the baby.'

Doing as she was told and glad to escape the glares from her furious mama, Cece hurried up to the bedroom that was hers and fed her daughter.

Later, with the baby full, changed and fast asleep. Cece also bathed and changed into a nightgown. She crept across the hallway to the room Finlay had been put into and smiled tenderly when she saw him fast asleep in bed with King curled up beside him.

Going back to her own bedroom. She slipped into the sheets beside the baby and lay there staring at her. She knew she should have gone down to talk to Mama and Grandmama, but it required an energy she didn't have right now. She was exhausted and needed to sleep for the baby would be awake in a few hours.

Cece closed her eyes and thought of Ross. He would have found the note by now. What was he thinking? Would he be pleased she was out of his life? He didn't need the trouble she brought. She would give him the cottage as promised and no doubt he would soon forget her, as she must try to forget him.

Cece

~ ~ ~ ~

'Am I to be criticised for being shocked and disappointed?' Mama demanded to know the following morning.

Seated at the dining table for breakfast, Cece sipped her tea.

'No one is criticising you, Violet,' Grandmama said, dismissing the serving girl from the room. 'Your feelings are justified, I grant you.'

'I'm sorry, Mama,' Cece murmured, pleased that Finlay had eaten and taken King for a walk. 'None of this was ever meant to be found out.'

'I don't know what upsets me more, Cecelia! That you didn't trust me enough to come to me at the beginning when you were in trouble, or that you could easily hide all this from me now.'

'You were in Paris.'

'Yes, Paris, Paris! Not the moon!' Mama banged her hand on the table. 'You get yourself in trouble, you flee to the wilds of Scotland, you live in a cottage, with hardly a word to anyone, you take in some stray off the streets, and then you have a baby. Who have you become? You're not my Cece, not my youngest daughter who grew up barely doing a thing wrong! I would expect this of Prue, but not from you, *never* from you.'

'Will shouting solve anything, daughter?' Grandmama asked quietly, yet with a steeliness in her tone that said she'd had enough. 'Cece has done wrong, made a mistake. She's trying to put it right.'

'Who is the father? Can he not marry you?'

Cece gazed into her teacup. 'No.'

'He is already married,' Grandmama spoke.

Cece's head shot up. Monty was married? The look on Grandmama's face and slightest of nods, confirmed the truth.

'Married? You had a dalliance with a married man? Good heavens above.' Mama placed a hand on her chest in dismay. 'Does he know about any of this?'

'No.' Cece swallowed back the hurt that while her life had fallen apart, Monty was happily married. '*He* will never know.'

'What are your plans, my dear?' Grandmama asked her.

'I should give her up, I know that…' Cece's heart broke at the thought.

'Yes, that is the only sensible option.' Mama nodded, stirring her tea for the umpteenth time. 'We can find a good family.'

'That would be easier said than done, Violet.' Grandmama glared at her daughter. 'Cece has cared for the baby. Giving her up might have been hard enough had she not seen her since the birth, but now she has held her and fed her, then I would imagine giving her over to strangers would be severely traumatic.'

Mama's eyes widened. 'Then what do you suggest, Mama? Shall Cece keep the child? What do we tell people?'

Cece wanted to crawl into a hole. Everything she had wanted to avoid was happening.

'Cece.' Grandmama gave her a gentle look. 'What do *you* want to do? I don't mean what you think is expected, but what you want in your heart.'

'No!' Mama glared at them both. 'We cannot afford to be sentimental about this.'

291

'Be quiet, Violet. For heaven's sake this is our flesh and blood we are talking about, not a dog or a horse, but your *granddaughter* and my great-granddaughter.'

Mama grew red in the face. 'And what of Cece's life? The scandal, the whispered conversations, the child growing up as a bastard. Is that what you want for your *flesh and blood*?'

'Please, both of you, stop shouting,' Cece murmured.

Kilburn knocked on the door. 'Excuse me, madam, but there is a gentleman to see Miss Marsh.'

The blood drained from Cece's face. Who could want to see her? Had a friend seen her at the train station yesterday and thought to call on her? Was it Monty? Did he know something? But how could he?

'Did he give a name, Kilburn?' Grandmama asked.

'A Mr Ross Cameron.'

Cece whimpered. Ross!

'Show him to the drawing room, will you?' Grandmama held up a hand as Cece was about to protest. 'Go and speak to him. He's come all this way. It must be important.'

'Who is this Cameron?' Mama asked, eyebrows drawn together. 'Now isn't the time for calls.'

Cece placed her napkin on the table and rose from the table. She couldn't believe Ross had come to London.

'Cece?' Mama questioned.

'Violet, enough. Let her go,' Grandmama said. 'I'll explain.'

Knees shaking, Cece walked across the hall. Standing in front of the closed doors, she took a deep breath, willing herself to be competent and do nothing foolish like cry.

Head held high, she opened the doors and stepped into the drawing room. Ross stood by the large window overlooking the street. He wore a grey suit that fitted him well. He must have caught the overnight train to get to London this morning. Cece's heart swelled at the thought of him going to such lengths to see her.

'Ross,' she murmured, closing the doors behind her.

He turned, his smile hesitant.

She walked forward. 'I'm so surprised to see you.'

'I am surprised I remembered your grandmama's conversation about where she lived. I'm afraid I've knocked on a few doors this morning disturbing people.'

'Why have you come?'

'To see you. To take you home.'

'Take me home?' Breath suspended, she didn't want to acknowledge what his words meant.

Ross looked around the elaborate room, with its high moulded ceilings, the rich rugs, the gilt-framed paintings and silk wallpaper, the fine furniture and the prestige of living in the heart of one of London's fashionable areas. 'I can't give you all this.'

'I don't want all this.' It was true. London wasn't her home.

'All I have is a farmhouse and thousands of acres of mountain sheep land, oh, and a bossy sister.'

'And all I have is a ruined reputation, a baby, a Finlay and his dog, and some money.'

'I don't want your money. I have my own.'

Her eyes locked with his. 'And the rest?'

'The rest I'll take gladly.'

A sob caught in her throat. 'The scandal?'

'Och, the Scottish love a good scandal. It gives us a reason to get drunk and fight.' He grinned.

Hope fluttered in her chest. 'But I need love, Ross. Life is nothing without it.'

'Will you have mine then, Cece Marsh?'

A single tear rolled off her lashes. 'There's nothing I want more.'

In two strides he was lifting her up off the floor and hugging her tight. He kissed her with a passion only just controlled.

The door opened and Finlay came in with King. He stopped and stared at them before his face broke into a large smile. 'Mr Cameron!'

Ross put Cece down. 'Aye, lad. I've come to take you and Cece home to the farm.'

'And the baby?' Finlay's smile faltered.

'Aye and the baby.' Ross turned to Cece. 'Have you named our daughter yet?'

Our daughter.

Cece's heart exploded into a firework of love for this strong wonderful man. 'I've named her Elizabeth, after your mother.'

'Elizabeth… Thank you.' His hand cupped her cheek. 'We had better hurry up and marry and make you both Camerons then!'

'Can I be a Cameron, too?' Finlay's voice wobbled.

Keeping a tight hold on Cece, Ross opened his other arm to include the boy in his embrace. 'You most certainly can.'

Cece kissed Ross tenderly. 'I'll love you forever.'

He grinned. 'I certainly hope so!'

Author Note

Hello Readers,

I hope you enjoyed, *Cece,* book three of the Marsh Saga series.

Millie, book one, was a new era for me to write. I'd never written a story set in the 1920s before and had to research a lot about how women were stretching the boundaries of their independence and freedom. The end of WWI brought many changes, but at the bottom of it all, women were still expected to marry well and raise children. I wanted that for Millie because she is the oldest and would naturally lead the way for her sisters. Yet, I also wanted to show each sister as being unique.

Prue was a joy to write as she is very different to her sisters. They all have courage when needed and spirit, but unlike the others, Prue has a little of a devil-may-care attitude and is more reckless.

Cece is not like her sisters at all. She's at a time in her life when she doesn't know where she fits. Sending her to Scotland allowed her to find not only her true self, but also her true love.

In order, the books are: *Millie, Christmas at the Chateau*, a novella that fits between *Millie* and *Prue*, then *Cece* and finally *Alice*.

I hope you enjoy the series, which you can find on Amazon, or order from bookshops and libraries.

AnneMarie Brear
2020.

Cece

AnneMarie Brear

Cece

Manufactured by Amazon.ca
Bolton, ON

24501990R00176